The Synoptics

Copyright © 1982 by Thomas E. Crane
First published 1982 by Sheed & Ward Ltd
2 Creechurch Lane, London EC3A 5AQ
All rights reserved
Nihil obstat Anton Cowan, Censor
Imprimatur Philip Harvey, Bishop in North London,
Westminster, 12 February 1982
The *Nihil obstat* and *Imprimatur* are a declaration that
a book or pamphlet is considered to be free from
doctrinal or moral error. It is not implied that those who
have granted the *Nihil obstat* and *Imprimatur* agree
with the contents, opinions, or statements expressed
British Library Cataloguing in Publication Data
   The Synoptics: Mark, Matthew, and Luke Interpret
   the Gospel.
   1. Bible. N.T. Gospels—Commentaries
   I. Title
   226'.06   BS2555.2
   ISBN 0 7220 8711 X
Typeset in 11pt on 13pt Century Schoolbook
by Sprint Productions Ltd, Beckenham, Kent
Printed in Great Britain
by Biddles Ltd, Guildford, Surrey

Contents

Introduction: Rediscovering Biblical Spirituality — 1

1. The Gospel and the Gospels — 8
2. The Gospel *about* Jesus — 15
3. The Gospel *from* Jesus — 25
4. The Marvellous Element in the Gospel — 34
5. The Words of Jesus — 50
6. Mark's Gospel: an Overview — 61
7. Mark's Theological Message: the Mysterious Identity of Jesus — 76
8. The Traditions of Jesus' Origin — 91
9. The Literary Level of Matthew's Gospel — 106
10. The Theological Dimension of Matthew's Gospel: the True Israel — 118
11. Luke's 'First Account' — 139
12. Luke's Special Contribution: the Acts of the Apostles — 156
13. The Essence of Luke's Theology: Peace and Goodwill to all Men — 182

Conclusion: the Gospel and our Life-Style — 193

Appendix: Suggestions for Further Reading — 207

A Panoramic View of Mark's Gospel   211
A Panoramic View of Matthew's Gospel   217
A Panoramic View of Luke-Acts   225

Introduction

Rediscovering Biblical Spirituality

For whatever was written in former days was written for our instruction, that by steadfastness and by the encouragement of the Scriptures we might have hope. (Rom 15:4.)

It would not be realistic or true to say that the Catholic Church has neglected the Bible. As a matter of fact, Catholics have always had a special reverence for the Sacred Scriptures as the Word of God: Bible reading has been in every Mass and in our daily prayers since the early centuries of the Church's history. However, we must admit that, at least in the Western Church, the Latin Vulgate version of the Bible was the one recognized as the official version, even long after Latin ceased to be commonly understood. The result was that, even though we still had the Bible, and though at least the clergy were still reading from it every day, most of our Catholic people gradually became more and more separated from the familiarity with the Bible which had been common in former times. Some other groups of Christians reacted to this situation by producing translations of the Scriptures in their own languages. Sometimes their translations were good, but even so, they concentrated so much on the Bible that they lost sight of the fuller spiritual richness of the Church's living tradition and sacramental experience.

The bishops of the Catholic world worked during the Second Vatican Council (1962-5) to improve this situation. One of their principal activities during the four yearly sessions of this ecumenical council was the ceremony of enthroning the Gospel in St Peter's Basilica in Rome, carried out every morning before the conciliar deliberations. Thus the bishops made a public act of recognizing the supreme place which the Word of God must have in their ministry. In the Council's official statements about Divine Revelation and about the Sacred Liturgy, these bishops declared that we should improve our study of the Bible, and use it more to learn and spread the Word of God. This means, of course, that we need new translations in modern languages—and this is why we have moved away in recent years from our former reliance on the Latin Vulgate, and also from the old-style English translations which were based on it. The newly-produced translations which we use now are made from the ancient Hebrew and Greek manuscripts, which are closer to showing the original sense of the Bible than the Latin Vulgate. Besides that, the people who produced these new translations have tried to present the genuine meaning of the ancient Scriptures in a modern form of language which is readily understandable for English-speakers of the present generation. After all, there are several million people in the world who use English even though it is not their native language (in Asia and Africa, for example). The modern versions must serve these people too, by bringing to them the Word of God with purity and clarity, and, of course, with correctness of translation (such as the *Jerusalem Bible*, the *New American Bible*, the *New English Bible*, the *Revised Standard Version*, and the *Good News Bible*).

We are familiar by now with the system of readings from the Scriptures which we have at Mass and in the other sacramental rites. Besides these, we are finding a renewed depth of interest in the Scriptures, in the movement of charismatic renewal, in retreats and renewal programmes, in religious formation, in ecumenical contacts and other areas. As a result of all this, it seems that our Catholic people are coming to a renewal of the biblically-inspired spirituality which was widespread in the Church of former times, before it became obscured by later historical and cultural circumstances.

This does not mean that we consider the Bible to be the only source of our spirituality, however, or that we expect it to have the answer to every question. Rather, it means that we see the Scriptures as a vital part of our faith-life and of our spiritual experience, so that we draw guidance and help from them as we try to absorb the Word of God and respond to it in our daily activities. This applies to both testaments, of course, but it is more relevant to our Christian life-style from the perspective of the New Testament. Thus we see the Old Testament in the light of the New—as St Paul and the writers of the Gospels did before us.

The Gospel and the Gospels

With regard to the New Testament, we sometimes hear people speaking about it in terms of 'Gospels and Epistles' or of the 'Four Gospels'. This arrangement is based on the literary forms of these books, but it does not take into account the intentions or the messages of the human authors whom God inspired to produce them. This is why we speak more nowadays of the synoptics (Mark, Matthew, and Luke-Acts), or of the Pauline or the Johannine writings. When we group the books in this way, we can see better the basic outlook and message of each of the units, because we are considering them in terms of the people who produced them and gave them their theological content as well as their literary forms. Even though several people evidently contributed their share, either in the stage of the oral tradition before the writing, or to the editing and arranging of the written documents, nevertheless the principal message that comes through is that of

Mark, Matthew, and Luke in the synoptic writings, or that of Paul or John in their respective parts of the New Testament. So this way of grouping the New Testament books helps us to read them in terms of the special message intended by their inspired authors.

In the second century AD St Irenaeus, one of the most influential writers of the early Church, spoke of the 'fourfold Gospel' or the 'one Gospel in four forms'. This phrase reflects the basic unity of the four evangelists, and the one essential message which comes through in all of their writings. However, the really important point is not the number of the Gospels, but the 'Gospel essence' of the whole New Testament (including St Paul's letters and the remaining parts of the New Testament as well).

This 'Gospel essence' is what converted the crowds to Christianity on the first Pentecost (Acts 2) and throughout the following years and centuries. It was a genuine *kerygma* (or proclamation) that caught the attention of so many thousands, indeed millions, of people because it touched their lives and uplifted their spirits. Once these ancient peoples heard the central point of the Christian Gospel, they found that it brought them things that they wanted to see and hear—a message from a God who was interested in helping them, and speaking to them in a language that touched their experience, giving them things that rejoiced them, and promising them even more of the same for the future.

This is why we say that the core of the New Testament, and of the whole of the Christian faith and life-style, is the 'Gospel'—the 'good news'—from God, which calls for a response of trust, confidence, faith, hope, and love.

The Synoptics

The synoptic writings (Mark, Matthew, and Luke-Acts) have a special value for us because they give us a moving picture in written form, so to speak, of Jesus in his earthly

Introduction

ministry and in his Passover, and also of the work of the Holy Spirit in the early Church, as Luke depicts it in the Acts of the Apostles. When we look at these sacred documents from the point of view of literary analysis and of their historical origin, we find several layers of authorship in them. Even though we are principally interested in seeing the person of Jesus, his teaching and his saving work, we find that the tradition of this comes to us only through the ministry and witness of his disciples, whom he sent as apostles to 'teach all the nations' (Mt 28:19). Furthermore, the apostles then preached the message so many times and to so many different people that the oral tradition must have circulated in various forms for about a generation, probably in a fragmentary way for the most part, before anybody began to write it down systematically. As far as we can tell now, it seems that all or at least most of Paul's epistles were written and circulating before any of the present Gospels emerged in their final form. But eventually the followers of these apostles began to undertake the project of putting the apostolic tradition about Jesus into the form of written narratives, in order to make the picture of Jesus attractive, relevant, and instructive for their contemporaries who had never seen or heard him. Thus about a generation after Jesus had died and returned to the Father, and shortly after Peter and Paul had died in Rome as martyrs, the Church began to have written interpretations of the Gospel according to the evangelists, just as earlier they had had it in the oral witness of the apostles, and in the letters which Paul had written to his converts. The followers of St John preserved the teaching of their venerated patriarch and put it into writing later, towards the final years of the first Christian century.

Meeting the Authors

There are, therefore, three layers of authorship present in

Chapter I

The Gospel and the Gospels

The God of Abraham, Isaac and Jacob, the God of our ancestors, has given divine glory to his servant Jesus. *(Acts 3:13)*.

We use the word *gospel* so much that we probably do not think what we mean by it. We speak of 'living by the Gospel' or 'preaching the Gospel'—a speaker once mentioned the phrase 'Gospel priesthood' and was quite upset when a student in the group told him that the Gospels do not speak about priesthood! We also know that in the recent renewal of the liturgy we have a new emphasis on the liturgy of the Word, centered on the Scripture, and that in this the reading of the Gospel has the principal place—and that in more solemn celebrations the reading of the Gospel is enhanced by candles and incense.

Nowadays, as we work to renew our faith-life and to sort out the proportions of essentials and accidentals, we find that we must come closer to the Scriptures than we did before, and that we need to draw from them the spiritual nourishment and guidance that we crave. All of this means that we need to clarify what we mean by 'the Gospel'.

We have surely heard, and perhaps used, the phrase 'Gospel truth', to mean something that is really sure and reliably true. But, at the same time, what do we mean by 'Gospel'? And what do we mean by 'truth'? If we mean *true* in the sense of 'historically true', we may not be doing full justice to the essence of the Gospel. St Paul

Chapter I

speaks in his letters about 'my gospel' and 'the gospel that I preach', but he never goes into details about history when he uses these terms. This means that, when we speak about the Gospel as we find it in the New Testament, we must include the message and the oral preaching of St Paul and of the other apostles as well, even though Paul did not write what we would call a gospel. Besides this, Jesus himself preached the 'gospel', even though we do not claim to have anything that he wrote. Basically, therefore, the Gospel is something preached, as a personal message for the here and now and not merely something about the distant past.

Ultimately, then, we have *one* Gospel, even though it comes to us in several forms in the New Testament books. The one Gospel is essentially an announcement, or a message, from God himself, that offers *good news*, or spiritual uplift, and calls for a response in faith *here and now*. The Gospel is *to us*—and it is *now*! And it is the Gospel of the Lord! We would miss the point tragically if we failed to recognize this, and thought of the word as merely telling a story about the past, however holy and edifying that story may be.

When we speak in terms of numbers, we can use the word 'Gospel' in several ways, in addition to referring to the four documents which we attribute to the four evangelists. For instance, we can also speak of the oral Gospel and the written Gospel. Another way of looking at it is to speak of the Gospel *from* Jesus, or the message which he himself preached, and then of the Gospel *about* Jesus, or the one which his apostles and their followers preached after they had been touched by the Holy Spirit in the Pentecost experience.

The Gospel is Now

This can be confusing, perhaps, but it leads us to appreciate the neccesity of looking carefully at this very important word, and of looking for the true essence of the Christian Gospel. Of course, the original Greek word means 'good news', or a pleasant and uplifting message. The English equivalent of the word occurs already in the Old Testament, in the prophetic oracles of the Second and Third Isaiahs. We find these phrases there:

> Zion, herald of glad tidings... Jerusalem, herald of good news! (Is 40:9.)
> Him who brings glad tidings, announcing peace, bearing good news. (Is 52:7.)
> He has sent me to bring glad tidings to the lowly. (Is 61:1.)

This quality of 'good news' or 'glad tidings' is the essence of the word, and of the message which it proclaims. This means that when we speak of 'Gospel truth', we are not limiting ourselves to refer to something that is only a matter of past history, or of something that may have happened in a certain way in the distant past. 'Gospel' speaks to us now in the present situation of our own life, and offers us an uplift for our spirit in the midst of our life as it is today. This implies that we hear the Gospel in a spirit of faith, and that we respond to it as to a call that comes to us from God.

When the ordained minister (priest or deacon) finishes the reading of the Gospel passage in the liturgy, he proclaims, 'This is the Gospel of the Lord!' and we respond 'Praise to you, Lord Jesus Christ!' This is because we have the feeling that what we have just heard is something that brings us a saving message, and that comes to us ultimately from God himself, not to tell us a story only, but to enter into a vital relationship with us.

When Peter and the other apostles were transformed by the coming of the Holy Spirit in the event of Pentecost (Acts 2), they could not keep their enthusiasm to themselves, and they had to become proclaimers and witnesses of God's presence and action in their lives. This does not

Chapter I

mean that they gave a detailed account of what happened; it means, rather, that they called on people to recognize that God was coming to them there and then, and challenging them to be converted and place their faith in Jesus, whom the heavenly Father had raised from the dead to be their Messiah and Lord.

Jesus also preached the Gospel. There are several passages in the New Testament which speak of Jesus 'preaching the gospel [or the good news] of the Kingdom of Heaven' (Mt 1:14-15; Lk 4:43). And Jesus promised his disciples that they would receive a reward from God for making sacrifices for his sake and for the sake of the Gospel (Mk 10:29), and that the Gospel would be preached to the entire world (Mk 13:10; Mt 24:14; 26:13).

The Essence of the Gospel

The essential core of the Gospel, which the apostles preached, and which the Church has consistently believed and offered to the world, is that God has shown himself to men in Jesus, as a God of goodness, life, healing, peace, and help. God did this in Jesus' public ministry, and, supremely, in his passion, death, and glorification. In this God has shown that his power for goodness and life is greater than the power of any creature for death, evil, and sin. Jesus preached the Gospel of God's kingship, or rule, and in his words and his actions he offered a message of God's fatherly kindness and healing power. The response which Jesus called his countrymen to make, but which, ironically, they did not give him, was a conversion of heart which would make them relate to God as Jesus himself did, that is, with childlike confidence and unhesitating trust. The crowds consistently failed to respond as he called them to do, and Jesus saw that he would eventually have to die because of the hostility of the leaders. But, instead of trying to avoid this prospect, he accepted it with tranquillity, and the confident expectation that God would show his fatherhood and care by raising him up after he had offered him perfect service by accepting the death which men's sinfulness would inflict upon him. This was Jesus' own way of showing that the Kingdom of God cannot be impeded by human failure; Jesus knew that God's goodness and lordship were operating in him, but it was only after Easter and Pentecost that his disciples understood the whole thing, and became themselves preachers and witnesses of this very Gospel.

The picture of a friendly, fatherly, and loving God, and the promise of endless heavenly joy in his presence, mediated by his own Son—this is the Christian Gospel. It offered to the Israelites the fulfilment of their national destiny and the completion of their collective history, but they did not see it that way, and they missed the point of the Gospel which both Jesus and his apostles offered to them. As a result, the Christian Church became more and more widely separated from Israel, and became principally gentile, as it is now. Even among these gentiles, the Gospel made progress mostly among the lower classes of society—slaves and such—because it offered them something that gave them joy and promised them something that made hope seem worthwhile.

As the first Christian century wore on, and the Gospel continued to spread, it remained at the core of the Church's collective life; the early forms of the liturgy were built around the action of *eucharist*, which in Greek means 'thanksgiving'. From that day to this, the Church's principal collective act is this same one—giving thanks to God for the good news of his friendship and of the lifegiving power over death and evil which he has shown in his raised-up Son. This is why now, just as twenty centuries ago, our celebration of the eucharist is our official way of offering thanks to God, in response to his gift of the Gospel to us.

Chapter I

In the Books

We find the Gospel *about* Jesus in every book of the New Testament—so much so, as a matter of fact, that we may miss the forest because we see so many trees. On the other hand, only the four evangelists present the Gospel *from* Jesus, in the form of their moving narrative pictures of Jesus and his earthly ministry of teaching and marvellous works.

This means that the Gospel goes through various stages, and that we can follow it as it moves forward on different levels. There are three principal levels of this kind which will become apparent. First, there is—as we have said—the Gospel *from* Jesus, as he himself brought to his countrymen the uplifting message of God's fatherly lordship and rule. The second level of the Gospel comes in the preaching of the apostles, including not only Peter and John and the others of the Twelve, but also Paul, as he preached and taught through the letters which he addressed to his Christian converts. Eventually, a generation or more after the time of Jesus, comes the third stage of this process, as the evangelists undertook the project of interpreting the message of these apostles *about* Jesus, in the written forms which are familiar to us now as the four Gospels.

The synoptics, whom we intend to consider most directly here, made their contribution—writing down their interpretations of the apostolic Gospel—only some years after Paul had written his letters and died as a martyr in Rome. Mark appears to have been first, so that he deserves credit for being the originator of the written Gospel as an organized narrative or literary form. The Gospels of both Matthew and Luke show evidence that they were based at least partly on Mark's Gospel. A decade or two later, towards the end of the first century, some followers of St John—probably at Ephesus, in what is now Turkey—put his rendering of the Gospel into written form as what we now call the Fourth, or Johannine, Gospel.

Summary
From all this we should be able to distil some central points. First, the Gospel is much more than merely a history book about the past: it is God's living message to his people, here and now. Secondly, it is centered in Jesus, is mediated by him, and is inseparable from him. Thirdly, the Gospel is *Good News*, not a neutral or dispassionate news report, or a 'scientific' chronicle. It is an enthusiastic, committed witness, intended to stir our hearts as well as to captivate our minds and our fantasy or imagination, and raise them to God. Fourthly, the Gospel does its work only when we respond to it as Jesus and his apostles called people to respond, with faith and a confident trust in the goodness of God who gives the message, so that we share the attitude which St Paul manifested when he said to his friends in Greece: 'Thanks be to God for this unspeakable gift!' (2 Cor 9:15). Fifthly, when we accept the Gospel fully, it becomes the central driving force of our life, so that we relate to God as Jesus did, and our interest and our energy become entirely dedicated to bringing it to others, as the apostles did, and as Christian missionaries have been doing ever since.

Chapter II

The Gospel *about* Jesus

It is true, God sent his word to the people of Israel, and it was to them that the good news of peace was brought by Jesus Christ—but Jesus Christ is Lord of all men. *(Acts 10:36.)*

Before reading this chapter, study the following passages of the New Testament. Make a written note of any details which catch your attention:
 Acts 2:14-39; 3:11-26; 4:8-12; 5:29-32; 10:34-43; 13:16-41
 1 Cor 15:1-11
 Phil 2:5-11
 2 Tim 2:8
In all these texts, notice the central importance of the dying and rising of Jesus.

In essence the Gospel is the message of good news that comes from God to his people. But it comes, on one level, in the ministry of Jesus, and then, on another level, in the preaching and the witness of the followers of Jesus, including the apostles and the later generations of the Church—including even the Church of our own day.

We know, of course, that what we primarily want to find is the Gospel which Jesus himself preached. However, we must acknowledge that this message of Jesus comes to us only through his followers, most importantly through his apostles, since these were the 'inner circle' whom he instructed in a special way during his earthly ministry—and even after his resurrection. For this reason, we can learn a great deal by concentrating for a while on this

Gospel *about* Jesus, as we find it in the early preaching of his apostles, before the present Gospels came to be written at all.

Paul

Though he was not one of the original group of twelve, St Paul has an even greater prominence in the New Testament than some of the original twelve. His conversion and the account of his missionary journeys are familiar to us from the Acts of the Apostles. But, aside from those historical factors, his theological message is much more important. It is not a systematic or orderly kind of message; we have to work hard to piece it together, partly from the narrative scenes in Acts, and, even more, from the thirteen letters which the New Testament preserves under the label of the 'Pauline epistles'.

In order to do a complete study of Pauline theology, we would have to go through all these documents carefully and thoroughly, and see what Paul said to the new Christian groups to whom they were addressed. But, for the sake of brevity, we can summarize Paul's doctrine by referring to a few sample passages, such as Rom 1:3-4 and 2 Tim 2:8. Here, even briefly, as in a passing breath, Paul refers to the whole basis of the Christian faith which has become the most important thing in his life, and which he shares with his friends. Also in Gal 2:2 he mentions 'the Gospel which I preach'. It is the message of what, in contemporary theological terminology, we call the 'paschal mystery'—the mystery of God's power for goodness and for life, working supremely in the passion, death, and glorification of Jesus, and the effects that this has on the earthly life and future destiny of Christians. In 1 Cor 15:3ff, Paul reminds his friends of the tradition which he himself has received and then passed on to them, namely, that Jesus died, and then was raised up on the third day. Another memorable Pauline passage is the

Chapter II

lyric of Phil 2:6-11: the point here is the same, namely, that Jesus who was brought low in humble suffering has been raised high by God, so that now men should acknowledge him as their Lord.

This Gospel of the paschal mystery, therefore, is what we mean when we refer to the Gospel *about* Jesus. But it is more than merely an announcement: it is also a call to action on the part of those who hear it, and a challenge to them to respond to the call by an act of faith. In the Epistle to the Romans (chapters 5-8), Paul again speaks, this time at greater length, about the practical connection that exists between the paschal mystery of Jesus and the faith-life of Christians. He draws the parallel between Jesus dying and rising in the paschal mystery, and Christians who are joined to Jesus by baptism, since this represents, sacramentally, a co-dying with Jesus on the part of the newly-initiated members of the Church. This separates them, also sacramentally, from the power of evil, death, and sin, so that Christians live by God's power, given in and through the raised-up Lord Jesus, and, like him, they can never be dominated by the power of evil and death.

Peter

If we looked at 1 Peter, especially 1 3-3:12, we could see, this time under the name of the apostle whom Jesus designated as the leader of his Church, a similar message. Again the central point is the paschal mystery—Christ has died, Christ has risen, Christ will come again—and we are joined to his victory over death and evil by our baptism, which joins us to his Church and transforms our earthly life into a preparation, in hope, for heavenly joy.

Acts

In a more graphic way, St Luke, who produced both the third Gospel and also the Acts of the Apostles, presents the Gospel *about* Jesus as it comes in the *kerygma* (proclamation) of the early apostolic preachers. The first of these kerygmatic discourses which Luke presents is in Acts 2—the familiar scene of the first Pentecost. Transformed and dynamized by the newly-imparted Holy Spirit, Peter and the other apostles throw off their fear and confusion. As the representative of the others, Peter addresses the crowd in the square in Jerusalem, and now proclaims, for the first time, the Gospel of the paschal mystery: God has brought the new age which was promised in the oracles of the Old Testament prophets, such as that of Joel. This new age is centered in the person of Jesus whose ministry showed signs, wonders, and miracles by God's power. But the Jews killed him, and now God has raised him from the dead, so that he is now Lord and Messiah (or Christ). This is the supreme and definitive manifestation of God's lordship and power, showing that he has overcome the power of creatures for evil, death, and sin. Jesus, who was crucified, God has raised up (Acts 2:36), and the apostles present themselves as witnesses of this mystery.

In the next chapters (Acts 3-5) Luke describes a series of events which show God protecting his apostolic witnesses and demonstrating his life-giving and healing power through their ministry, as they witness to the Gospel. In Acts 3:13-26, after healing the crippled man at the Beautiful Gate of the Temple in Jerusalem, Peter speaks again (in the second kerygmatic discourse). Again he proclaims the message of the paschal mystery: God has glorified his servant Jesus (Acts 3:13, 26), by raising him from the death which sinful men had inflicted on him, and the same divine power has healed this crippled man through the ministry of the apostles. The leaders of Israel object, and try to prevent the spread of his Gospel and to stop those whom the apostles are converting. But the message goes on, presented again in Acts 4:8-12 and yet

Chapter II

again in Acts 5:29-32, both times to the ruling council of the Jews (the Sanhedrin).

The Gospel moves to the gentiles, as Peter preaches to Cornelius in Acts 10, especially in Acts 10:34-43. Here the leader of the Church speaks again of the new age which God has given his people—a Gospel (Acts 10:36), offered through Jesus, the prophet rejected and brought low by men but now raised high by God as Lord of all who are to have salvation through faith in him. Paul preaches to the Jews in Damascus in Acts 9:22, and to the Jews in Antioch of Pisidia in Acts 13:16-41. He turns and preaches to the gentiles, first in Lystra (Acts 9:22), and then, more fully, in Athens (Acts 17:22-31). In these addresses to gentiles there is a notable change: whereas the earlier discourses were replete with terminology and images drawn from the Old Testament, Paul obviously is aware that he cannot expect the gentile pagans, sophisticated and cultured as some of them are, to recognize the biblical allusions which are familiar enough to Jews who have been brought up with the Old Testament. So he adapts the form of his preaching, by omitting Old Testament terms, and even quotes from Greek poets (Acts 17:28). But, even here, as he prunes away expendable Old Testament images and terms, the indispensable essence of the Gospel remains (Acts 17:31). Paul proclaims that God has raised up Jesus from the dead, and calls upon his hearers to have faith in this raised-up Lord, through whom God will judge them, and all men.

Also in Acts, Stephen, in his dying moments, witnesses to the same Gospel. Jesus, the prophet rejected by his own countrymen, is now glorified as the 'Son of Man' in heaven at God's right hand (Acts 7:51-56). In the next chapter Philip instructs the Ethiopian by interpreting to him the prophetic oracle of the Second Isaiah (Is 53:7f), to the same effect, giving him 'the Good News of Jesus' (Acts 8:35).

The Gospel which these apostolic preachers present is always that of the paschal mystery: God has shown his power for goodness and life supremely, by raising up Jesus from the dead. Along with the announcement there is the call for a personal response. This must be a response, first of faith, and then of practice—a life-style governed by conversion to the power of God as he has shown it in the paschal mystery, and dynamized by the Holy Spirit whom the raised-up Lord has sent to animate his followers and make them witnesses of this same mystery.

The Paschal Mystery and the Old Testament

When we speak of 'the paschal mystery' we are already using Old Testament terminology. *Pascha*, or *pesach*, means 'the Passover', which was—and still is—the principal feast of the Jewish year, commemorating the 'passing over' from slavery in Egypt, through the trials of wandering in the desert, to the new life of freedom in the Promised Land of Canaan. Jesus' death occurred at the time of the Passover celebration (in the Springtime, March-April). This is why the apostolic preachers, including St Paul, and later the evangelists who produced the written Gospels, use so many terms and images drawn from the Exodus tradition and the Passover observance to speak of the paschal mystery (the 'passover') of Jesus. St Paul writes in 1 Cor 5:7: 'Christ, our Pasch, has been sacrificed,' and speaks in the same passage of the unleavened bread which was a basic feature of the Jewish Passover ritual. St John, in his Gospel (Jn 1:29), calls Jesus the 'Lamb of God'. Again, in the Calvary scene (Jn 19:31), the same evangelist speaks of the broken bones of the thieves and the unbroken bones of Jesus; he then quotes Ex 12:46, which gives the ritual directives for eating the Passover lamb, and requires that it be a lamb without blemish, with no bones broken. In 1 Cor 10:4 Paul

Chapter II   21

draws—rather fancifully, it would seem—a parallel between Jesus as the source of life for Christians and the water-giving rock which Moses struck in the desert during the time of the Exodus (Num 20:7-11).

At first it may not seem that there is much of a connection between the paschal mystery of Jesus and the whole Exodus event of Israel. But the parallel goes beyond the mere coincidence of the dates—it is very strong at the level of the symbolic importance of both realities. In the one, as in the other, God showed himself by his acts of goodness, making his chosen servant (or servants) 'pass over' from bad to good, from death and oppression to life and peace. Similarly, both had to pass through a trial, the desert on the one hand, and the agony of death and desolation on the other. Of course, there are differences too: the Exodus showed God's plan to care for a whole people, whereas the paschal mystery shows his care for Jesus (and his care for the whole Christian people too, of course). Also, Exodus was an earthly passover, from the land of Egypt, through the land of the Sinai desert, to the land of Canaan. But the Passsover of Jesus is moral and spiritual, as he goes from the earthly reality of his ministry and passion, through the tragedy of death, to the heavenly reality of God's eternal presence. Similarly, for Christians who are 'in Christ', sharing in the paschal mystery is a passing over from the slavery of sin to the spiritual freedom of being children of God, ruled not by foreign power but by the Holy Spirit who has been given to us.

There are several more Old Testament themes that are prominent in the Gospel of the paschal mystery. These are: the *Kingdom of God*; the *Servant*, or the *Suffering Servant of God*; the *Son of Man*; the *Rejected and Vindicated Prophet*; the *New Covenant*; the *Day of the Lord*; etc. The apostolic preachers, who were all Jews, had been brought up on the Old Testament scriptures and were thoroughly familiar with these themes. It should be no surprise, therefore, that they used this biblical style of language to express their new Christian faith and their new Gospel. But, by the same token, this was a new way of quoting and interpreting the ancient and familiar Scriptures—and so it constituted a novel and unauthorized departure from the sacred Jewish traditions. It was a basic tenet of the early apostolic preaching that the entire Old Testament points to Jesus, and is completed in him. Understandably, this increased the resentment and the antagonism of those Jews who remained unconverted (which was most of them). Now there were two ways of reading the Old Testament—the old traditional way, and the new Christian way, which saw the whole Old Testament in terms of Jesus! So there were hostilities and disputes, which continued to increase the distance between Judaism and the Church, until eventually the Church became more gentile than Jewish, as it is now.

But this brought problems too. We see, especially in the letters of St Paul, some examples of the effort which he makes to present the paschal mystery to gentiles, without relying on the Jewish terminology of the Old Testament scriptures, since he knew that he could not expect them to recognize or understand the references. We have already seen the example of the scene in Acts 17, in which Paul preaches the Gospel to the gentiles, in Athens, without quoting or using biblical terms. Likewise, in 1 Cor 15, he struggles at great length to interpret for his Greek converts the theme of the resurrection of Jesus. Without speaking of Passover, or Suffering Servant, or Son of Man, he uses the analogy of the seed—a universally recognizable symbol of life (1 Cor 15:35ff). The seed must be buried and subjected to the dampness of the earth before it breaks out in the form of a plant—new life comes from death, not only for the seed, but also for all who will draw their nourishment from the fruit of the newly-produced plant. Here the Gospel bridges the gap between the Jewish style of Old Testament language and the wider patterns of gentile expression! Paul also breaks into the terminology of athletics (1 Cor 9:24; Phil 3:24), and of military armour (1 Th 5:8; Eph 6:14; etc), as he searches for new terminology which will make the same Gospel intelligible and appealing for gentiles.

The Paschal Mystery in the Church

Eventually, as time went by, it became the ongoing project of the whole Christian Church to take the Gospel of the paschal mystery, which is the core of Christian faith, and express it in a way that is intelligible and also practical enough to be liveable for people in their everyday experience.

The principal vehicle for this effort in the Church is the liturgy. If we stop to think about it, the main liturgical action of the Church's year is the Easter Vigil ceremony, in which the Church celebrates the paschal mystery in signs and symbols. The language of the ritual is replete with references to the Exodus (the Red Sea, the passover from death and slavery to life and freedom, etc) and to the water of baptism, because it is by this vehicle that Christians become members of the Church, and thereby sharers in the paschal mystery of Jesus.

Every Sunday is, for Christians, a miniature of Easter; every Mass and every other sacramental action is likewise a renewal of God's victory over evil in the passover of Jesus. As we celebrate the sacraments throughout our lives, all the important events of our life-experience come to be touched by this mystery, and by the Gospel. It begins with our initiation into the Church in baptism and confirmation, and extends through to the sanctification of our death in the funeral rite, which is also animated by the Church's hope in God's compassion, that he will bring his deceased servants to share in the heavenly glory which he has conferred on his raised-up Son.

Summary and Conclusion
Therefore, our daily life in the Church is a continual sharing, by faith, in the paschal mystery of Jesus. With or without the terminology of the Old Testament, and with or without the analogies that St Paul develops, the core of Christian life, on the practical level, is the task of accepting God's message—his Gospel of peace—and cooperating with his plan to conquer the evil and sin that touch our lives, by his power of healing and life-giving goodness. The struggle of Christian morality and spiritual experience is a share in Jesus' trial—always an effort, because of the tension which results from the conflict of our religious experience as the basic realities clash in us: the goodness of God and the satanic evil of sin. The Gospel about Jesus' Passover is God's guarantee that we are to have a share in his ultimate victory, after we complete the trial of our earthly pilgrimage which is our Passover, and our desert experience.

1. Why did the early apostolic preachers emphasize the dying and rising of Jesus?
2. How does the phrase 'paschal mystery' relate the Old Testament to the New Testament?
3. How does St Paul adapt his terminology to the culture of the gentiles?
4. What is the relationship of the dying and rising of Jesus to the everyday life of members of the Church?
5. How is the paschal mystery observed in the formal activity of the Church?

Chapter III

The Gospel *from* Jesus

Jesus toured all Galilee. He taught in their synagogoues, proclaimed the good news of the kingdom, and cured the people of every disease and illness. *(Mt 4:23.)*

Study the following passages before proceeding to read this chapter. Write down any details or features which particularly come to your attention:
  Mk 1:14f
  Mt 4:12-23
  Lk 4:14-43
  Mk 4:1-34
  Mt 5-7; 8f
  Lk 17:20f

We have already made the point that, although we want to find the Gospel which Jesus himself preached, we can find it only in and through the message which his apostles and their followers preached about him. This is why we see that it is necessary to distinguish between the Gospel *from* Jesus and the Gospel *about* Jesus. The Gospel *about* Jesus is, as we have seen, what we called 'the Gospel of the paschal mystery': God has shown himself as a God of goodness and life, in Jesus, and supremely in his passion and glorification, and calls on all men to come to him by faith in Jesus the Raised-up Lord.

The Gospel *from* Jesus is in the four Gospels themselves. St Paul has just about nothing at all to offer on this subject, because his whole message is centered on the paschal mystery and how it affects the life-style of Christians. But all four Gospels, and especially the Synoptics, present a narrative picture of Jesus in the public ministry which preceded his passion. In this public ministry Jesus appears as the prophet who announces to his countrymen the Gospel of the Kingdom of God. Mark is the first to show this picture: 'Jesus appeared in Galilee proclaiming the good news of God... The reign of God is at hand.' (Mk 1:14f.) Mt 4:12f shows the same thing, but, in typical Matthaean fashion, there is also a text from the Old Testament to accompany the scene. It quotes the oracle of Is 9, to the effect that, when Jesus came to preach in Galilee, it was the coming of the great light that Isaiah had mentioned in that oracle. In Mt 4:17 Matthew gives Jesus' words: 'The kingdom of heaven is at hand.' (Matthew prefers to say 'heaven' rather than 'God' because he follows the Jewish practice of respecting the divine name so carefully that he even avoids mentioning it.) Also, in Mt 4:23, he shows an even more complete picture of Jesus both preaching the good news (the Gospel) of the kingdom of heaven, and curing people of their diseases and illnesses. Luke varies the presentation somewhat, showing in the first scene of Jesus' public ministry his visit to Nazareth. There, in his own hometown, Jesus participates in the synagogue worship, and applies to himself the words of the Third Isaiah's prophetic oracle (Is 61:1ff), about the one sent by God to bring good news (or gospel: see Lk 4:18), quoting Is 61:1. At the end of the same chapter (Lk 4:43) Luke shows Jesus saying: 'I must announce the good news of the reign of God, because that is why I was sent.'

Synonyms
This phrase, then—'the gospel of the kingdom of God'—, becomes for us the summary of the message which Jesus

Chapter III

himself preached to his own countrymen. We must search out the essence of this theme, however, because various words appear as synonyms, and because the various contemporary versions of the Gospels also express the theme in alternative forms of translation. Essentially, 'Kingdom of God' is not a theme which Jesus originated. It is perhaps the central theme of the whole Old Testament and of the sacred tradition of Israel, because it means, ultimately, God's fatherly lordship accepted by his trusting people—i.e, the perfect relationship between God and his people. So, whatever equivalents we find in our contemporary versions of the Bible—*Rule of God, Reign of God, Kingdom of Heaven,* or some similar phrase—they all eventually come down to this.

In the Old Testament

Back in the time of Moses (1250 BC), God formed his people in a covenant relationship with himself, at Mount Sinai. The Israelites accepted God's dominion over themselves (his rule, or reign) and pledged that: 'Everything the Lord has said, we will do.' (Ex 19:8.) From that event onwards, the rule of JHWH, the God of Moses, over Israel was in effect. As time went on this same God showed that he was also able to direct the destinies of the people of Egypt, Canaan, and other nations as well, so that he alone—not Baal, or Ra, or Marduk, or any other deity which the ancient peoples worshipped—was truly Lord of Israel and of all men.

Unfortunately, there was a wide gap between the theory and the practice. The history of Israel's time in the desert, and later in the promised land of Canaan, shows that these people were never as dedicated and loyal to the service of this God as he called them to be. The oracles of the prophets, and the accounts which we have in the Old Testament books of Samuel, Kings, and Chronicles, show repeatedly that the later generations forgot the covenant which their ancestors had entered into with JHWH at Sinai. The theological formula was simple: the Israelites suffered endless troubles and eventual exile because they had failed to earn God's favour by maintaining their side of the Sinai covenant which Moses had mediated to them. If they had served God loyally, in the way that their ancestors had committed themselves—and them—to do, their life would have peaceful under his powerful providence and protection.

Promise

After a while the prophets began to speak more of a future era in which God would come again to his people, purify their hearts, conquer their enemies, and restore their earthly prosperity under the leadership of a new king—a king who would be a sort of latter-day David, successful and victorious in everything as David had been in his day. Other oracles spoke of the future leader as another prophet like Moses (Dt 18:15-18). In this ideal future age, God would lavish upon his people and outpouring of favours which would surpass their imagination and their expectations: a great banquet, and an end to all pain, illness, famine, and war. All of Israel's enemies and oppressors would be conquered, and subjected to the rule of JHWH; Israel's one God would be accepted and served by all the nations of the earth, who would stream to Jerusalem to offer him gifts and homage in the restored Temple there.

By the time of Jesus, a fresh wave of nationalism was in the air in his homeland. The enemies, on the socio-political level, were now the Romans, who had occupied the land of Palestine and made it into a suffering province of their vast empire. On the cultural level the enemies were the Greeks and the Egyptians, because their way of life was attracting the interest of too many Jews, especially younger Jews, and was making them forget and

Chapter III

abandon the ancient traditions which they had inherited from their ancestors. The conservative movement of the Pharisees and Sadducees had emerged about a hundred years before Jesus' time, as an attempt to preserve the Jewish tradition and prevent it from being extinguished by foreign enemies on the one hand, and, on the other, by internal indifference on the part of the Jews themselves. In order to keep their ancestral tradition alive, these leaders emphasized the most obvious elements of them— the external rites and customs which were most readily identifiable as signs of Judaism. These were customs like circumcision, the dietary laws, the feasts and fasts, the use of such things as prayer-shawls and 'phylacteries', ritual washings, observance of the Sabbath rest, and countless other practices.

We probably fail to do justice to these leaders because we see them principally in a negative way, as the enemies of Jesus in the Gospels—and so they were, true enough. But the basic purpose of their movement was laudable: if it had not been for them, Judaism might simply have disappeared altogether! The great weakness of these traditionalist leaders was that they had reduced Judaism to a matter of external observances, with themselves as the models of virtue to be imitated. In this they had lost sight of the fundamental attitudes of fidelity, filial piety, and covenant love which the teaching of Moses and the oracles of the great prophets had inculcated as the vital core of religion. In such oracles at Dt 6:4-9, Micah 6:6-8, and Jer 31:31-4 we can see clearly the themes of love and commitment which were too often absent from the religion of the Pharisees and their other colleagues.

This is why Jesus never attacked Judaism as such, or the Law and the Prophets. In fact, in his Sermon on the Mount Jesus even declared: 'I have not come to do away with the Law and the Prophets, but to make their teachings come true' (Mt 5:17). Similarly, he told his disciples in the same context: 'If your virtue goes no deeper than that of the scribes and Pharisees, you will never get into the kingdom of heaven!' (Mt 5:20)—that is, you will never have the kind of relationship with God that he wants you to have, and which the true Israel must have, according to the full meaning of the Old Testament.

Jesus' Gospel of the Kingdom of God (or of Heaven) presents the essence of religion as God teaches it in the Old Testament—a fatherly God who shows himself in life-giving and healing goodness, and whose lordship (or kingdom, or reign) is accepted eagerly by his own people as trusting children. As he preached this Gospel, Jesus offered his people a kind of religion which they had not seen before, and which they had not heard preached to them by their conventional leaders. Thus the Gospel of the Kingdom of God is present in Jesus' words as he preaches, and also in his marvellous works, as in them he shows God's healing and life-giving power freely offered for the good of men. It is present, too, in his own personality, for Jesus shows the perfect relationship with God—that of a trusting and loving son who communicates in fidelity and obedience with a loving and provident father.

All this was in the Law of Moses and in the oracles of the other Old Testament prophets. But it was not in the teaching of the official leaders, and one of the great tragedies of human history is that the leaders of God's own people failed to recognize his message when it came to them in the mission and person of Jesus. The scribes, the Pharisees, and the Sadducees were entrenched; and their influence was pervasive. Jesus could get a response of enthusiasm, certainly—people would accept the benefit of his healings eagerly enough. But he could not get them to show a real conversion of heart, which would have led them to deepen their religion from the self-righteousness of their own works to the interior piety of God's own children trusting in the goodness of their Father.

Because of the challenges and rebukes which God levelled at them, the leaders decided that there was not enough room in Israel for these two kinds of religion, and that Jesus had to go. (Mk 3:6; Mt 12:4; Lk 19:47.) Jesus was well aware of this opposition, and could see that he would have to come to the ultimate confrontation—a confrontation in which, because of their strategic superiority, these leaders would prevail and cause his death.

But there are also precedents for this in the Scriptures! Jesus knew the tradition of his people. He knew the Old Testament themes of the Servant of God (Ps 16:10); of the Rejected Prophet (Is 8); of the Suffering Servant (Is 52-3); and of the Son of Man (Dan 7). In all these images the power of God ultimately prevails and vindicates his suffering servant, by raising him up after he has been brought low by the forces of human sinfulness, and of death itself. And, because he knew it to be the embodiment of these biblical images, Jesus could face the prospect of death calmly, saying: 'The Scripture must be fulfilled' (Lk 22:37), and feeling assurance that, once his enemies had done their worst, God would do his best. Three times in the Gospels Jesus predicted that he would walk the path of the Son of Man (Mk 8:31; 9:31; 10:33), humiliated and oppressed by men, and then vindicated and raised up by God as the lord of his oppressors. Even as he walked with his disciples to Gethsemane, Jesus told them that he would be struck down and then raised up (Mk 14:28).

And so it was! We come full circle: Jesus preached the Gospel of the Kingdom of God, and the Kingdom of God was then supremely manifested in him! As the Suffering Servant of God, and as the Son of Man, he received the supreme award—the Father raised him up by his right hand, so that now he is Messiah and Lord, as Peter proclaimed on Pentecost. (Acts 2:36.)

Yet, once we see this Gospel of the Kingdom of God worked through as a living reality in the person of Jesus, we see too some new dimensions that were not at first apparent. We now see that the Kingdom of God is not a political matter, or an area to be identified exclusively with the temporal fortunes of the Jewish nation, as it had appeared to be in the Old Testament era, and even in the expectations of some Jews in Jesus' own time. Jesus sees the Kingdom as God's lordship over all: God gives the rain and the sunshine to everyone (Mt 5:45), and 'many will come from the East and the West, and they will find a place at the banquet in the kingdom of heaven with Abraham, Isaac, and Jacob' (Mt 8:11). Jesus' Gospel of the Kingdom of God was purely religious and moral, therefore, not political and social; and it was universal, not merely identified with Jewish nationalism. Furthermore, a new dimension of the Kingdom of God showed itself in the glorification of Jesus, because his disciples could now see that the Kingdom of God goes beyond the framework of our earthly experience and includes life after death. Resurrection is not a return to earthly existence in space and time, but a real passover, through the desert of death, to the promised land of the Father's heavenly presence. The Risen Lord whom the apostles experienced in the first Easter had burst the confines of earth, of space and time, and of all creation, to arrive at the fullness of the Kingdom, which is heaven!

When they applied this to their own lives, and to the experience of the Church in general, the apostles came to see that the life pilgrimage of Christians on earth is not the whole of the Kingdom of God, but merely a sign or a preliminary phase of it. This is why the bishops of the Second Vatican Council (1962-65) declared that the Church is not the Kingdom of God on earth, but is rather

Chapter III

the sign of the Kingdom of God (*The Church in the Modern World*, para. 39).

We live in the Church by the power of God, as he has shown it to us in and through Jesus; we are now animated and led by the Gospel of the Kingdom of God which we see enfleshed in the public ministry of Jesus, and manifested supremely and definitively in his passion, death, and glorification. When our earthly pilgrimage of sharing in his passover is completed, we will come, through the mystery of our own death, to resurrection—into the fullness of the Father's heavenly presence. Then we shall see the things that he has promised us.

1. What did Jesus mean by the phrase 'Kingdom of God' (or 'Reign of God')?
2. How was this theme present in the Old Testament?
3. Why and how did the message of Jesus conflict with the teaching of the recognized religious leaders of Israel?
4. How do the works of Jesus form a part of his message?
5. Was Jesus' 'Good News of the Kingdom of God' a new message for his contemporaries?

Chapter IV

The Marvellous Element in the Gospel

The large crowd of the disciples began to thank God and praise him in loud voices for all the great things they had seen. *(Lk 19:37.)*

Read the following New Testament texts; note in writing anything which catches your attention:
2 Tim 2:8: Paul's Gospel
Mt 1f; Lk 1f: God's marvellous providence operates before the ministry of Jesus
Mk 16:1-6; Acts 2:1-13; 16:16-34: marvels occur after the ministry of Jesus
Mk 4:35-5:34: a 'cluster' of miracle stories
Mt 8f; 11:2-5; 12:22-8: Jesus explains his own works.

There is a strong current of scepticism in the contemporary air about the miracle stories of the New Testament—and about those of the Old Testament as well, for that matter. One influential school of thought speaks of 'demythologizing' the Gospels, i.e, removing their 'mythical' or 'fictional' elements, which are supposed to be unacceptable to the so-called 'scientific' world-view of 'modern man'.

If we start out with the assumption that we can remove the marvellous element from the Gospel, then we no longer have 'good news'—no longer have something wonderful, something worth getting interested in or excited about, in our religious experience. The element of marvel, or miracle, is a part of the very essence of the Gospel, as it is of the Old Testament.

However, we must still admit that we cannot look at these ancient traditions of the Bible with the same kind of fact-oriented scientific certitude that modern historians usually expect. For the most part it is simply not possible to prove or to disprove the historical character of the miracle traditions. To do that we would have to have some concrete evidence that simply is not there. In fact, this shows us the very nature of these biblical traditions—they are essentially religious, or *gospel*, traditions. In other words, they are *kerygma*—declarations of faith passed on by word of mouth from generation to generation, and even from century to century. The validity of these faith-formed declarations derives from the reliability of the tradition itself, and from the witness of the persons who transmit it, rather than on the experience or the critical judgement of those who receive it. As a matter of fact, those who present the gospel tradition in faith expect that their hearers will also receive it in faith, not with the detached indifference of people who read a newspaper or hear a television report.

This applies to the Old Testament as well as to the New Testament. Today the Jews still preserve the traditions of Moses and of the great Exodus from Egypt, not because they can verify all the historical or geographical details by scientific analysis, but simply because this is the core of their collective religious identity. Similarly, we Christians place our faith in the Gospel, marvellous as it it, because in it and through it God has spoken his message to us.

All this means that we will never absorb the real religious essence of the Gospel, or of the Old Testament, if we are unable to go beyond the outer layer of the narrative and relate by faith to the divine message which comes to us in the witness of the evangelists. We should not conclude from this that we must accept all the miracle traditions as if they were as factual as normal historical records—or that we are justified in denying that any of the miracle-stories of the New Testament are historically based. Rather, we must conclude that we are not speaking here on the level of space and time only, or of things which are entirely under the control of human effort. We are listening *in faith* to those who pass on to us their declaration made *in faith*, that God has communicated himself in the special events which the tradition witnesses.

Some object that this is to avoid the issue—that we must either affirm the historical character of the miracle tradition, or deny it. But we can do neither; what we have to do is to recognize the *religious*, or *gospel*, character of the tradition as a whole, as well as of the individual parts of it. Then we either share the religious experience of those who witness this faith to us, or we do not.

The Works of Jesus

Naturally, we need some kind of understanding of the works of Jesus. As far as the miraculous, or marvellous, element is concerned, we probably fail to go far enough in recognizing it—we think of Jesus' works of healing and curing, or walking on the water, or the like. But there are other marvellous aspects to his ministry as well, such as his compassion towards sinners (Lk 7:36-50; Jn 7:53-8:11), including the fact that he even prayed for his killers (Lk 23:34) and accepted his death with an equanimity that elicited the amazement of the Roman centurion (Mk 15:39). Perhaps we do not expect to see these things as miracles because they do not appear to be spectacular reversals of the order of nature, or intrusions by God into the ordinary course of created events. But that is not the essence of a miracle. The real essense of a miracle is, simply, that in an external event the eyes of faith see the presence and power of God addressed to believers. The

Chapter IV

ancient peoples who produced the Bible had a simpler view of the world than we have; without our emphasis on 'scientific' analysis of the visible world, and on unchangeable 'laws of nature', they saw the whole universe as the product of divine genius and power. Pagans attributed this power to their various gods and goddesses; the Israelites, including Jesus and his apostles, attributed it to JHWH, the God who came to their ancestors, to Moses, and to the other prophets, and who spoke to them in the events of their life-experience.

Jesus himself explained his own works. John the Baptist was puzzled by the things that he was hearing about Jesus, so he sent his friends to ask him: 'Are you "he who is to come"?'. Jesus replied by appealing to his own works and his own preaching: 'The blind recover their sight, cripples walk, lepers are cleansed... and the poor have the good news preached to them.' (Mt 11:2-5.) Jesus explained who he was by reference to what he was doing! And, in doing this, he applied to himself the substance of some of the most powerful oracles of Book of Isaiah. In these passages the Old Testament prophet promises his people that God will lavish upon them an outpouring of his favours which will surpass their wildest imaginings or expectations:

> But your dead shall live, their corpses shall rise;
> Awake and sing, you who lie in the dust.
> For your dew is like a dew of light,
> and the land of the shades gives birth. (Is 26:19.)
> On that day the deaf shall hear the words of a book;
> And out of gloom and darkness, the eyes of the blind
>   shall see. (Is 29:18.)
> Then will the eyes of the blind be opened,
> The ears of the deaf be cleared;
> Then will the lame leap like a stag,
> And the tongue of the dumb will sing. (Is 35:5.)

In the same scene Jesus also says to John's representatives: 'The poor have the good news preached to them' (Mt 11:5). This is an allusion to another Isaian oracle (Is 61:1-3), in which the prophet sees himself sent by God to tell his own Jewish contemporaries that God will bless them with good news and with joy. We see this 'good news' as the 'Gospel of the reign (or kingdom) of God' which Jesus brought to his countrymen as the essence of his message. Jesus speaks of this preaching of 'good news' as one of his principal tasks (Lk 4:43).

All these things in the Isaian oracles were to be visible signs that God would be showing his healing favour and his goodness to his people—that his kingdom, or 'reign', was now present and operating in their midst. So, when Jesus alluded to his own marvellous works (Mt 11:5), he was saying, in effect: 'my works are signs to you that the Kingdom of God which the Old Testament prophets promised in their oracles has now come to you, and is present here and now in front of your eyes!'

Jesus' marvellous works were not mere displays of power for their own sake—this would have been no more than entertainment, or even magic. The works that Jesus performed were consistently benign, helpful, life-giving, uplifting, reassuring, and pacific. (The Gospels show one or two exceptions to this, but, as we shall see in due course, we can probably understand why.) The essential thing about Jesus' marvellous works, therefore, is not whether they happened or not—nor is it a matter of our trying to reconstruct them in precise detail (which we cannot do). Rather, the essential thing—consistently maintained by the Gospel tradition—is that God showed himself in a marvellous, or miraculous, way in the public ministry of Jesus. Thus his works, including his preaching, like his personality, were signs addressed to faith, showing the Kingdom of God, and challenging people to respond in faith, by a conversion of their hearts, and with

Chapter IV

confident trust in the fatherly God who was speaking to them in and through Jesus.

Other Miracles

If we begin from the realization that the marvellous works of Jesus are signs of the Kingdom of God present in the midst of people, then we can see that, in addition to those marvellous events which come in Jesus' own ministry, there are other marvels which are associated with him but which do not come directly from him or through him. Fundamentally, these Jesus-associated signs are an extension of the same divine message (the Gospel of God's Reign), since they draw their significance entirely from the fact that they are associated with him and with the Kingdom of God which was present in him.

Some examples of this latter category of Jesus-associated miracle-events are the cosmic signs which occur at the moment of his death (Mt 25:51ff; etc.), and his resurrection from the dead, which, strictly speaking, is an act of the Father. Other Jesus-related miracles are the several presented by Luke in the Acts of the Apostles: these include, besides the Pentecost event in Acts 2, the various displays of God's power and providence such as the healings, the marvellous releases of the apostles from prison, and the other manifestations of God's saving power working in and through the new Church. This type of Jesus-associated miracle applies, too, to the marvellous elements which add lustre to the Infancy Gospels of both Matthew and Luke (Mt 1f and Lk 1f).

The common element in all this is not that Jesus works miracles, but rather that God the Father shows himself primarily in and through Jesus—directly in Jesus' own ministry, and indirectly in the events which draw their significance from the fact that they are associated in some way Jesus or with his Church. The modern distinction between natural and supernatural events simply did not exist in the minds of the ancient peoples who are represented by the Bible. These ancient peoples did not have any difficulty, as people have today, in seeing that all events show divine power in one way or another. This, again, is why we simply cannot prune out the miraculaous and non-miraculous elements of the Gospel: ultimately, there is nothing in the Gospel which is not marvellous, which does not show God to faith.

Even the distinction betwen 'historical' and 'non-historical' does not fit here. The marvellous elements of the Jesus-event are too big to be confined within the limits of this kind of terminology. If 'history' refers essentially to what people did in time past, then, according to that definition, most of the marvellous elements of the Bible do not belong to such a category. Miracles are acts of God, not merely 'human events'; furthermore, miracles show that there is no closed order of space and time which is immune to God's presence and power. God can show himself when, where, to whom, and in whatever manner he chooses. The fact that he does is what makes things miracles!

The Tradition
Even as we hold that miracles are real and possible, we can still find clues in the Gospels which show us some features of the evangelists' literary styles and of their own individual ways of interpreting the miracle tradition.

1. Mark
Taking Mark's Gospel as the first of the four, as most commentators do nowadays, we cannot help noticing the vivid style with which he usually embellishes the dramatic character of his narrative. His very first miracle-story is the one in which Jesus expels the evil spirit from a man (Mk 1:23-8), and it is richer and more imaginative than anything in some neutrally-phrased news report. Mark

gives the 'shriek' and the words of the possessed man himself, the sharpness and the authority with which Jesus addresses the unclean spirit: 'Be quiet! Come out of the man!' (Mk 1:25)—and then the second 'shriek', as well as the enthused reaction of the crowd, who see it all as 'a completely new teaching in a spirit of authority' (Mk 1:27). In the next chapter Mark describes the paralysed man, the roof, the unspoken interior thoughts of the scribes, and the man picking up his mattress and walking home—all as vividly as in a movie. (Mk 2:1-12.)

In these miracle scenes Mark shows his originality and his narrative skill. He could have presented a dry catalogue of Jesus' works, but instead he re-presents the events with a clarity of detail which makes some commentators suggest that Mark is reproducing in a written form the eye-witness reminiscences he had received in Peter's preaching—things he had heard many times over as he accompanied Peter on his apostolic travels. This may or may not be the source of the narrative detail, but, whatever Mark's source, he presents the scenes impressively and marvellously.

Perhaps the best of Mark's miracle-stories are the group of four which he presents as a cluster in Mk 4:35-5:43. In the first scene—the calming of the storm—Mark adds the small details of the waves splashing into the boat (Mk 4:37), of Jesus asleep 'in the stern' of the boat and of his head resting 'on a cushion' (Mk 4:38), and of the wind dying down and 'everything grew calm' (Mk 4:39). These features of the evangelist's narrative strengthen the dramatic character of the scene, and highlight the marvellous and mystifying power of Jesus.

In the Gerasene incident which follows the storm at sea, Mark adds the rich detail of the possessed man who broke his chains (Mk 5:3f) and 'screamed and gashed himself with stones' (Mk 5:5), and of the dialogue between him and Jesus (Mk 5:7-10). There is a powerful simplicity in

Mark's picture of the man once he is cured, 'fully clothed and perfectly sane', now blessed with wholeness. The entire incident of the pigs, which accompanies the healing, may perhaps be a secondary embellishment of the narrative—it is not an essential part of the episode, certainly, and in fact it is one of the few works of Jesus which we can hardly call benign. Jesus' power over the evil spirits is a sign of the presence of the Kingdom of God, but his destruction of someone's source of livelihood is another matter entirely! This is not typical of the character of Jesus' works. However, if we recall that swine's flesh was unclean according to the Law of Moses (Lev 11) we may see this act as another illustration of Jesus' expulsion of evil power—as another sign of the presence of God's reign in him and in his ministry. By seeing the scene in this way we may perhaps come closer to understanding the intent of the evangelist who was interpreting the tradition with its original Jewish nuances.

We can also learn something from the two accounts of Jesus feeding the crowd (Mk 6:34-45; 8:1-9). Some commentators explain the two accounts by saying that they simply represent two feedings. But we should notice the similarity of detail in the whole sequence of scenes which accompanies the feeding: there is a water scene, a lake crossing, a confrontation with the Pharisees, a healing in foreign territory, and more. This suggests that the second sequence of scenes (Mk 8:1-26) is really a doublet of the first sequence (Mk 6:34-7:37), and that Mark decided to preserve both renderings as they came to him—perhaps in the form of two written fragments—either because he did not think there was any good reason for *not* preserving both, or because he preferred to preserve both fragments rather than to let one be lost for ever. Matthew follows Mark in both passages (Mt 14:13-21; 15:32-9), but Luke gives only one rendering of the loaves miracle in his Gospel (Lk 9:10-17). John also has only a single form of the tradition in the fourth Gospel (Jn 6), although he embellishes it with the scene of Jesus' walk on the water and his lengthy discourse on the Bread of Life (Jn 6:16-24; 25-58).

2. Matthew

This introduces us to the way in which the individual evangelists have interpreted the Jesus-tradition differently according to the manner in which it came to them through the ministry and witness of the apostles. Matthew's literary and theological technique can be seen from the way in which he clusters together ten miracle stories in chapters 8 and 9 of his Gospel. Taken together like this, the ten scenes are Matthew's way of showing the Kingdom of Heaven present in the *works* of Jesus: they correspond to the Kingdom of Heaven present in the words of Jesus which Matthew has just presented in the Sermon on the Mount in the immediately preceding chapters (Mt 5-7). Furthermore, we should be surprised to note that Matthew shows two possessed men cured across the lake (Mt 8:28) in the land of the Gadarenes, whereas Mark speaks of only one man cured in the land of the Gerasenes (Mk 5)! There can be no doubt that Matthew is presenting essentially the same tradition, because he shows it along with the storm at sea. Quite evidently, therefore, Matthew has reproduced the entire block of Mark's material, but in his own way. The little girl whom Jesus goes to help is already dead in Mt 9:18, whereas in the earlier rendering of the scene in Mk 5:23 she is only 'critically ill' until she dies in Mk 5:35-43.

Not only that, but Matthew has reproduced Jesus' act of healing the blind man of Jericho (Mk 10:46-52) by showing *two* blind men in the same incident (Mt 20:29-34), and by giving the whole scene a second (or first) occurrence in the miracle-cluster in Mt 9:27-31! In short, where Mark has Jesus healing one blind man, Matthew has intensified the marvellous element by quadrupling the healing! Once again, there can be no doubt that he is presenting essentially the same tradition, because of the similarity of the dialogues, in which Jesus is called 'Son of David' on each occasion (and only here, except for one other unrelated instance in Mt 15:22). What is more, Matthew also doubles his presentation of the possessed mute (Mt 9:32-4; 12:22f). These, too, are both accounts of a single incident, as we can see from the dialogue about 'Beelzebub, the prince of demons' which occurs in each account (Mt 9:34; 12:24), and from the fact that in both renderings of the tradition the Pharisees make the same objection. The variations between the two scenes, which are understandable in terms of oral tradition and narrative style, are not greater than the similarities, so that the 'singleness' of the incident of Mark's original presentation in Mk 3:20-30 is undeniable.

Along with his tendency to intensify the marvellous element, Matthew also simplifies narrative and dramatic details. He condenses the incident of the demoniacs to seven verses (Mt 8:28-34) where Mark had presented the scene much more vividly in twenty verses (Mk 5:1-20). The double account of the miracle-within-a-miracle—the dead girl and the woman with a haemorrhage—is reduced to nine verses in Mt 9:18-26, in contrast to Mark's richer rendering of the tradition in the twenty-three verses of Mk 5:21-43.

Matthew also adds some marvellous elements which are not found in Mark at all, such as Peter's walking on the water (Mt 14:28ff), which Matthew adds to Mark's rendering of the walking-on-water tradition (Mk 6:45ff). Similarly, only Matthew has the puzzling incident of Peter and the coin in the fish's mouth (Mt 17:24-7). This scene does not appear typical of Jesus' Gospel of the Kingdom of Heaven, and some commentators suggest that it may represent an interest of Peter's followers, who wanted to emphasize his closeness to Jesus, and also Jesus' own respect for the Temple. If this is so—and it cannot be known for certain—it shows that the incident is a later expansion of the original miracle tradition.

3. Luke

Luke also interprets the miraculous aspect of the Jesus-tradition in his own way. The Infancy Gospel is the obvious area in which we can compare Matthew and Luke, but not Mark or John. Luke's miraculous scenes in this section of his Gospel include the marvellous conceptions and births of both John the Baptist and Jesus. Elsewhere in his Gospel Luke presents the wondrous catch of fish at the beginning of Jesus' public ministry (Lk 5:1-11). Luke is the only one of the synoptic evangelists to show this, although there are some affinities between this Lukan passage and the passage in Jn 21 (which, incidentally, occurs after Jesus' resurrection, and emphasizes the Beloved Disciple, whereas Luke's scene puts greater emphasis on Peter). Luke presents Jesus' healing of the centurion's servant (Lk 7:1-10) which Matthew also has (Mt 8:5-18), but adds dialogue which shows his obvious favour for the Roman—and this touch typifies the gentile orientation of Luke's whole theological message, as we shall see more clearly later.

In many ways Luke remains close to Mark, whose Gospel he is evidently using as a source for his own work. But he adds some miracle stories which are in none of the other Gospels, such as those of the cure at Naim (Lk 7:11-17), the healing of the stooped woman (Lk 13:10-17), and the cleansing of the ten lepers (Lk 17:11-19). These passages underline Luke's interest in showing that God's favour comes, through Jesus, to women and outcasts. Another feature of Luke's style is his omission of the scene in which Jesus causes the fig-tree to wither and die. Mark has this in Mk 11:12-25, and

Matthew copies it from Mark—but Luke does not have it at all, perhaps because he found it too offensive and violent. Such an explanation would be very much in keeping with the generally sensitive style of Luke's whole theological presentation.

4. Acts

We have already briefly considered the miracle scenes in the Acts of the Apostles, including the Pentecost event in Acts 2. Luke, it seems, has included in this second volume of his work a number of miracle stories which show the Gospel of the Kingdom of God becoming intertwined with that of the paschal mystery—of it continuing in the new Church, after Jesus had completed his earthly mission and returned to the Father's heavenly presence. Indeed, in addition to the healings which he presents, Luke gives us the apparently vindictive incident of the deaths of Ananias and his wife Sapphira (Acts 5:1-11). Even though this scene is not typical of the benign character of the Gospel tradition in general, or of Luke's theological approach in particular, it is in essence an illustration of the irresistible might of the Holy Spirit, who overcomes the evil power of falsehood and surpasses the deceptive power of human sinfulness. When we see the scene in this theological way, and in the light of the theological nature of the whole pattern of Luke-Acts, we can conclude that Luke is consistent here with his basic purpose.

Perhaps the principal marvel that Luke presents in Acts is the one that is least recognized. This is the fact that, by Luke's day, the Church had spread so far, and so fast, in spite of so many obstacles from within and without. It seems that this is a fact which had impressed Luke profoundly, and he tried to explain it to his friend Theophilus (Lk 1:1; Acts 1:1). And this shows that Luke, like the other evangelists, had worked to adapt the Gospel tradition which had come to him from the early apostolic

6. John

Most commentators agree that the fourth Gospel is so different from the synoptic Gospels that we should study its special vocabulary and style separately. However, here we can at least note briefly that the fourth Gospel has its own form of the miracle tradition, but that it prefers the term 'sign' to the term 'miracle'. There are seven of these 'signs', and all of them are in the first part of the document, which we can call the 'Book of Signs' (Jn 2:1-12). These are: the two Cana miracles (the wedding miracle and the healing of the royal official's son); the sabbath healing, the loaves miracle, and the walking on water; and then the healing of the blind man and, finally, the raising of Lazarus. Of course, when we say that there are these seven signs, we are not meaning to minimize the one great sign of the resurrection of Jesus—but that comes at the end of the document, along with the several epiphanies of the risen Lord and the marvellous catch of fishes, and these are in a class by themselves and illustrate the more numinous character of the entire Johannine message over against that of the Synoptics. Because of this special flavour characterizing the Johannine Gospel there are symbolic overtones to these signs which are not so evident in the synoptic miracle scenes. Even so, however, they are all life-giving, and they all call for faith in the person of Jesus and in the divine life which he has come from the Father to offer to men.

Summary and Conclusion

In summary we should be able to conclude that the miracle—or marvellous—element is inherent in the very nature of the Gospel. We cannot sort out and separate the marvellous and non-marvellous elements; every word of the Gospel is just that—Gospel. It is the amazing and awesome good news. God shows himself to us this way in Jesus, and invites us to respond to him in faith and in our life-style.

There are details of the miracle stories which we are simply not able to reconstruct on the level of historical precision, because the evangelists did not intend to speak on that level. But the level that counts is the level of faith, which sees God presenting himself in Jesus, in the Church, and in other persons and events as they derive their significance from being associated with Jesus in some way.

It represents one extreme to reject the historical credibility of the whole miracle tradition; it represents the other extreme to maintain a purely defensive or apologetic stance over the real historical character of every detail in that tradition. The important point is not to try and maintain that this or that is, or is not, a matter of historical fact from the distant past of New Testament times; the important point is to believe that this is *Gospel* for us in the present, as we see and hear the evangelists interpreting the witness of the apostles about God's message given in Jesus. The very fact that God should undertake to do such a thing, for us, is already marvellous!

1. What is the essence of a marvel (or miracle) in the Bible?
2. Do marvels necessarily involve a suspension of the laws of nature?
3. If the evangelists are not intent on recording details historically, what is it that they are trying to emphasize when they describe miracle scenes?
4. Can we separate 'miracles' from the rest of the Gospel tradition?
5. Can you give two examples of how each synoptic evangelist interprets the marvellous element in the Gospel?

Chapter IV

6. How should we answer an objector who says that the Gospels are not true?

Chapter V

The Words of Jesus

With many such parables he spoke the word to them, as they were able to hear it, and he did not speak to them without a parable. *(Mark :33f.)*

Read the following passages, with an eye to the form and style of expression. Notice any inconsistencies or additions, and make a written note of them for future study:
  Mt 5-7: Jesus' 'Sermon on the Mount';
  Mk 4:1-34 and Mt 13:1-52: some parables of Jesus (notice especially Mk 4:43f and Mt 13:34f);
  Mt 10:5-42: notice especially the change of tone beginning at 10:16;
  Mk 13; Mt24f; and Lk 21:3-35: Jesus' last instruction to his disciples;
  Lk 10:25-35; 15:1-16, 31: some uniquely Lukan parables.

Both Mark (Mk 4:33) and Matthew (Mt 13:34) state in their Gospels that Jesus spoke 'in parables, and without parables he did not speak to them.' We may wonder whether we should interpret this literally, or whether, like so many other things in the Bible and indeed in the ancient world in general, this is a hyperbole which we should take with a pinch of salt. The matter becomes more problematic if we think of a parable as a story, or as 'an earthly story with a heavenly meaning', because it is obvious that not everything Jesus said was a story.

In any case, it is remarkable to see just how wide is the

Chapter V

variety of Jesus' sayings that we have in the Gospels—
and we cannot help noticing that many of his sayings are,
as we have just seen, not stories. There is the Sermon on
the Mount, which is three chapters and 111 verses long
(Mt 5-7), with a counterpart only twenty-nine verses long
in Luke's Gospel (Lk 6:20-49)—and in Luke it is not a
sermon on a mountain at all, but simply a 'great sermon'!
There is the cluster of four parables which Mark preserves
in the fourth chapter of his Gospel, and which Matthew
has expanded to a cluster of seven in his section on the
parables of the Kingdom (Mt 13). Again, there are the
beatitudes—not only the familiar ones from the Sermon
on the Mount (eight in Mt 5 and four in Lk 6), but also
several others, such as 'Blessed is he who is not scandalized in me' (Mt 11:6) and 'Blessed are those who hear the
word of God and keep it' (Lk 11:28). Along with these
beatitudes there are the 'woes' or rebukes which Jesus
utters in the Great Sermon of Luke 6:24ff, and his seven
'woes' against the Pharisees in Mt 23 (also in Lk 13:37-
54). Mark gives a collection of Jesus' words of rebuke
against the Pharisees in chapter 7 of his Gospel, but these
are not in the form of 'woes'. There are, too, the so-called
'pronouncement stories', which have a saying of Jesus as
their punch-line: for example, the scene of the coin of
tribute which culminates in Jesus saying, 'Give to Caesar
the things that are Caesar's, and to God the things that
are God's' (Mk 12:13-17). A second example of a 'pronouncement story' is the scene in Mt 8:18ff, in which Jesus
replies to the prospective disciple: 'The foxes have lairs,
and the birds of the air have nests, but the Son of Man
has nowhere to lay his head.'

Each of the three synoptic evangelists concludes his
picture of Jesus' public ministry with the lengthy scene of
the eschatological discourse, or the last instruction which
Jesus gives to his disciples in Jerusalem. Jesus here
encourages them to persevere in the face of the trials

which will come to them after his departure. The fourth Gospel, of course, as we have already seen, is in a class by itself—and for several reasons. As far as the words of Jesus are concerned, the fourth evangelist specializes in lengthy discourses—so much so that he usually accompanies the 'sign' scenes of chapters 2-12 with lengthy discourses. These several discourse passages in most cases start out with the character of a dialogue between Jesus and his interlocutors, but soon—imperceptibly—the interlocutors recede, and the dialogue becomes a monologue of Jesus. This is the case with the scenes of Nicodemus (Jn 3), of the woman at the well (Jn 4), of the Bread of Life discourse (Jn 6), and of others. The final one of these Johannine discourse sections is the Last Supper discourse, which continues for almost five chapters (Jn 13-17). However, when we analyse it closely, we can see that this results from the work of the evangelist himself, and perhaps too of an editor following him, adding sayings of Jesus to the original form of the discourse and so making it as long as it now is.

There are also some individual sayings of Jesus, like the ones in Mk 2:18-22 about nobody fasting while the bridegroom is present, sewing a new patch on an old cloak, or pouring new wine into old skins. All these appear to be quite universal sayings, however: they are the kind of sayings which Jesus could have repeated from the ordinary folk wisdom of the ancient world. We could say the same of the parable of the sower, or of the parable of the lamp hidden under a basket (Mk 4).

Another category of saying of Jesus is what is known as the 'floating word', such as the one in Mk 4:9: 'Let him who has ears to hear me, hear!' Mark has this same saying a second time in the same chapter (Mk 4:23). Matthew, who follows Mark, preserves the sense of the saying, but varies the form a little to become: 'Let everyone heed what he hears!' (Mt 13:9; and again a second time in the

Chapter V

same chapter, Mt 13:43). Moreover, Matthew has already given this same saying of Jesus in Mt 11:15, in a different context. Luke has the same saying, in substance, in Lk 14:35, in a context that is again different from that of either Mark or Matthew. Besides, substantially the same saying is present yet again in the Book of Revelation, and seven times at that (Rev 2:7, 11, 29; 3:6, 13, 22; 13:9). The saying of Jesus about many being called and few chosen (Mt 22:14) also seems to be a 'floating word', since it has no necessary relation to its context. Another example of this kind of saying of Jesus is the one that occurs in both Lk 14:11 and Lk 18:14, about the exalted being humbled and the humble exalted.

Lastly, we have another puzzling kind of saying which St Paul attributes to Jesus in Acts 20:35: 'It is better to give than to receive'. The odd thing here is that this saying of Jesus does not occur in the Gospels or anywhere else in the New Testament!

Synonyms

This all suggests that there are not only many sayings of Jesus in the Gospel, but also many kinds or forms of his sayings. However, the Greek text of the Gospels is quite consistent in using the word *parabole* to describe Jesus' sayings. Besides, as we have already seen, Mark and Matthew say that Jesus spoke 'only in parables'.

But it is surprising to see how the translators of our various contemporary versions of the New Testament translate this Greek word. They use a wide variety of equivalents, in addition to often rendering it simple as 'parable'. In Lk 4:23 Jesus refers to 'the *proverb*, "Physician, heal yourself"'. This is the rendering of *parabole* which we find in the *Good News Bible* and in the *New American Bible*, although the *Jerusalem Bible* has 'the *saying*'. Mk 7:17 speaks of the 'proverb' which Jesus has just spoken concerning the things that go into and come out of a man (this is the NAB rendering, though in this case the GNB has 'saying'). The same word comes across in Lk 5:36, in the context of a new patch on an old coat, as 'figure' in the NAB and as 'parable' in the GNB. Mt 13:33 says: 'He offered them still another *image*', i.e, that of the yeast puffing up the dough, whereas the *New International Version* says 'still another *parable*'. Luke also renders *images* when he gives Jesus' words about the blind leading the blind (Lk 6:39, NAB), although here the GNB gives 'parable'. Mt 24:33, following Mk 13:28, has Jesus saying: 'Learn a *lesson* from the fig tree' (NAB and GNB), whereas Lk 21:29 has 'parable' in the corresponding section of his Gospel. Mk 3:23 speaks of 'examples', and in Mk 4:30 Jesus asks: 'What *comparison* shall we use for the reign of God?' We may also recall the older version which said that Jesus spoke in 'similitudes', though this word has gone out of use in ordinary spoken English. Heb 9:9 and 11:19, by the way, have *parabole* in the Greek text, which is translated as 'symbol' in the NAB and as 'figuratively speaking' in the JB.

In short, the evangelists use one Greek word (*parabole*) to cover just about every saying of Jesus, whether it is a story, proverb, figure, image, lesson, example, comparison, symbol, or similitude. From this we should conclude that we must see a parable as more than merely a story with a lesson, since, though some parables of Jesus are in the form of a story, many are not.

In the Old Testament

We can derive some help for understanding this situation from the Old Testament, which uses the Hebrew word *mashal* in several ways. The Book of Proverbs has this word in its title in the Hebrew text. The Hebrew text of Ps 78:2 says 'I will open my mouth in a *mashal*', where the Greek text uses the word *parabole*. The NAB and JB render this as 'parable', but the GNB translates 'I am going to use *wise sayings*'. The lengthy dialogue (twenty-five chapters) which Job conducts with his three friends is a *mashal* in the Hebrew text (Job 27:1; 29:1). The prophet Ezekiel takes abuse from his fellow Israelites because he speaks 'riddles', 'parables', and 'allegories', all of which are *mashal* in the Hebrew text (17:2; 21:5; 24:3).

From this rather flexible use of the word *mashal* in the Hebrew text of the Old Testament it would seem that the essence of the term has to do with an important or weighty saying, whatever form that saying might take. This is really what Jesus' sayings are, too—they are examples of *mashal* because they always make an important point. But the closest Greek equivalent that the evangelists could find was *parabole*, which really has a somewhat different meaning, since—strictly speaking—it indicates a comparison or likeness. When we notice the variety of words which the modern Enlish translators use to render the Greek *parabole*, we should be able to see that they are trying to show that the words of Jesus take many forms—but that they are, in one way or another, weighty, important, and memorable.

As far as the form of Jesus' words is concerned, he uses word-pictures which speak the graphic language of the imagination (this is the whole point of *images*). This was the typical manner of speaking in the ancient Orient—and in much of the Orient it is still typical today. Semites are not 'logical' as westerners are: they think and speak, not so much in abstract concepts, but in the concrete terms of what is familiar and recognizable. It is for this reason that Jesus spoke of coats, fish, seeds, weddings, kings, and servants: then, when he had won his hearers' attention to the word-pictures, he was able to raise their attention to the heavenly things that he wanted to illustrate by his parables (or comparisons). And so his word-pictures *are* 'parables': each of them makes a point which is, somehow, comparable to his Gospel of the Kingdom of God.

From the Old Testament references which we have looked at we can see that Jesus did not invent this way of speaking. Parabolic speech was—and to some extent still is—the ordinary style of language in the Orient, for people there speak in images and in the 'concrete'. Then, from these everyday images, they draw the comparisons, approximations, and—sometimes—contrasts which they want to put across. God is a shepherd, a king, a fortress, and a rock; Israel is a flock, the sheep of his pasture; God and Israel relate to each other on the basis of a covenant; God speaks his word, forms man out of clay, and walks in the cool of the evening.

When we put together the language of images and comparisons, which is the essence of the parable, with the manner of using weighty *mashal* sayings to make an important point or to teach, we have the style of the ancient Orient in general and of Israel and the Old Testament in particular—weighty sayings in the form of word-pictures. Jesus naturally used this style traditional to his people, but he used it to present is own message—the Gospel of the Kingdom of God. Even to mention the Kingdom or Reign of God is already a parable—the description of something divine in terms that people can recognize from their own earthly experience of monarchy. But God's reign is not a matter of geography or politics as it would be in any human kingdom: it is a moral relationship between God and his people which goes beyond the national and temporal interests of the Israelites and extends to all humanity.

Jesus could, perhaps, have spoken of the rule of God over his people in abstract, conceptual terms. But if he had, we would be much the poorer, lacking the richness of his images. His word-pictures tantalize and attract: there is always something puzzling and unusual about them—a surprise ending, or a reversal of expected situations—which makes the hearer remember the picture in his imagination, and ponder it, to draw out the lesson gradually for himself.

The Message

The message that comes through in these word-pictures of Jesus is, in one way or another, his Gospel of the Kingdom of God. But no picture ever shows the whole reality, and each saying of Jesus illustrates only one aspect or fact of God's rule. It is only by putting them all together, in context, that we can come to a more or less complete and unified understanding of Jesus' message.

The principal theme, which is that of the *lordship of God*, comes across in the sayings which the evangelists have clustered together in Mk 4 and Mt 13. The theme of *discipleship* comes across in the sayings about hidden treasure (Mt 13:44ff), the unmerciful servant (Mt 18), and the good Samaritan (Lk 10:30-37). *The coming judgement of God* dominates in the cluster in Mt 24f about the faithful and the drunken servants, the ten maidens, the silver pieces (or talents), and the sheep and the goats. The theme of *God's mercy for sinners* can be seen in the short saying in Mk 2:17: 'People who are healthy do not need a doctor; sick people do. I have come to call sinners, not the self-righteous.' The word-picture of the vineyard workers who receive equal pay for unequal work (Mt 20:1-16) is not about social injustice, but about the *generous Lord* who gives his subjects more than they deserve or expect. Luke is especially fond of speaking about *God's compassion towards sinners*, and he collects together the sayings of Jesus about the lost son, the lost sheep, and the lost coin (Lk 15). All these make the same point, namely, that God shows his compassion by forgiving and accepting those who are separated from him by their sinfulness.

The Evangelists Interpret Jesus' Words

In different ways each of the synoptic evangelists has worked to group together the sayings of Jesus in order to present them in some kind of organized manner. Matthew presents Jesus preaching the Sermon on the Mount (Mt 5-7) to his disciples; Luke shows Jesus speaking some of the same words (Lk 6:20-49) partly to his disciples and partly to those who were oppressing his disciples! Mk 4 shows that Mark has preserved both Jesus' parable (or saying) about the sower and the explanation of it, which probably derives from the primitive apostolic Church. Matthew expands on Mark's presentation, adding the text of Is 6 (Mt 13:14f); he then adds more words of Jesus about eyes seeing and ears hearing (Mt 13:16f) which are suggested by the use of those image-words in the Isaian text. Matthew also contributes the parable of the wheat and the weeds (Mt 13:24-30), together with the allegorical interpretation of it which also probably comes from the early Church rather than from Jesus himself.

We can compare the royal wedding banquet of Mt 22 with the great supper scene of Lk 14. Both seem to be essentially the same parable. But Matthew has added the king's anger and his act of burning 'their city' (Mt 22:7), and also the wedding-garment scene which is extraneous to the original parable and does not occur at all in the Lukan passage (Mt 22:11ff). In addition to this, Matthew has also added the 'floating word' of Jesus about many being called and few chosen (Mt 22:14).

These elements provide us with clues to the literary techniques of the synoptic evangelists, who have interpreted the apostolic tradition about Jesus as it came to them in the Church and adapted it to make particular points for their contemporaries. Mark has gathered four parables or sayings of Jesus in chapter 4 of his Gospel; Matthew has taken this cluster and expanded it to a group of seven images in Mt 13, whereas Lk 8 has only two of Mark's original four parables (those of the sower and the lamp). However, Luke has a group of his own in Lk 15 (the lost son, the lost coin, and the lost sheep), since these three familiar images occur only in his Gospel.

The Eschatological Discourse, or Last Instruction, is another example of the evangelists' attempts to interpret the words of Jesus. Mark was first, with his rendering of the discourse in thirty-seven verses (Mk 13). Matthew reproduces the Markan passage almost identically (Mt 24), but then adds a group of sayings or parables which are related to the instruction through the theme of being alert and ready to face the judgement of the master when he returns to demand an accounting (the ten maidens, the silver pieces or talents, and the sheep and the goats [all Mt 25]). The result is that Matthew's rendering of the discourse is ninety-seven verses long against Mark's thirty-seven verses. Luke also adapts the Markan discourse, in his case by adding the details about the coming siege of Jerusalem (Lk 21:20) and the practical warning to the disciples against 'drunkenness and worldly cares' (Lk 21:34).

John

There are also some special features which characterize the words of Jesus as they are presented in the fourth Gospel. We have already referred to the arrangement of dialogue and monologue. In addition to this there is the special connection of the discourses to the signs: the words of Jesus in the lengthy discourse sections explain the actions which he has just performed, such as the Bread of Life discourse following the loaves sign (Jn 6), or the emphasis on light and seeing after Jesus has healed the blind man (Jn 9). Again, there is the rich profusion of peculiarly Johannine 'parables' or 'figures' which describe Jesus as *word*; *water*; *bread of life*; *light*; *gate of the sheepfold*; *shepherd*; *lamb*; *vine* (with *branches*); *king*;

etc. Even though these images are obvious and familiar, all of them are the special and unique contribution of the fourth evangelist—but, it should be noticed, they do not all appear as words spoken by Jesus, sometimes occurring as having been used by another person to refer to Jesus.

Conclusion

We may conclude by noting, as we did before we came to the words of Jesus, that each of the evangelists tries to interpret Jesus' sayings as they have come to him in the early apostolic Church's living tradition. By grouping, arranging, and rearranging these sayings, the evangelists have here and there varied the picture, in order to present to their circle the person of Jesus and his message of God's Rule. The link that joins the written Gospels with the spoken words of Jesus is, of course, the experience and witness of the apostles: these men were the privileged companions who were allowed to learn the mysteries of the Kingdom from the Word made flesh. It was they who passed on the words of their teacher as they remembered them. Eventually these remembered words came to the evangelists, who incorporated them into their Gospels as we now have them.

1. How is parabolic speech characteristic of the ancient Orient?
2. Why do the evangelists preserve the parable form of Jesus' words?
3. How should we understand the expression of the evangelists in Mk 4:43f and Mt 13:34f?
4. How does Matthew re-arrange the words of Jesus which he has taken from Mark's Gospel?
5. What are the aspects of the Kingdom of God which show up in the words of Jesus?
6. Why and how did the evangelists include in their Gospels the Last Instruction of Jesus to his disciples?

Chapter VI

Mark's Gospel: an Overview

Then Jesus began to teach his disciples: 'The Son of Man must suffer much and be rejected by the elders, the chief priests, and the teachers of the Law. He will be put to death, but three days later he will rise to life.' *(Mk 8:31.)*

Allow yourself about an hour to an hour and a half. During this time read Mark's Gospel through at one sitting. Do not stop to puzzle out the problem passages which may catch your attention; instead, note them down in writing for later study. Try to get a feel for the document as a whole. Think for a day or so about what you have discovered in Mark, and only then go on to read this chapter.

Most of us become familiar with the Gospels from hearing sections of them read aloud in the liturgy, especially at Sunday Mass. However, such a process is necessarily fragmentary, for we hear only a few verses at a time; moreover, we seldom notice how the individual passage which we hear read aloud fits into the pattern of the Gospel as a whole. This situation is still further complicated by the fact that we are accustomed to thinking of the 'life of Jesus' as a kind of composite, drawn from what may or may not be in all four of the Gospels. As a result we do not become familiar with the special pattern of each Gospel, or with the distinctive message displayed by each evangelist in the way he composed his document to show the power of the Gospel to his circle of friends in the early Church.

Nowadays we are moving away from an oversimplified view of the Gospel—and of the whole Bible, for that matter—as a mere history book. As a consequence we are finding it increasingly necessary to look for the theological patterns and literary features of each Gospel. Moreover, we have to work to figure out how these documents speak to us in our own day, challenging us and calling us to build our life-style as a response to the Gospel message. In recent years a major help has come in the shape of the new Lectionary, which concentrates on just one of the synoptic Gospels for each year of the three-year liturgical cycle. (The fourth Gospel gets special attention every year during the Easter season.) This means that we can make a systematic effort to study one of the synoptic Gospels each year. If we do this with the help of reliable study-aids, we should gradually come to see each of these Gospels as a whole, and then we should be able to discern more and more clearly the special 'stamp' which each of these evangelists puts on his document.

Mark's Gospel as a Whole

As we have just found out, to read Mark's Gospel 'once over lightly', from beginning to end, without stopping to analyse details, doesn't take more than an hour or an hour and a half, since it covers only about twenty-five pages in most Bibles (sixteen chapters). As we do this, we may well get the impression of a biography of Jesus, in the form of a moving-picture narrative. The whole thing speaks the language of faith, and of the marvellous presence of God in Jesus. By the same token, of course, it presumes that whoever reads it will read it with the same attitude of faith.

There are varying opinions about exactly where the main sections of Mark's Gospel are, but, whichever

Chapter VI

version of the Bible we read, most of them explain the structure of the document in biographical or geographical terms. There is, first of all, the cluster of three scenes which Mark has put together to form the 'introductory triptych': the preaching mission of John the Baptist, Jesus' baptism by John in the Jordan river, and his trial in the desert (Mk 1:1-13). Then there is the public ministry of Jesus in Galilee and in its environs (Mk 1:14-9:50). In this section Jesus gathers his new disciples around himself, and preaches the Gospel of the Kingdom of God, first in his native neighbourhood of Galilee (Mk 1:14-7:23), and then in the gentile areas which are adjacent to Galilee (Mk 7:24-9:50). Mark makes a definite shift of the geographical setting in chapter 10, which describes Jesus' journey to Jerusalem (Mk 10:1-52). The rest of Mark's Gospel is set in Jerusalem. First of all (Mk 11-13) there is Jesus' Jerusalem ministry, ending with his final address to his disciples (the 'eschatological discourse', or last instruction); then comes the 'paschal mystery' section, in which Mark gives his rendering of the tradition of Jesus' passion, death, and vindication (Mk 14-16).

The last chapter of Mark is problematic, because we are not sure exactly where it ends. Most Bibles show Mk 16:1-8 set apart from the rest of the chapter as authentically the work of Mark the evangelist. But the ancient manuscripts which are translated in our contemporary versions do not all agree on the last verses of Mark: many have Mk 16:9-20 (which is usually called the 'longer ending'), but others have different endings. The NAB gives three different endings for Mark; other versions give the 'longer ending' (16:9-20) in the body of the text and then supply one or more of the alternative endings in italics (the RSV does this), or set apart by itself (as in the NEB), or in a footnote (as in the GNB). In any case, in Mk 16:1-8 the evangelist does not show the risen Lord, but rather tells of the experience of the women who visit the tomb on the first Easter morning and learn from the 'young man in a white robe' that Jesus has been raised up.

This rapid overview of Mark's Gospel can help us in a negative way, by making us aware of how many things Mark has *not* presented in it. There are no scenes of the birth and infancy of Jesus; no Sermon on the Mount; no *Our Father*; no prodigal son parable; and no crucified thieves. There is also no appearance of the risen Lord (except in the alternative endings which, as we have just seen, are not really part of the original document at the evangelist composed it). But if we are to come close enough to the Gospel to get a feeling for its internal dynamic and its theological essence, then we must look for its positive 'special features': this approach will show us how Mark's Gospel differs from the other Gospels, and also how Mark himself interprets the apostolic teaching that has come to him—how he has 'tailored' it, so to speak, as a message to his friends and circle.

Main Features

As for the positive features of Mark's Gospel, we cannot help but notice at the start its brevity. As we have already seen, it is only some twenty-five pages long. It has only fifteen complete chapters, plus the problematic sixteenth (however many verses this last may have). We have also noted that Mark's opening scenes show Jesus as already adult, coming to John the Baptist to receive the symbolic washing (Mk 1:9). Mark is interested, therefore, in depicting the public ministry of Jesus, as well as his passion and death, and the women's Easter-morning experience of the 'empty tomb'. This is all very concrete and 'down to earth'. There is nothing in Mark's opening scenes about Jesus' ancestors or origins. And at the end, in the last chapter, Mark does not show the risen Lord. Some

Chapter VI

commentators, it is true, and some Bibles in their footnotes, maintain that Mark did originally conclude his document with a presentation of the risen Lord to his disciples—but this can only be conjecture. As it stands now, Mark's own verses at the end—before the 'alternative endings' were added by later editors to provide a smoother termination—do not depict the person of Jesus as risen from the dead, though they do present the 'risen Lord' tradition.

The whole Markan style puts more emphasis on narrative than on discourse. There are only a few sections in which Mark presents anything like a speech or discourse of Jesus. These are the parables in chapter 4, Jesus' rebuke of the Pharisees in chapter 7, and his last instruction to the disciples in chapter 13. The rest of the document is characterized by a fast-moving narrative style. Mark uses a technique of 'clusters' to join together a number of similar elements. For instance, he 'clusters' five conflict stories in Mk 2:1-3:6. He also forms a 'cluster' of four parables of Jesus in Mk 4:1-34, following it with another 'cluster' of four miracle stories in Mk 4:35-5:43. Jesus' words of rebuke to the Pharisees in Mk 7:1-23 are another example of the evangelist's use of this technique. And if we look carefully at Mk 8:34-10:52 we see that Mark has here brought together Jesus' words on the ethical demands of the Kingdom of God; instead of scattering Jesus' ethical teachings throughout the Gospel, Mark has collected them in this one section as Jesus' private instruction to his disciples. There is another 'cluster' of conflict stories in the 'Jerusalem ministry' section (Mk 11:27-12:34); and the 'eschatological discourse' (Mk 13) is really another 'cluster', in which Mark gives Jesus' sayings to his disciples on the coming trials and the end of the age.

Another clue to Mark's style comes from his use of 'sandwiches'. In Mk 3:20-35 the evangelist presents two incidents about Jesus' relationships with his family, with another scene—about 'Beelzebub'—in between them. The miracle story of the daughter of Jairus in Mk 5 is in two scenes, between which Mark has placed another miracle story (that of the woman with the blood)—again like a 'sandwich'. We see the same thing happening when Mark gives the fig-tree incident in two passages (Mk 11:12ff and 11:20:25) but breaks the continuity of his narrative by inserting between them the scene of Jesus cleansing the Temple (Mk 11:15-19).

Mark also appears to be interested in offering his readers translations of the Aramaic words and phrases which he quotes on Jesus' lips. In Mk 5:41 *Talitha cumi* means, as the evangelist explains, 'Little girl, I tell you to get up!' (GNB translation). In Mk 7:11 he explains that *Corban* means 'given to God', and in Mk 7:24 that Jesus' word *Ephphatha* spoken to the deaf man in the territory of the Ten Towns means 'Be opened' (JB). *Abba* in Jesus' agony prayer is 'Father' (Mk 14:36), and *Eloi, Eloi, lama sabachthani* means 'My God, my God, why have you forsaken me?' (Mk 15:34; NAB).

Along with this deliberate and consistent effort to make his message intelligible for those whom he apparently does not expect to be familiar with Jesus' native language, Mark also takes pains to explain Jewish customs. In case his readers may not know who the Pharisees are or what they do, the evangelist interprets their customs in Mk 7:34. He explains the monetary value of the widow's mite (Mk 12:42); the nature of the Feast of Unleavened Bread (Mk 14:12); and the necessity of buring the body of Jesus on the 'Preparation Day' before the onset of the Sabbath (Mk 15:42).

All these features of Mark's Gospel may have escaped our notice the first time through, but, as we become increasingly sensitive to such details, we begin to see that there is a deliberate plan—and a specific message—in

Chapter VI

Mark's document. As yet we may not be quite ready to figure it out, but at least we can be sure that this document is too carefully composed to be a mere 'historical' chronicle. It is a special theological message—the *Gospel, about* Jesus and *from* Jesus—presented now for the first time in history, in a new literary form. Mark's document is 'narrative theology'.

The Earlier Gospels

When we piece the clues together, we may venture the conclusion that Mark composed his Gospel in about 65AD. This means that the primitive apostolic Church's oral tradition about Jesus had already been in circulation for about a generation.

As we have seen, we find the oral gospel *about* Jesus in the kerygmatic discourses which St Luke presents in the words of the apostolic preachers in Acts, and also in the letters which St Paul addresses to his new Christian converts. We have already had a brief look at these texts of the New Testament, and the point was made that their message is primarily the Church's Gospel *about* Jesus, i.e, the Gospel of the paschal mystery of his passion, death, and vindication. This early level of the apostolic tradition says very little about Jesus' earthly life before the days of the first Holy Week. True, St Paul writes in Gal 4:4 that Jesus was 'born of a woman, born under the Law', but all that this means is that Jesus was human and that he was Jewish. Elsewhere (Rom 1:3; 2 Tim 2:8) he calls Jesus a descendant of David, but it is difficult to tell whether Paul means this historically or metaphorically. Even if we take it historically, it does not say much about Jesus' earthly life.

In Acts 10:37ff Peter expands on the paschal mystery Gospel and adds a short summary of Jesus' public ministry:

Jesus of Nazareth, beginning with the baptism which

John preached... God anointed him with the Holy Spirit and with power, and he went about doing good works and healing all who were in the grip of the devil, and God was with him.

But even this description of Jesus' earthly activity before Holy Week is brief, general, and strictly theological: it says everything about Jesus' public ministry in terms of its religious essence, but virtually nothing about it in terms of what we would today call 'historical detail'.

This leads us to a remarkable conclusion. There must have been a great number of Christians who lived outside Palestine—both gentiles and Jews—who were converted to the Church through hearing of the Gospel *about* Jesus' paschal mystery, but who lived and died without knowing in any appreciable detail what we would recognize as a 'biography' of Jesus! Before Mark wrote his Gospel there was no systematic written description of the earthly Jesus—of his origin, birth, and infancy, even of his teachings or his works of power. St Paul says nothing about these things in his letters. Such early converts must have heard innumerable times the message of Jesus' passion, death, and glorification—but even that was presumably given to them orally rather than written and read out to them. For that matter, to the best of our knowledge even Paul was not present in Jerusalem in the first Holy Week, so what he does say about Jesus' passion and glorification is not from his own visual experience: it has come to him, rather, in the oral form of the apostolic tradition. Paul himself acknowledges this in 1 Cor 15:3ff.

This should help us to appreciate Mark's creative originality, and the importance of his contribution to the evolving collection of documents which now make up the New Testament. He deserves more credit than he usually receives for being the first to 'invent' a gospel as a brand-new literary form. Thanks to him and his literary technique the Church possessed, for the first time, a word-picture of the earthly Jesus and of his public ministry before the days of the great Holy Week. Indeed, this seems to be the meaning of the phrase which we find as the opening verse of his Gospel: 'The beginning of the good news about Jesus Christ Son of God' (Mk 1:1). Does Mark mean that this is where we start the document, i.e, that this is the first verse of the first chapter ('the beginning') of the written Gospel? Or does he mean, rather, that this is the background which led up to the Church's message (good news) about Jesus, who is the Messiah (the Christ)?

This latter interpretation seems to do better justice to the evangelist's intention, because it means that 'good news' in this verse does not refer to Mark's own document or to Jesus' preaching, but rather to the Church's witness—to the message which the apostles and their Christian friends proclaim. The 'beginning' is not merely this first verse of the first chapter, but the whole series of events which led up to Jesus' Passover, even though nobody knew how they fitted together until after Jesus came to be known as 'the Risen Lord'.

After Mark

According to a widely-shared consensus among commentators, the Gospels of both Matthew and Luke are based on that of Mark. This view shows a certain tension, so to speak, between contemporary Gospel scholars on the one hand and, on the other, the view which was dominant until recent times to the effect that Matthew's Gospel was first. St Augustine suggested in the fourth century that the idea of the priority of Matthew was based on the superior dignity of Matthew as an apostle, whereas both Mark and Luke were merely 'evangelists' and therefore inferior to Matthew! John's Gospel, of course, was, and still is, considered to be the last of the four to be written, and for this reason comes last—and latest—in the series.

Matthew

In the light of the evidence of the Gospel texts themselves, then, it seems that, of the four Gospels as we now have them, Mark's was the first to be written. Some commentators say that the apostle Matthew wrote a document before Mark wrote his Gospel: that may be so, but, even if it is, what we now call Matthew's Gospel was produced by a later editor, who revised Mark's Gospel using Matthew's earlier document as well as some other source material available to him.

Mark's Gospel is notably different from Matthew's for having none of the careful artistic touches which characterize Matthew. Mark has nothing to offer about Jesus' birth or origin to compare with Matthew's masterful Infancy Gospel (Mt 1-2). The familiar chapters of Jesus' Sermon on the Mount are from Matthew (Mt 5-7), but there is nothing like it in Mark. Similarly, the beautiful 'cluster' of the seven Parables of the Kingdom is from Matthew (Mt 13): we can see here, as already remarked, that Matthew has kept the form parables of Mark's earlier cluster (Mk 4:1-34), but enlarged the collection to a total of seven. Matthew has added various other words and deeds of Jesus as well, with the result that his Gospel (at twenty-eight chapters in length) is almost twice as long as Mark's (sixteen chapters). At the end, Matthew clearly differs from his predecessor in presenting the apparation of the risen Lord to the women (Mt 28:1-10), and also the final scene in which the risen Lord appears to the hesitant disciples in Galilee and sends them out on the mission, thereby making them 'apostles' in the proper sense of the word ('those who have been sent').

Matthew evidently shares a great deal of Mark's attitude towards Jesus, both as the rejected prophet of the public ministry and as the glorified Christ of the paschal mystery. However, it may well be that Matthew wanted to say something special of his own, different from what

Chapter VI

Mark had said, for otherwise he would scarcely have had reason to take the trouble to revise Mark's Gospel so carefully. We will have occasion to consider Matthew's special message later, but for the present it is sufficient to note that Mark's message must have been clear to Matthew, who both shared it and went beyond it.

Some commentators reject this explanation, insisting that Matthew's Gospel was written before Mark's, and that Mark has somehow abbreviated Matthew. Indeed, St Augustine expressed this opinion as long ago as the fourth century! However, this objection seems to be based largely on a prior desire to maintain the 'traditional' opinion as an end itself—Matthew before Mark—coupled with a refusal to accept the clues which the text of Mark offers. Furthermore, if we were to accept the priority of Matthew's Gospel to that of Mark, we would have to explain why Mark had chosen to abbreviate what would then have been the earlier document, and, in so doing, to omit some of its best parts. For instance, how could we explain Mark's omission of the glowing beauty of Matthew's Infancy Gospel, with the Magi and the Holy Innocents? Again, why would Mark have bypassed Jesus' prophetic teaching in the Sermon on the Mount? And what reason could we give for Mark's having chopped up Matthew's cluster of seven Parables of the Kingdom (Mt 13) and reduced it to a group of only four parables, in a different setting and in a different context (Mk 4)? Most convincingly of all, why should Mark have failed to show the risen Lord in the last chapter of his Gospel? Or to preserve the impact of the earthquake scene and its effect on the tomb guards? (Mt 28:1-4.)

For all these reasons we may feel confident that we are on solid ground in insisting that our present Matthew is based on our present Mark. But it still remains for us to work out what the special message is which Mark fashions and offers in his new literary creation—the special message which, apparently, was not quite enough for Matthew, so that Matthew had to elaborate his own document with his own different emphases.

Luke

St Paul mentions his friend Luke three times in his letters (Col 4:14; 2 Tim 4:11; Philm 24—in the latter two instances along with Mark). Luke is the gentile convert and author whom commentators generally credit with the only bipartite work in the New Testament (Luke-Acts). Naturally, Acts is not based on Mark's Gospel, since Acts talks about things not mentioned by Mark; but Luke's Gospel does show clear signs of Mark's influence.

Luke takes over from both Paul and Mark the kerygmatic Gospel of the paschal mystery as the controlling core of the Christian proclamation. Paul was the apostle to the gentiles, and the universalism which characterizes Paul's preaching and letters was also of special interest to Luke, who found this theme to be prominent also in Mark's picture of Jesus. However, Paul was a relative newcomer to the apostolic fellowship, and he was unable to speak of the earthly life of Jesus or of Jesus' public ministry simply because he had not experienced it as the original twelve apostles had experienced it. So this is another element which Luke found helpful in Mark's Gospel, and he adapted it to his own special purpose. Nevertheless, Luke must also have wanted to go beyond Mark's Gospel, for he added to it an abundance of other elements which had come down to him in the apostolic tradition. Mark had not spoken of Gabriel's visit to Mary, or of the shepherds of Bethlehem; he had not spoken of the widow of Naim, or of the word-pictures of the lost sheep, the lost coin, and the lost son. Luke is the only evangelist who has these, and in all the sections in which they occur he surpasses Mark in terms both of literary style and theological emphasis.

Matthew may have written before Luke, or Luke before Matthew. It does not matter too much which of these Gospels came first, but it appears fairly certain that both Matthew and Luke used Mark's earlier Gospel as well as a number of other source materials which were available to them. It also appears fairly certain that neither Matthew nor Luke used the other's work—perhaps neither even knew that the other existed

The suggestion has been made that, just as Matthew wrote before Mark, so Mark really set out to compile his Gospel by selecting and adapting elements from both Matthew and Luke. We can reject this proposal for essentially the same reasons as those we offered for holding that Mark did not abbreviate Matthew's Gospel.

John

It is not very difficult to see the substantial differences between Mark and the fourth Gospel of John. On the superficial level, there is the factor of quantity—the fourth Gospel is five chapters longer than Mark's. But the real differences are more basic. The more 'spiritual' style of language in John is a matter of symbol, image, nuance, atmosphere, and a mood of mystery, whereas Mark is—as we have said—blunt, concrete, and vivid, as well as faster-moving.

There is a point of contact between these two Gospels at the beginning of Jesus' public ministry, in that they both speak of John the Baptist as the one who was the occasion for Jesus' emergence from the obscurity of his hidden life (Jn 1:19ff; Mk 1:2-11). Similarly, they both speak of Jesus' wondrous act of feeding the crowd in the wilderness with a few pieces of bread and some fishes. However, Mark gives two renderings of this scene (Mk 6-8), whereas the fourth Gospel gives only one (Jn 6). Besides this, the Johannine rendering presents Jesus' lengthy Bread of Life discourse along with the feeding scene, and this is in obvious contrast to Mark's simpler presentation of the wondrous feeding on its own. Both evangelists also present Jesus' walking on the water as part of the same sequence of scenes (Mk 6:45-50; Jn 6:16-21). And, of course, both evangelists present, as the concluding chapters of their Gospels, the Paschal Gospel of Jesus' Passover. But John's Gospel shows the risen Lord presenting himself to the women and to the disciples (in chapter 20 as well as in the appendix, chapter 21) with a special slant in favour of the Beloved Disciple, who, presumably, is the apostle John himself. Mark's Gospel, on the other hand, appears to represent more the prominence of Peter, not only in the paschal mystery chapters, but throughout the whole document.

The Johannine Gospel sets its own tone right from its opening verses, which form its Prologue. Here the evangelist draws his readers' attention to the lofty eternity of God and to his creative and life-giving Word, which became flesh and dwells among men. Throughout the fourth Gospel this more 'spiritual' idiom prevails, and is remarkably different from the concreteness of the Markan style. Furthermore, the lengthy discourse passages of John show a more mature and articulate level of theological expression than Mark, which remains closer than the fourth Gospel to the earlier form of the apostolic preaching as we have seen it in Paul's letters and in the Acts of the Apostles.

Summary

This harvest of clues which we have observed in Mark's Gospel should carry us well beyond the external levels which may well have occupied our attention earlier. We should be ready now to read Mark again, but this time more deeply, and to recognize that Mark's interest is not at all limited to presenting of a mere 'biography' of Jesus, or to guaranteeing the details of time and place which are

Chapter VI

of such important to our contemporary idea of 'history'. Mark's Gospel was never intended to be a history book! It is, first and foremost, a Gospel. What we need to do, therefore, is to figure out how Mark interprets the Gospel, so that we can grasp the special theological message that he presents in his document as he addresses it to his friends in the first generation of the primitive apostolic Church.

1. How is the beginning of Mark's Gospel different from the beginnings of the other Gospels?
2. What does the evangelist mean by the first verse of his Gospel?
3. Can you recognize any of the literary 'clusters' or 'sandwiches' which Mark includes in his document?
4. Did you notice any sayings which seem to represent the mind and the message of the evangelist himself rather than those of Jesus?
5. Is Mark graceful and delicate in his literary style?
6. Does Mark's Gospel seem to be later than Matthew's?
7. Is it necessary to say that Peter was the principal source behind Mark's Gospel?

Chapter VII

Mark's Theological Message: the Mysterious Identity of Jesus

But they did not understand what this teaching meant, and they were afraid to ask him. (Mark 9:32.)

Read Mark's Gospel through again, this time with an eye to the special theological clues which the evangelist includes. Notice especially the following features:
  Mk 1:11; 9:7; 15:39: the identity of Jesus
  Mk 8:31; 9:31; 10:33f: Jesus' predictions of his coming death and vindication
  Mk 8:34; 10:43f: discipleship according to the mind of Jesus

Mark had inherited already about a generation of the Church's apostolic tradition by the time he undertook his project of interpreting that tradition for his friends in his new document. For that reason he had certainly absorbed the emphasis on the paschal mystery as the core of the Church's faith. Even though it is not until the final chapters of his Gospel that he gets to show the great scenes of Jesus' passion, death, and burial, and of the women's Easter experience at the empty tomb, the theological emphasis of these final chapters is really the starting-point for Mark's own message. Like all the apostles and evangelists, Mark is first foremost a witness of the Gospel of the Risen Lord.

But it would appear that Mark has heard people—

Chapter VII

Christians, and perhaps pagans as well—asking such questions as: 'How can you expect us to accept as Lord and Messiah a criminal who was executed by the Roman governor for treason, and rejected by his own people as a false propphet?' 'How can this Jesus be the "Christ", or the "Messiah" that God sent to his people, if they were unable to recognize him?' This document is Mark's attempt to provide an answer to questions such as these.

We have noticed that Mark translates Aramaic words and phrases and interprets Jewish customs. Furthermore, of all the disciples, Peter stands out in Mark' Gospel with special prominence (the evangelist mentions Peter explicitly more often than any of the other disciples). These clues in the text itself seem to accord with the ancient tradition which holds that Mark was a disciple of Peter, presumably in Rome, and that he wrote down the things which he had heard from Peter about Jesus. This means that Mark was passing on—in some fashion, but not necessarily word for word—what he had learned from Peter. We may assume that Peter spoke Aramaic, and possibly some Greek; in consequence, Mark had the task of transmitting this message in the common form of Greek which was the vernacular language in much of the ancient world during these decades of the first Christian century.

This may explain what Mark means by the opening words of his document. Most of our versions translate this first verse of the first chapter as: 'The beginning of the Gospel [or 'good news'] of Jesus Christ, the Son of God.' But, as we have already seen, the real meaning goes somewhat beyond the literal sense of the words. What is 'the Gospel' of Jesus? What is 'the beginning' of the Gospel? How and why is Jesus 'the Christ'? In what way is he 'the Son of God'? The 'Gospel' or 'good news' is the Church's proclamation of the paschal mystery—and now he, Mark, is going to explain how it all started.

This explanation makes good sense. The word *gospel* occurs only six times in Mark's document (Mk 1:1; 1:14f; 10:29; 13:10; 14:9), and in each case it means, not a written work, but an oral message about the salvation which God offers to men through Jesus. This in its turn suggests that everything which Mark presents in the course of his message is related directly, in one way or another, to what he plans to show in the final chapters. If we use our imagination and pretend that we are reading Mark's Gospel backwards, as if we were looking through the reverse end of a telescope, and so starting with Jesus' passion, death, and resurrection, we would then see his public ministry in the light of these dominant realities. And this would bring us close to seeing Mark's plan: he is reading, or showing, the public ministry of Jesus in the light of the paschal mystery,

This exercise does require imagination, because it means that the Jesus whom Mark depicts in the public ministry is really the glorious Lord whom the Father has raised from the dead! But, after all, how could it be otherwise? As far as Mark and the apostolic Church are concerned, there is only one Jesus, and he can never be anything but the Risen Lord! Even when Mark shows Jesus being baptized by John the Baptist, or tested in the desert (Mk 1:2-13), it is the glorious Lord whom he shows being baptized and tested. This same principle runs through Mark's whole document. This is the glorious Risen Lord, the Son of God, as he walked and talked, preached, and healed—but nobody knew who he was, except God and Jesus himself, and the evil spirits who realized that they did not belong in his presence.

Mark's Christological picture, therefore, is a 'split-level' picture. We see this from the beginning because we already know the end of the story—but nobody in the picture saw it as we do! Essentially Mark is describing, in one graphic scene after another, the fact that nobody recognized or understood Jesus' real identity. As we become more attuned to Mark's idiom and to the style of his language, we find that he is presenting at one and the same time two completely opposite pictures of the person of Jesus. In more systematic terms we call these two pictures the 'high' and 'low' Christologies: Jesus is simultaneously the lowly and rejected prophet, the Suffering Servant of God, and also the supremely glorified Risen Lord, the Christ and the Son of God! The real mystery is not that Jesus is one or the other, but that he is both—and at the same time. The mystery surpasses human comprehension, and that is why Mark shows that nobody whom Jesus meets understands the mystery of his 'veiled' identity. Mark insists that Jesus cannot be understood or appreciated in human terms. The only correct way to understand Jesus, or to relate to him, is God's way.

The key to grasping this mystery, and the light that makes it recognizable, is the glorious vindication that came to Jesus in his resurrection. Nobody could recognize him during his earthly presence because nobody saw him as God saw him—people were simply too human in their view of Jesus! Mark's message is not only a report on this identity of Jesus as a reality of the past, but also a challenge for those who receive this message, or read this document, in the present—an assurance that Jesus lives as the Risen Lord, and that he will show himself in his Second Coming (the *parousia*).

The Gospel of the Paschal Mystery and the Kingdom

Our evangelist has undertaken to show the connection between the Gospel of the Kingdom of God, which Jesus preached, and the Gospel of his passion and glorification, which eventually became the hallmark of the Church's witness. These two messages, or Gospels, came together only in Jesus' own person. Jesus preached to his countrymen that God was preparing to show them his goodness and providence. Nobody understood or accepted his message in the way that he intended it to be understood and accepted. Eventually Jesus realized that his own people would put him to death. But this is the turning-point: Jesus accepted the inevitability of his own death, because he was sure that in it God would show his lordship—the reign of God would show itself supremely in his, Jesus', own trial! God would show in his suffering servant that his power for goodness and life was greater than the power of any creature for sin, evil, and death.

And so it was! That is how Mark answers his questioners—how he can maintain that a rejected prophet is the glorious Messiah, even though nobody could understand or recognize the fullness of Jesus' identity, because people failed to see him as God saw him, and as he saw himself!

The Introductory Triptych (Mk 1:2-13)

John the Baptist appears as a herald and a prophet, calling his countrymen to repent of their sins and prepare to face God's coming judgement. Jesus arrives on the scene and accepts the symbolic washing which John administers. But, as he comes out of the water, Jesus has an 'inaugural experience'—something like those of Moses (Ex 3), Isaiah (Is 6), Jeremiah (Jer 1:4-19), and Ezekiel (Ezek 1-3). He sees the Holy Spirit coming to him, and he hears God's voice speaking to him as his Son—in words which reflect the 'Son of God' theme of Ps 2:7 and the 'Servant' theme of Is 42:1 and 44:1f. During his solitary retreat in the wasteland, Jesus experiences the tensions and trials of a son and servant who must work out and act out this identity, as one whose life is claimed and guided entirely by God, not by Satan.

Nobody Knows (Mk 1:14-8:26)

Mk 1:14-3:6 In three phases Mark now shows Jesus as the

Chapter VII

beloved Son whom God has claimed as his own in the baptism voice. Jesus preaches the Gospel of the Kingdom of God (Mk 1:143f) and calls upon his fellow Galileans to respond with a conversion of heart. He brings the Kingdom of God in his works, which are manifestly signs of God's healing power and life-giving goodness. But the response is never what it should be: nobody reconizes Jesus in faith for what the baptism voice has declared him to be (the evil spirits recognize God's presence and power in him, but this recognition is not an act of faith; it is merely an awareness that they do not belong to his presence). After a series of conflicts (Mk 2:1-3:6) the leaders decide to destroy him because his idea of religion does not accord with theirs.

Mk 3:7-6:6 In the face of this hostility Jesus continues to preach and to bring to his neighbours in Galilee the message of God's benevolent lordship. Evil spirits cannot remain in his presence. He heals souls as well as bodies, and teaches in word-pictures which illustrate various aspects of God's rule (Mk 4:1-34). But nobody is converted. Even his own chosen disciples do not understand his teaching. In his own home-town he is rebuffed by his neighbours: they too are human, since they see him merely as 'the carpenter, the son of Mary' and not as the prophet sent by God. Their unfaith pains him. (Mk 6:6).

Mk 6:7-8:26 No matter. Jesus carries out his mission. He sends his chosen group of twelve followers to do what he has been doing himself; their mission becomes an extension of Jesus' own work, and an implicit foretaste of what his disciples will do after his resurrection. But there is trouble ahead. The figure of John the Baptist hovers over the scene again, as 'forerunner'—the prophet calling his people to conversion, and killed for his loyalty to the word of God. Jesus feeds the crowd in the wilderness and walks on the water, but his disciples cannot grasp the point of it all. The confrontation with the Pharisees (Mk 7:1-23) is a contrast between two views of Judaism: Jesus holds firm for following the mind of God, and rebukes these leaders for being so wrapped up in their human pietism that they make it an end in itself and become hypocrites by imposing it on others as a burden, instead of helping them to know God as Friend and Father.

The Turning-Point (Mk 8:27-30)

At least the disciples should understand by now, and Jesus asks them what they think. Peter speaks on behalf of them all, and says precisely the wrong thing: 'You are the Messiah!' (Mk 8:29). This may look like the right answer, but Jesus is not satisfied with it: instead of commending Peter for giving the right answer, Jesus rebukes him and forbids him to speak to anyone about him (Mk 8:30). Peter may not speak to anyone about Jesus because he does not yet know how to speak about him correctly!

Peter has been favourably impressed by Jesus' marvellous works of power, and now he optimistically expects that Jesus will inaugurate a new 'messianic age' of peace and power for the people of Israel. But he has not understood Jesus! Jesus has never claimed to be the Messiah. What he is, nobody sees; what he has not claimed to be, that is what Peter thinks he sees. What Peter says is not enough; he has much to learn.

Jesus knows that he must die with his identity still unrecognized and unappreciated. But he also knows himself and the identity which the baptism voice assigned to him (Mk 1:11). Because of this he can accept calmly the fate that looms ahead of him, foreshadowed by that of John the Baptist (Mk 6:14-29). The lordship of God will manifest itself supremely in his death. God will raise up

Chapter VII

the 'Son of Man'. Jesus says this no fewer than three times in Mark's Gospel (Mk 8:31; 9:31; 10:33).

Jesus is not inventing the 'Son of God' term here. He draws it at least partly from the bizarre apocalyptic of Dan 7:1-14. This late Old Testament book is confusing because of its fantastic imagery and obscure terminology, but this figure of the puny and helpless 'Son of Man' which occurs in Daniel's vision represents the people of Israel, oppressed and persecuted by enemy nations which are larger and more powerful than itself. But the plan and decree of God is that, eventually, the underdog 'Son of Man' (which, in this scene, is Israel) is to be lifted up from misery and subjection, and become the lord of those who have humiliated him.

There are some other texts, both biblical and extra-biblical, which speak of the 'Son of Man', including some of the prophetic oracles of Exekiel (Ez 2), where the term means a man who is humble and lowly in the presence of God's over-powering majesty. So Jesus can use the term to describe himself, because he knows that he is to be both low (oppressed by men) and high (raised up by God as lord of his oppressors). Between this turning point of his Gospel and the end of the document, Mark shows Jesus using this term 'Son of Man' no less than a dozen times to describe his own identity. Peter wants a lordly Messiah, but Jesus knows that there can be no Messiah who is not a Suffering Servant and a Son of Man, just as there is no acceptance for a prophet among his people—even though later events prove that he was right.

Jesus Instructs the Disciples (Mk 8:31-13:37)

This interview and dialogue between Jesus and Peter is Mark's way of showing that the public ministry of Jesus is finished. From now on the crowds and the leaders are no longer prominent. Mark shows Jesus concentrating on his relationship with his chosen band of twelve confused and uncomprehending disciples. The crowds have been unconverted; the leaders are hostile; Jesus' own relatives do not understand or appreciate him. The disciples must be the ones to carry on after Jesus is killed. But they have to learn what discipleship means. If they do not comprehend the identity of Jesus, they cannot comprehend the meaning of their own vocation!

Now the second main point of Mark's theological message begins to emerge: discipleship means following Jesus in the paschal mystery of suffering and glorification. Now that Jesus has described himself as 'Son of Man', who must be brought low by men and then raised high by God, he tells the disciples that they must walk the same path (Mk 8:34-37). By giving these words of Jesus here, Mark certainly makes the identity of Jesus relevant to his contemporaries. The Gospel as Mark presents it is therefore not merely an edifying story; it is a call and a challenge to share in Jesus' cross, with confidence that this will lead to a share in his glorification.

Even so, the fullness of Jesus' identity continues to elude the disciples, in spite of their goodwill, which never succeeds in overcoming their incomprehension. Jesus shows them a glimpse of his veiled glory in the Transfiguration, but they remain confused (Mk 9:2-8); they fail to see that Jesus must be not only radiantly glorious (as he is in the Transfiguration scene), but also the rejected prophet like Moses, Elijah, and John, the recently executed baptizer. These same disciples need to learn how to pray and trust in the Father's powerful providence; when they learn that lesson, they will be able to overcome evil spirits like the one that they cannot yet expel (Mk 9:14-29).

It is in this section of his Gospel that Mark has collected and assembled the words of Jesus on the ethical demands of the Kingdom of God and of discipleship. These words of Jesus are not for the crowds in general

(Mk 9:30), much less for the hostile leaders, because there is no point in teaching the meaning of discipleship to those who show no acceptance or conversion of heart towards Jesus' message. For the second time Jesus describes his role as that of the 'Son of Man', although the mystery continues to be too much for these puzzled fishermen (Mk 9:31ff). Jesus instructs them now on cross-bearing, on following his example and professing his message (Mk 8:34-38); on childlike simplicity and trusting in God's fatherly providence; on serving others and avoiding human 'gimmicks' which blur the true Word of God; on the danger of being deceived by wealth and looking for prestige without accepting the necessity of sacrifice, and of serving others according to Jesus' example (Mk 9:33-10:45).

As we read this section of Mark's document, we may get the impression that Mark is to some extent interpreting—selecting some of the words of Jesus on various moral matters which are not all on the same level of importance. This may be, but, if it is, it only helps us to see what we have been saying—that the evangelist is working here to 'interpret' the Jesus tradition which he has received from Peter and, presumably, from other members of the apostolic fellowship as well, in order to impress upon those who are to read this document that the Gospel is a practical guide for their daily life-style.

Jerusalem (Mk 11-16)

All of the remainder of Mark's document is set in the city of Jerusalem. And the reaction of Jerusalem to Jesus is totally negative, in one way or another. The crowds optimistically acclaim him as a new David (Mk 11:10), just as blind Bartimaeus did at Jericho (Mk 10:48), presumably because, like Bartimaeus, they are encouraged by Jesus' reputation as a Galilean wonder-worker. But both Bartimaeus and the crowds have missed the point!

They look for wonders, but they do not recognize the presence of the Kingdom of God. They show no interest in following a Suffering Servant, or the example of humble trust in God which the cult represents. (Mk 11:2-7). Jesus has come to the capital to suffer in loneliness, and to be raised up in vindication by God as the 'Son of Man', but nobody understands except God and Jesus!

Jesus' 'ministry' in Jerusalem is not much of a ministry. Mark has apparently 'telescoped' the tradition here, in order to emphasize the one thing he wants to emphasize—that Jesus' whole experience in the capital was a series of confrontations and misunderstandings. The prophet from Galilee runs into conflict with everyone: with the unpraying crowds who mill about in the Temple courtyard (Mk 11:15); with the chief priests and the scribes (Mk 11:27); with the Pharisees and Herodians (Mk 11:13-17); and with the Sadducees (Mk 11:18-17). All these leaders practise and preach a sadly distorted form of Judaism, and mislead God's people by their hypocrisy (Mk 12:38ff); the right kind of religion, Jesus says, is the humble and trusting service of God which the poor widow shows in her simplicity, rather than the showy formalism and the self-righteousness of works upon which these leaders rely (Mk 12:38-44).

Farewell Words (Mk 13)

The Eschatological Discourse, which Mark here presents as Jesus' last instruction to his puzzled disciples, is confusing, mainly because it speaks of the future on several levels at the same time. Another complication comes from the fact that Jesus uses a number of apocalyptic terms drawn from the Old Testament tradition and adapts them to his own situation and to that of the disciples. Mark is also intent himself on adapting the lessons of this instruction to his own contemporaries.

In the first place, there is the imminent prospect of

Jesus' own execution, which anyone with half an eye can see coming, in the light of all the conflicts which have been going on during this Jerusalem ministry. These have been building up into a crescendo of hostility towards Jesus, and there has to be a catalyst—as the evangelist has already foreshadowed as early as Mk 3:6 (the remote plot of the leaders against Jesus). Then there is the next stage of the future, which is that of Jesus' own vindication: this Jesus confidently expects to receive from the Father, as he has said in the three Passion predictions (Mk 8:31; 9:31; 10:33). But there also has to be a future time of trial for the uncomprehending disciples, who must expect to follow Jesus on the path of the Suffering Servant and of the Son of Man (Mk 13:9f). Here Mark appears to be retrojecting on to the lips of Jesus himself some of the experiences which were to come to the disciples in the years following Jesus' own trial, so that, in hindsight, these tribulations of the disciples appear in their true light—as the share which the disciples must have in Jesus' trial, and which must precede their share in his vindication.

But Jesus is still the Son of Man, and after all the trials there will be the raising up and the glory. Jesus will come again, as he has already said in Mk 8:38. This *parousia*—which St Paul described several times in his letters, some years before Mark wrote his Gospel—will be a cause for either hope or fear, depending on whether those who are to face it are disciples or unbelievers. That the *parousia* will come is sure, but when it will be is not given to men to know (Mk 13:32). The last exhortation that Jesus leaves with his disciples at this point is a call to persevere in hope, waiting for god's relieving hand (Mk 13:37).

The Paschal Gospel (Mk 14-16)
In his representation of Jesus' passion Mark emphasizes

the theological principles which he has already established in the earlier chapters of his document. They are the same as the central themes of the apostolic *kerygma*: God, as provident Father, is the principal character, showing his power for life in the struggle of his Suffering Servant. This shows the operation of the biblical patterns of the rejected prophet, the Son of Man, and the Suffering Servant—'the Scripture must be fulfilled', as Jesus says (Mk 14:28, 49, 62). The supper is to be the memorial of his handed-over body and his poured-out blood, and a foretaste of the messianic banquet which God will later give to the disciples, as the Isaian oracles promised long ago (Is 25:6; 55:1f). Judas' treachery shows Jesus as the victim of the unfaithful friend, like the psalmist who sang Ps 41:9. Jesus accepts the arrest, but the disciples resist because they do not understand the mysterious way in which the biblical patterns are to be worked out. They still do not see the picture God's way.

Eventually Jesus dies in anguish, deserted even by his chosen disciples. But at the very moment of his death God shows his presence, in the signs of the darkness at noon and the splitting of the veil of the Temple (from the top down, in a way that could not be human), symbolizing his rebuke of those who have erred tragically in their malice. Even as he dies, Jesus is loved and publicly vindicated by the Father in these great signs, which are superhuman in their magnitude. The Roman soldier standing near Jesus now sees and says what Jesus' own people failed to see and say: 'Clearly, this man was the Son of God!' (Mk 15:39). Only now can it be said as, in retrospect, all the pieces fit together in the light of the paschal mystery: Jesus' life and death show the biblical patterns in operation. He is God's chosen one, but nobody saw it until he was dead—and then it was a pagan, a Roman, who got the message!

Chapter VII

The Women at the Tomb (Mk 16:1-8)

Perhaps Mark wrote more than these eight verses of the last chapter. Some commentators are satisfied that he did not, on the ground that what he says in these eight verses is quite enough to make the point he wants to make. The other school of thought suggests that Mark wrote more, probably about the Risen Lord coming to Peter and the other disciples, perhaps in Galilee—but that somehow this ending perished, and that later editors added the present endings in order to make the whole thing finish more smoothly. This latter explanation makes good sense, and is respectable as a hypothesis—but it can never be more than a hypothesis, because it is essentially an interpetation of what just is not there.

We have to be satisfied, therefore, with the eight verses that are in all the reliable manuscripts, and in all our contemporary versions of the Bible as well. And in these verses Mark shows that nobody was expecting Jesus to be raised up. Nobody expected the stone to be moved. The women went to the tomb of Jesus with the intention of performing the ritual of anointing his body, which they had had to postpone because of the onset of the Passover rest (Mk 15:42). The presence of the 'young man sitting at the right' (Mk 16:5) surprises them, but his message sends them completely out of their wits! 'He has been raised up!' But they are surprised only because they had not understood Jesus' identity as God understood it, and Jesus himself understood it. Now, in hindsight, all the pieces fit together. This is the answer to the questions which have been put to Mark: Jesus is Lord and Christ now, just as he was God's son and servant at the beginning, as the baptism voice had said—but nobody understood, because nobody saw him God's way. Now that he has been raised up, as 'Son of Man', the Kingdom of God, which Jesus proclaimed and preached, has been supremely manifested in his own person—and the God who can shown himself in this way is worthy of the faith of his disciples.

1. Was Mark trying to be a historian? If not, what was he trying to be?
2. Why does Mark show Jesus enjoining silence about himself (Mk 3:12; 5:43; 7:36; 8:30; etc)?
3. Why does Jesus rebuke and correct Peter's enthusiastic description of him as 'the Messiah'?
4. Why does Mark translate Aramaic words and explain Jewish customs (Mk 5:41; 7:11, 34; 15:34; 7:3f; 12:42)?
5. What is the theological significance of the events which occur at the moment of Jesus' death (Mk 15:33-9)?
6. Where and how does Mark suggest the meaning of discipleship

Chapter VIII

The Traditions of Jesus' Origin

Jesus Christ, a descendant of David, who was a descendant of Abraham. *(Mt 1:1.)*

Read the Infancy Gospels (Mt 1f and Lk 1f). Compare them with each other; notice what they have in common, and which scenes are unique to one or the other. Read also Jn 1:1-18 and see how it compares with these two Infancy Gospels.

When we look through the earliest parts of the New Testament, as far as we can reconstruct them, we find that they present Jesus as an adult; there is nothing in these levels of the primitive apostolic Church's tradition about the details of Jesus' earthly origin.

The Early Tradition

In the early levels of the Gospel tradition Jesus himself emerges when he comes from Nazareth as a grown man to be baptized by John the Baptist. He goes about his public ministry, preaching the Gospel of the Kingdom of God, but saying nothing about his own origin or birth. Similarly, the early witness of the apostolic preachers, as Luke preserves it in the Acts of the Apostles, speaks of Jesus principally in terms of the paschal mystery of his Passion and Glorification. As for the earlier phase of his earthly life, there is only Peter's brief mention in Acts 10:37ff, about 'Jesus of Nazareth beginning in Galilee with the baptism that John preached'. So here, even when we do have a reference to Jesus' earthly life before the first Holy Week, it goes back no further than to the beginning of his public ministry and to the occasion of John's baptizing ministry.

Paul As we mentioned earlier, even the body of the Pauline letters offers remarkably little about Jesus' earthly life before the central events of the first Holy Week. In Gal 4:4 Paul says, in passing, that 'when the designated time had come, God sent forth his Son, born of a woman, born under the law'. But this means no more than that God made Jesus to be human and to be Jewish. In Rom 1:3, and again in 2 Tim 2:8, Paul speaks of Jesus as 'a descendant of David', but we have to work to figure out whether Paul is speaking historically or figuratively here. Either way, he tells us little in specific terms about Jesus' origin.

Mark If we follow the school of thought which accepts Mark as the first of the present four Gospels, we cannot help noticing that the document comes from an evangelist who does not appear anxious to speak about Jesus' birth or early life at all. Mark opens his Gospel with Jesus as an adult. In the course of it he shows a fleeting scene of Jesus in his relationship with his mother and his other relatives (Mk 3:21, 31-5). Again, in the scene of Jesus' unsuccessful visit to his home-town of Nazareth, the townspeople say: 'Is this not the carpenter, the son of Mary, a brother of James and Joses and Judas and Simon?' (Mk 6:1-6.) Matthew takes this scene over from Mark (Mt 13:53-8), but it does not really refer to Jesus' birth or origin, except that it gives some names (the 'brothers' and 'sisters' can mean his kin, his relatives in the extended family pattern of the ancient Orient, without necessarily meaning children of Mary). Luke also adapts this Markan passage, but he adds the favourable response of the people in Nazareth: 'Is this not Joseph's son?' (Lk 4:22.) Incidentally, Luke also provides a genealogy of Jesus (Lk 3:23-38)—but, as we shall see later, this is more theological than biographical.

John The fourth Gospel has a short scene (Jn 6:42) in which Jesus' countrymen say: 'Is this not Jesus, the son of Joseph? Do we not know his father and mother? How can he claim to have come down from heaven?' This passage adds the name of Joseph, which also occurs in Jn 1:45, but, even so, there is really nothing here beyond what is contained in the earlier documents.

Of course, when we speak of the fourth Gospel, we must take note of the special contribution it makes to the New Testament in the form of its Prologue (Jn 1:1-18). This certainly speaks of Jesus' origin—his origin as the Word which was with God from the very beginning, and was God, and became flesh and dwelt among us. But here we see a clear example of the lofty and 'spiritual' character of Johannine language. This evangelist is not really trying to speak about Jesus' origin in human terms: his whole point is that Jesus is more than human—that he is nothing less than the eternal and life-giving Word of God, come to earth in human form. But, whatever else we may say about the Johannine Prologue, or about the fourth Gospel in general, it derives in any case from a later period of the New Testament era (about 95AD), and so does not represent an early stage of the apostolic tradition.

This all means that the tradition of Jesus' earthly origin, and of his birth and infancy, did not form a recognizable element of the message of Jesus himself, or of the early preaching of the apostles. Jesus preached the Gospel of the Kingdom of God, and his apostles preached the *kerygma* of the paschal mystery. When these apostolic preachers spoke of Jesus' earlier earthly life—his life before the first Holy Week—they spoke of his adult ministry. But they were more interested in the mystery of his resurrection, and in the consequences which flow from it, than they were in what preceded it in time. The terminology which we find in these early levels of the apostolic tradition mentions Mary as Jesus' mother and Joseph as his father, but that is about all the detail that we have in the New Testament—except for the opening chapters of Matthew and Luke. And these chapters represent a more mature stage of the early Church's theological perception and understanding of Jesus.

We have, of course, already made the point that we need to be cautious in trying to work with the kind of terminology which we find in the early tradition. This problem surfaces, for instance, when we endeavour to work out whether the title 'Son of David' (Mt 10:47f) is symbolic or biographical in the strict sense, or whether people used the term at that time without analysing how they meant it. Since Jesus and his apostles (including Paul) were Jews, we may tend to expect that they would use the terms of the Old Testament as a principal content of their vocabulary, and that they would apply these terms to Jesus without questioning whether they fitted on the level of what we would call 'biography' or 'history' in the contemporary sense of those words.

Mark had his own purpose in mind when he composed his Gospel, as we have already seen. But his purpose did not require him to speak of Jesus' life further back than the beginning of his public ministry, following his baptism. If we date Mark's Gospel about 65AD, this shows the state of theological tradition in the primitive apostolic Church at this period of the first Christian century: it would seem that the question of Jesus' birth, origin, and infancy was not of pressing interest to the people who brought the apostolic tradition to this stage of its development. The Church was intensely interested in the paschal mystery, and, as Mark's Gospel shows, there was by now the beginnings of an interest in Jesus' public ministry—insofar as it was seen in the light of his eventual glorification, and insofar too as it could show recognizable norms for discipleship. But a whole generation—the first generation of the Church—appears to have lived and died without being much instructed, or even especially interested, in Jesus' birth or infancy.

For this reason we find ourselves compelled to be satisfied with what we find in the Infancy Gospels of Matthew and Luke. And we have clues which indicate that these two evangelists worked independently of each other, neither seeing the other's document as he wrote his own—although we think that they both used Mark's Gospel and some other common material as well.

Theological Character

People sometimes speak of these chapters as 'infancy narratives', as they speak too of the concluding chapters of the Gospels as 'Passion narratives'. This terminology appears inadequate, however, because it fails to do justice to the essential character of the Church's early tradition as *gospel*—as 'good news'. And, since what we have here is a picture of Jesus which flows from this oral tradition, we should speak rather of 'Infancy *Gospels*', just as we should also speak of the concluding chapters as 'Passion (or Paschal) *Gospels*'.

This distinction may seem over-subtle, but it does help us to recognize an essential fact which characterizes the Infancy Gospels: they are not scientific records in the modern sense, but rather parts of the theological messages which Matthew and Luke present in their overall Gospel documents. We can never absorb the full meaning of the Infancy Gospels if we separate them from the rest of these two documents and reduce them to 'historical accounts' in our own modern sense.

We see the Infancy Gospels in their proper persepctive, in relation to the rest of Matthew's Gospel or to the whole two-part complex of Luke-Acts, if we see them as a kind of 'backward bridge'. This means that, since the core of the Gospel tradition is the proclamation of the paschal mystery, the Infancy Gospels are a link which joins the first Holy Week, and the public ministry of Jesus, with the Israel of the Old Testament which preceded him. We suggested before that we should try to use our imagination and pretend to see the Gospels *backwards*—through the opposite end of a telescope, so to speak. The first Holy Week and Easter then appear in the front line; behind them comes Jesus' public ministry, and then, even further back in time, the Infancy Gospels. In this way the opening chapters of Matthew and Luke show how Jesus' earthly origin, birth, and infancy join this whole Gospel to the Old Testament people of Israel, in continuity with their sacred history.

This theological purpose is evident in both Infancy Gospels (Mt 1f and Lk 1f). But, aside from this essential agreement on the theological level, it is remarkable that these two renderings of the Infancy Gospel coincide in only a very few details. We may not normally be aware of this fact, because we are accustomed to thinking of the 'Christmas story' as a whole, without stopping to analyse whether one detail or another—the shepherds, for example, or the Magi—comes from Matthew's Gospel or from Luke's. But once we take a careful look as these two pictures, we can quite readily see that, on the narrative level, they are in agreement on the names of Jesus, Mary, and Joseph, and on Betheleḥem as the birthplace of Jesus—but on very little else. This is because the two evangelists orient their Gospels differently, Matthew aiming his message at Jewish Christians, and Luke addressing himself to gentiles (converts or potential converts).

Matthew

The overall purpose of Matthew's whole Gospel is to show to Jewish Christians that the completion of Israel's destiny and the fulfilment of the Old Testament Scriptures are now visible in the Christian Church, which carries on the true Judaism as Jesus proclaimed and lived it. This theological message already begins to take shape in the opening chapters (Mt 1f): there are repeated citations of Old Testament texts, and, in addition to these, there are many more references which are merely implied. In fact, the whole Matthaean Infancy Gospel is such a 'collage' of Old Testament themes and images that this is ultimately the essential meaning of it: the Kingdom (or Lordship) of God which was visible in the Israel of the Old Testament is now present and operating in Jesus, and was so even before his birth.

Matthew presents six units here. The first two—the genealogy and the relationship of Joseph to Jesus—make up the first chapter. Then the three units of the Magi, the flight into Egypt, and the massacre of the Innocents (Mt 2:1-18) all go together as elements of the infancy of Jesus. The final unit—the return from Egypt and the settling in Nazareth (Mt 2:19-23)—could be seen as part of the cluster of preceding scenes, but it can also stand alone, since there is a pause which suggests that some time has elapsed before Joseph returns to his homeland with Mary and the child Jesus.

The Genealogy (Mt 1:1-17) In the opening verse of his Gospel Matthew immediately makes the point that Jesus continues in the line of the Old Testament figures who were instruments in God's plan for his people. The rather obscure line of descent shows that Jesus is born of the great family of God's chosen people, in the line of Abraham, the great patriarch, and of David, the great king. The genealogy leads to Joseph, but then we notice the careful phrasing of Mt :16: 'Joseph, the husband of Mary. It was of her that Jesus who is called the Messiah was born.' There must be some point to the fact that Matthew does not say simply, 'Joseph was the father of Jesus'.

Joseph (Mt 1:18-25) Whatever the explanation of the puzzling forty-two generations may be (Mt 1:17), Matthew apparently finds it necessary to dwell for a while on Joseph and his relationship to Jesus. Matthew is evidently aware of the tradition of the virginal conception of Jesus, although he does not mention it explicitly (just as he does not mention Jesus' birth explicitly, either). But this presents a problem for the evangelist: how can Jesus be a descendant of Abraham and David if he was virginally conceived (since Jewish genealogies follow the male line)? Matthew finds the answer in Joseph as the 'legal' father of Jesus, and this is what he emphasizes. Mary is the mother virginally, in terms of the prophetic oracle of Isaiah (Is 7:14). Matthew cites this text according to the Greek version, which says 'virgin', and Joseph accepts God's command to exercise the legal prerogative of the father by marrying Mary and giving her son the name 'Jesus' (which means 'saviour'). (Mt 1:24f.)

The Magi (Mt 2:1-12) Matthew seems to have been strongly influenced by the prophetic oracle of Is 60 in presenting the scene of the Magi. These eastern visitors personify the foreigners whom the Isaian oracle envisions as coming to pay their respects to Israel's God in Jerusalem. Precisely because they are gentiles, they foreshadow the fact that eventually the Gospel will move away from the unconverted false Israel and be given instead to other people. (Mt 8:11f; 11:20-24; 21:33-46; 28:19.)

The Innocents (Mt 2:13-18) The murderous cruelty of Herod the Great is fully in accord with the description of his reign which we have in the extra-biblical writings of Josephus Flavius, the Jewish historian of the first century AD. There is no indication of how many babies were among the 'Holy Innocents'; but the essence of the scene is not in the quantity of the killings, but in the outrage that this kind of report should provoke. The fabric of Matthew's message is woven on two threads here. The first thread is the constant working of God's providence, which shows itself in a succession of miraculous interventions—the same God who acted in the Old Testament is acting now in the earthly origin of Jesus. The second thread is one which will recur throughout his Gospel: any Jew who knows the Scriptures will see the biblical patterns operating in Jesus. Just as Jesus is a descendant of Abraham and David (Mt 1:1-17), and also virginally conceived according to the Isaian oracle, so too is he now protected from the murderous jealousy of a foreign king as the baby Moses was protected in Egypt (Ex 2:1-10). The mournful wailing of the mothers of the murdered babies suggests to Matthew another biblical image—the mourning of Rachel, which Jeremiah mentions in his oracle (Jer 31:15ff).

Nazareth (Mt 2:19-23) Matthew concludes his Infancy Gospel with another allusion to the Scriptures, based on the fact that Jesus lived in Nazareth. This time, however, he rather overreaches himself by referring to a non-existent Old Testament prophecy! There is no passage in the prophetic books which reads according to the wording which Matthew gives in Mt 2:23. It would seem, then, that the evangelist is here indulging in a play on words. The word *nezer* occurs a few times in the Hebrew text of the Old Testament, meaning 'bud' or 'shoot' or 'blossom' (Is 11:1; 53:2). Moreover, there is also a tradition in the Old Testament about the 'Nazirites', who were men specially consecrated to God from the time of their birth (Lev 21:12; Jdg 13:5). It seems that Matthew has 'blurred' these passages in order to suggest that there is a biblical element—somewhere—in the fact that Jesus lived in Nazareth.

Once we have become accustomed to Matthew's 'theological accent' we can understand why he tries so hard to use biblical terminology in his scenes of Jesus' earthly origin. He wants to make his message intelligible to Jews, and they will readily recognize the pattern and style of his language. Matthew is not being logical in a strict or philosophical sense, or historical in the modern 'biographical' sense. He is being 'biblical'—which means that he talks about Jesus in the language of the Scriptures, to show his Jewish readers that Israel's sacred history, preserved in the Old Testament, is also visible in Jesus—and visible continuously from Jesus' birth. Matthew will go on to show the same divine presence in Jesus' public ministry, in the first Holy Week, and then in the mission of the apostles whom the Risen Lord sends out to witness to him and his teaching. Eventually, when we come to a more detailed study of Matthew's Gospel as a whole, we will see how consistent he is in interpreting the Jesus-tradition in a thoroughly Jewish way, for those Jews who have become converts to Christianity.

Luke

The first thing to notice about Luke's Infancy Gospel is the careful parallel which he has drawn in his first chapter between the two annunciation scenes and the two birth stories. Jesus and John the Baptist, who were associated

Chapter VIII

together in life and death, are here also associated in the marvellous events of their births. This theme of the miraculous providence of God permeates Luke's presentation and gives it a glow of peace, joyful wonder, and gentleness. The same qualities will continue to be present, if somewhat unevenly, throughout Luke's bipartite work (the Gospel and the Acts of the Apostles). Then, in addition to these parallels, the third evangelist also gives us the scenes of Jesus' presentation in the Temple as a baby and of his being lost and later found there as a twelve-year-old boy.

In the parallels, which he has constructed by using earlier narrative traditions, Luke seems to be anxious to show that John the Baptist is of great importance—but that Jesus is of even greater importance. Both are destined, in God's mysterious plan, to be prophets who will have to die because of their fidelity to God's word. It is possible that Luke was, in his own day (about 80AD), acquainted with surviving disciples of John the Baptist, and wished to attract them to become Christians by showing that God destined John to be the 'forerunner' of Jesus.

All the personalities of Luke's Infancy Gospel represent the best piety of the Old Testament Israelites. Mary herself appears here as a simple and humble daughter of Abraham, a faithful member of her people. Zechariah, Elizabeth, Joseph, the shepherds, Simeon and Anna, and the doctors of the Law all present a picture of Jewish piety at its purest, as they serve the Lord patiently and await the peace and salvation which God promised to his people through the ancient prophets. The goodness and simplicity of these characters of the Gospel picture contrast starkly with the treacherous hypocrisy of the Pharisees and the other leaders, who eventually kill Jesus and go on to persecute his disciples.

The four canticles are a special feature of Luke's

contribution to the New Testament. Yet it may surprise us to notice that, when we inspect these songs carefully, there is nothing specifically 'Christian' in any of them except the context itself, which Luke supplies by including them in his document. Mary's Song (Lk 1:46-55) is so similar to the Old Testament Song of Hannah (1 Sam 2:1-10) that some commentators think it is based on it—and this opinion seems difficult to fault. Zechariah's *Benedictus* (Lk 1:68-79) appears to have been originally a song in honour of John the Baptist (Lk 1:76): perhaps John's followers sang it in memory of their martyred hero before Luke adopted it and included it in his Infancy Gospel. The Song of the angels at Bethlehem is only one verse long in its present form, but it may originally have been the opening verse of a longer song which eventually perished, so that now only these few words survive. In his Song of Peace (Lk 2:29-32), which has something of the flavour of the Second and Third Isaiahs, Simeon thanks God for letting him experience the salvation which will eventually reach out to the gentiles.

The Genealogy (Lk 3:23-38) Luke's genealogy of Jesus is not a part of his Infancy Gospel, since he puts it in the context of Jesus' baptism at the age of thirty. However, we can look at it briefly, since it deals with Jesus' origin. The first thing that we notice about it is that it is quite different from the genealogy which appears in the first verses of Matthew's Gospel. Even if we took the time to compare the names of Jesus' ancestors in these two lists, we would be forced to the conclusion that they are so different that we simply cannot reconcile them. The two evangelists have evidently drawn their material from different sources—sources which do not agree with each other. However, this only goes to show even more clearly that both evangelists have intentions which are primarily

Chapter VIII

theological rather than, as we would say nowadays, 'statistical'. The two genealogies go in opposite directions because, as we have said, the two evangelists were addressing different kinds of people. Matthew starts out by mentioning Abraham and eventually traces the line of descent to Joseph, and, through him as Mary's husband, to Jesus. But Luke starts out with Joseph as son of Heli (Lk 3:23) and traces the line of descent backwards in time. After he has traced Jesus' family line back to Abraham (Lk 3:34), he keeps on going even further back until he shows that Jesus is a member of the great universal family of Adam (Lk 3:38), who was God's child too, as Luke says in the last phrase of the same verse.

This genealogy gives us a better picture of Luke's own theological purpose than the Infancy Gospel itself. The reason for this is that there is a great contrast between the gentile orientation of Luke's bipartite work as a whole and the heavily Jewish 'flavour' of his first two chapters. We can see the same peculiarity in the first chapters of Acts, which are also more thoroughly Jewish than the orientation towards the gentiles which comes through in the rest of the book. This all suggests that Luke has used this Jewish-Christian material which has come to him from such sources and adapted it to suit his special theological purpose, which is to show God's saving friendship coming through Jesus and his Church to the pagans of the gentile world. It is a matter of historical fact that Jesus and his Church emerged from the people of Israel, and it is this simple historical fact which Luke draws attention to by making use of these Jewish and Jewish-Christian traditions. Once he has finished presenting his Infancy Gospel, Luke is more original and indeed creative in his 'Adamic' genealogy of Jesus: by this he shows that, even though Jesus is from Israel, he is also a brother to all gentiles, since, like them, he is a descendant of Adam.

Conclusion

For a long time, indeed for several centuries, the popular piety of Christians of the Western culture has been more interested in the story of Christmas than in the mystery of Easter. In a way this is understandable, of course: the baby, the manger, and the other details are more tangible and recognizable than the unseen glory of the resurrected and ascended Lord, and the invisible power of the Holy Spirit working in the Church. However, this tendency has led to a tension between popular piety and the 'centre of gravity' of the New Testament and of the liturgy, since these build on the paschal mystery as the 'beginning' or core of the Gospel and Christianity. This 'beginning' is not the first page or the first chapter, like the beginning of a book; rather, it is the centre which unifies and gives meaning and direction to all the other parts. This has been one of the principal concerns of specialists in liturgy, theology, and biblical exegesis during the present generation—from about the end of the Second World War, in fact. They have been trying to bring about a shift of emphasis, so that our piety will eventually be centered in the mystery of Easter as the 'beginning' of our relationship with God, with the Christmas story as a prelude. If and when this effort succeeds, we will be better able to see the proportions, and our liturgical experience will have been brought more into harmony with the message of the New Testament writers.

1. *How do the Infancy Gospels of Matthew and Luke compare with the Prologue of the fourth Gospel?*
2. *What is the predominant feature of Mt 1f?*
3. *Do you see any inconsistency in the description of Jesus in Luke's Infancy Gospel?*
4. *Why does Luke show such strong Jewish features in his Infancy Gospel?*
5. *How does Luke emphasize the Holy Spirit in his Infancy Gospel?*

Chapter VIII

6. Which Infancy Gospel emphasizes Joseph more? Which emphasizes Mary more? What is the reason for this?

Chapter IX

The Literary Level of Matthew's Gospel

Many will come from the East and the West and sit down with Abraham, Isaac, and Jacob at the feast in the Kingdom of heaven. *(Mt 8:11.)*

Read through Matthew's Gospel at one sitting, as you did that of Mark. Allow yourself about an hour and a half for this. Notice the material which has been adapted from Mark. Notice also Matthew's systematic presentation of the words of Jesus in five discourses (Mt 5-7; 10; 13; 18; 23-5), the 'clusters' of miracle stories (Mt 8f), and the 'clusters' of conflicts (Mt 11-13; 21f). And see how frequently Matthew cites the Old Testament.

We sometimes hear or read that Matthew' Gospel consists of five booklets based on the five-book structure of the Law of Moses in the Old Testament. A principal reason for this explanation is the fact that Matthew presents five discourse sections, with five speeches of Jesus on five different aspects of the Kingdom of Heaven (as Matthew prefers to call the 'Kingdom of God', avoiding, in typical Semitic fashion, the mention of the sacred name of God).

However, this explanation does not seem to be correct, since it fails to account for the fact that Matthew puts his Infancy Gospel (Mt 1f) at the beginning of his document and his rendering of the Paschal Gospel at the end (Mt 26-8). So there are really seven panels or sections, not five—and the number seven seems to be a favourite device of this evangelist, since he groups various things in sevens (the seven beatitudes, the seven petitions in the *Our Father*, the seven parables of the Kingdom, the seven woes uttered against the Pharisees, etc).

But we must certainly acknowledge that Matthew has exercised a remarkable degree of literary artistry. He has quite evidently been influenced by Mark's Gospel, and by another document which many commentators call 'Q' (this 'Q' was apparently also used by Luke, though not by Mark). In addition to these two sources the evangelist also used some further source material which is peculiar to his Gospel, and which is therefore simple called 'M'. This 'M' material includes such things as Matthew's Infancy Gospel, some of the sayings of Jesus, and the Risen Lord scenes in his last chapter. Whatever else we may say about these elements of Matthew's Gospel, they are peculiar to him.

Aside from the Infancy Gospel at the beginning and the Paschal Gospel at the end, Matthew has indeed composed five booklets in the central section of his document, each of which contains a narrative segement followed by a discourse segment (or 'speech') of Jesus. There is another discourse section in Mt 23, in which Matthew gives Jesus' 'woes' against the Pharisees, but this leads straight into the lengthy Eschatological Discourse (or Jesus' Last Instruction to the disciples) in Mt 24f, so that the two discourses make up one long section.

All this is on the literary level, of course, and not on the theological level. But there are so many useful clues in the literary structure of Matthew's Gospel that it is worth our while to go through the whole document at this level in order to see how the evangelist has adapted the apostolic tradition to the situation of his own contemporaries who are to receive his message. After we have done that we shall put the clues together and try to find the basic theological message which Matthew presents.

The First Panel: the Infancy Gospel (Mt 1f)

We have already taken a brief look at both Matthew's and Luke's Infancy Gospels. By looking again at Matthew's we should be able to notice the rich profusion of biblical images which he has drawn from the Old Testament. It becomes steadily clearer that Matthew is more interested in speaking about the origin of Jesus theologically than in describing his birth in what we would call, in the modern sense, historical terms. There are pictures here both of the ancient Israelite ancestors of Jesus, who appear in the genealogy (Mt 1:1-17), and also of some gentiles, whom the Magi (in the opening verses of Mt 2) represent.

Also, from the beginning, the God of Israel is present at the birth and infancy of Jesus, as he was present to his people in the ancient past and in the days of these ancestors. This means that Matthew wants to show the continuity between Israel's ancient ancestors and Jesus. From the outset of his Gospel Matthew wants to portray the God of Israel as present and active in the conception and earthly origin of Jesus just as he had been present to his people in the early days of their sacred history. We can only appreciate the religious and theological importance of these chapters if we keep them in the evangelist's own perspective, i.e, as a bridge linking Israel's ancient history (in the Old Testament) with the events that come with Jesus and, eventually, since it is the Risen Lord who will send them out as his witnesses to the gentiles (Mt 28:16-20), with the apostles and with the whole Church.

The Second Panel (Mt 3-7)

Each of the five central panels (or 'booklets') of Matthew's

Gospel has a narrative segment followed by a discourse segment. In the first of these five panel Matthew for the first time shows that he is following Mark's lead by his presentation of the introductory triptych (Mt 3:1-4:11) to show the beginning of Jesus' public ministry. Here, again, are the preaching of John the Baptist, the baptism of Jesus, and Jesus' forty-day retreat in the desert, with the accompanying trials and his struggle with Satan. However, we can also see that Matthew fills in the scenes more than did Mark, so that he expands to twenty-eight verses what Mark presented in only thirteen (Mk 1:1-12). There is then a brief narrative of Jesus' gathering of his first disciples (the two pairs of brothers, Simon and Andrew, and James and John) as he now comes to Galilee and begins preaching the Gospel of the Kingdom of Heaven. Matthew makes the point that Jesus' message was characterized by this theme and that it came to the people of Galilee like a ray of sunshine (Mt 4:11-17); to bring this out, he quotes the 'darkness-light' themes of the oracle of Iasaiah (Is 9:1ff).

The first discourse segment comes in Mt 5-7, as the evangelist presents Jesus preaching his Sermon on the Mount. This is a major clue in showing the independence of Matthew's plan: he borrows from Mark's Gospel, but he has his own picture to offer, and he departs from Mark when and where he finds it necessary for his purpose. We should notice also that each of the five 'speeches' of Jesus ends in the same way: 'When Jesus had finished these words...', and that the next panel then begins with a narrative segment.

The Third panel (Mt 8-10)

It is surely no accident that there is now a shift from words to action. Whereas the previous panel, dominated by the Sermon on the Mount, shows Jesus mainly as a preacher, or as the prophet of the Gospel of the Kingdom, Matthew now groups together ten miracle stories to show Jesus as the wonder-worker. There are echoes of Mark's Gospel here again, in Jesus' healing of the leper and his curing of Peter's mother-in-law, and the summary (Mt 8:16-17); however, Matthew has enlarged on the Markan base by adding the cure of the centurion's servant in Capernaum, and his citation of the Isaian oracle (Is 53:4) in Mt 8:17. The next cluster of three miracles also draws from Mark, although Matthew has changed the sequence. Here Jesus calms the storm, curses two demoniacs across the lake (in Mk 5 there is only one!), and cures the paralysed man. There are some sayings in Mt 9:9-17 and then another cluster of four miracles. This cluster is unique because the third and fourth miracle stories are doublets of cures which Matthew also has elsewhere in his Gospel: the cure of the two blind men in Mt 9:27-31 is both a doublet and also a doubling of the incident of Bartimaeus of Mk 10:46-52 (cf Mt 20:29-34), so that what was one cure in Mark becomes four cures in Matthew! The possessed mute cure of Mt 9:32-34 is also a doublet of the same incident in Mt 12:22ff.

After this comes the discourse segment, as Jesus sends his disciples to extend his mission of bringing the Gospel of the Kingdom of Heaven, by doing the same works of preaching and healing. The speech which Jesus gives this time we can call his Missionary Discourse (Mt 10:5-42), although it seems to be a missionary discourse proper only in Mt 10:5-15, since from verse 16 the tone changes. This is another clue to Matthew's literary technique. He constructs these 'speeches' of Jesus by 'clustering' or stringing words of Jesus which are related on the basis of a similar theme or of a key word or phrase. In Mt 10:16 the key phrase seems to be 'I am sending you...' The panel ends with the standard transitional formula of Mt 11:1.

Chapter IX

The Fourth Panel: the Negative Response (Mt 11-13)

At first glance it may seem difficult to find a common denominator to these passages of the fourth panel. However, the literary structure is clear enough—narrative in chapters 11-13, and discourse (seven parables of the kingdom) in chapter 13. The transitional formula comes in Mt 13:53. A strong negative element begins to show up here, as Jesus faces up to those who are responding to his message the wrong way. John the Baptist does not understand who Jesus is or what he is doing (Mt 11:2-19). Jesus rebukes the unconverted generation of his countrymen, and reproaches the unconverted towns of Israel (Corazin, Bethsaida, and Capernaum). There is a series of confrontation with Pharisees and scribes, and the Pharisees begin to plan Jesus' destruction (Mt 12:14). Jesus stands apart from all of these, and even from his natural family (Mt 12:46-50). He is the gentle and suffering 'servant of God' (Is 42:1-4), as Matthew applies another Isaian oracle to him (Mt 12:18.21)—and, incidentally, the oracle says that the suffering servant will give the gentiles reason for hope. This is another clue to Matthew's message: the Gospel of the Kingdom of Heaven, which Jesus preaches, will eventually go beyond Israel, to the gentiles.

In the light of this literary pattern, the cluster of seven parables of the kingdom in Mt 13 is more than merely a collection of Jesus' stories about the Kingdom of Heaven. Perhaps if we were to see or hear these parables separately they would have their individual meanings to offer, but, when we see how Matthew groups them in this context, they take on a collective meaning which derives from their position in the unfolding rhythm of the document. There is a certain negative note here: much of the seed which the sower puts out is lost; the weeds will be burned and destroyed; many of the things caught in the net will be thrown away. Those who find the buried treasure or the precious pearl are prepared to part with what they have because they have found something better. And there is a powerful contrast between the smallness of the mustard seed and the bigness of the plant which it eventually produces. Mark had a smaller cluster of four parables (Mk 4), but Matthew has expanded this to seven, adding not only more parables but also a fairly lengthy text from the Old Testament oracle of Isaiah (Is:6:9f) in Mt 13:14-15, and a lengthy explanation of the meaning of the parable of the wheat and the weeds. He also adds some sayings of Jesus (Mt 13:16-17) which are related to the preceding verses on the basis of the related themes of 'eyes/see' and 'ears/hear' in the Isaian oracle.

This means that Matthew has grouped in this middle panel a number of elements from various sources to show, in one way or another, that Jesus has received a predominantly negative response to his message. People are unconverted, ignorant, or hostile. But, as Jesus says in the parables, the inner dynamic of the Kingdom of Heaven will take its course and produce fruit anyway. Human failure cannot impede the coming of the Kingdom of Heaven!

The Fifth Panel: the Church Emerges (Mt 14-18)

In the next panel Matthew again shows shows that he is following Mark's Gospel, but that he does not allow it to dominate him. Again, too, he goes beyond Mark by adding more details. He adds, in the narrative area, some special emphasis on Peter: in the walking on the water (Mt 14:22-33); in Peter's confession and the conferral of the keys (Mt 16:16-20); and in the puzzling incident of the coin in the fish's mouth (Mt 17:24-7). Then there is another speech of Jesus (Mt 18), in which he instructs the disciples on being as children, on scandal, on fraternal correction and forgiveness, and on praying together. In the light of the negative character of the previous panel

(Mt 11-13), it seems that Matthew is now beginning to show how the Church emerges, as Jesus turns more to his disciples, led by Peter, and prepares them to be the true Israel, built on foundations of faith like the faith of Peter (Mt 16:16).

The Sixth Panel: the Shift to Jerusalem (Mt 19-25)

On the narrative level of this panel, Jesus and his disciples head for Jerusalem—walking, of course—, and Jesus instructs them along the way, speaking of the ethical demands of the Kingdom of Heaven. For the third time Jesus predicts his suffering, death, and vindication, describing himself as the 'Son of Man' (Mt 17:22; 19:18). The mother of Zebedee's sons, James and John, requests special honours for them, and this prompts Jesus to express his teaching on service to others being of greater importance than seeking prestige or favours. In the capital city of Jerusalem the entire narrative is characterized by a series of conflicts and confrontations between Jesus and the leaders of his people. This grows to a crescendo, demanding some kind of resolution, which will not be long in coming. Even though Matthew is again dependant on Mark's Gospel here, we can see that he adds, from another source, Jesus' parables about the two sons (Mt 21:28-32)and about the royal banquet and the wedding garment (Mt 22:1-14). All three of these images suggest that others will receive the benefit which the originally intended receivers have forfeited. This is also an indication that Matthew wants to show the gentiles coming into God's plan after Israel has responded negatively to Jesus.

In the discourse section of this panel there are really two speeches of Jesus distinct from each other. The first speech rebukes the Pharisees in particular and the unconverted Israelites in general (Mt 23), and the second is Jesus' eschatological discourse (or last instruction) given to his disciples (Mt 24f). Jesus starts the first speech with some words to the crowds and to his disciples (Mt 23:1-12), warning them against the misleading example of these inadequate teachers, and he then addresses seven 'woes' to the Pharisees themselves (Mt 23:13-31). These 'woes' are in the same style of rebuke as those of the prophetic oracles of the Old Testament (e.g, Amos 5f; Is 5; 10): Jesus tells the leaders of the punishment that will come to them for their persecution of him and his disciples, and for their failure to accept the true Kingdom of Heaven which he has brought to them. The last three verses of the chapter (Mt 23:37ff) constitute another oracle in prophetic style, in which he rebukes Jerusalem for its lack of conversion.

In the Eschatological Discourse (Mt 24f) it is obvious that Matthew has reproduced the corresponding text of Mark (Mk 13) almost word for word. In this passage we see another example of the evangelist's literary technique: he follows his Markan source quite closely in Mt 24:1-37, but from that point on he adds sixty verses of sayings and parables of Jesus, related to the context on the basis of the theme of the need to be watchful and ready for the master's return and for his coming judgement. Here Matthew inserts the parables of the wise and foolish maidens and of the silver pieces or talents, and the scene of the final judgement with its imagery of the sheep and the goats (Mt 25). Much of this 'sayings' material is also in Luke, but none of it is in Mark; we conclude from this that both Matthew and Luke have taken it from the 'Q' document which must be assumed to have been available to them but not to Mark.

The Seventh Panel: Matthew's Paschal Gospel (Mt 26-8)
The first time we read through Matthew's concluding panel we see the influence of the Markan source which has also been prominent in the earlier sections of Mat-

thew. There is the Prelude (Mt 26:1-46), which includes: the plot against Jesus; the anointing at Bethany; Judas' treachery; the Last Supper, with Jesus' act of instituting the eucharistic memorial; and the agony at Gethsemane. Then comes the arrest (Mt 47-56) followed by the two trials, the Jewish one first (Mt 26:57-75) and then the Roman one with the torture (Mt 27:1-31); after that there is the execution of Jesus (Mt 27:32-56) and his burial (Mt 27:57-61), with the priests arranging for guards to be placed at the tomb (Mt 27:62-6). In this part of the Paschal Gospel Matthew's individuality goes beyond its Markan source in frequent references to the Scriptures (both explicit and implicit), in the detailed emphasis on Judas, and in the scenes of Pilate's wife and his washing of his hands.

At Calvary Matthew produces a master stroke: he reproduces from Mark the great signs of the darkness and the Temple veil being split, but he greatly intensifies the scene by adding apocalyptic details about the earthquake, the graves being opened, and the dead walking in the streets (Mt 27:51ff). He again shows his individuality with his description of the tomb guards, who are to recur in the following (and last) chapter. These details are all peculiar to the Matthaean rendering of the Paschal Gospel, and in one way or another they emphasize that everything which see here is in accordance with the patterns recognizable from the Old Testament Scriptures. They also highlight the guilt of Israel's leaders, whom Matthew depicts as dishonest and treacherous because their intention was to destroy Jesus regardless of legality or truth.

The three segments of Matthew's final chapter describe the tomb scene, the bribing of the guards, and the mission of the apostles. In all these segments Matthew shows his independence of Mark, since Mark's Gospel does not introduce the Risen Lord at all (except in the later additions to Mk 16 which, as we have seen, are not by Mark himself). Matthew resumes the language of cosmic portents here, recalling his description of the signs which occurred at the moment of Jesus' death. Again there is an earthquake, and again there is a mention of the tomb guards. But in Matthew the Risen Lord appears and speaks first to the women and only then to the apostles. The bribing of the tomb guards by the priests is yet another reference by Matthew to the basic malice which he attributes to these leaders of Israel. Finally, the Risen Lord's sending of his apostles to 'all peoples everywhere' brings the document to an end on a note of universalism, and carries the Gospel message beyond the confines of Israel, which has not accepted it.

Conclusion

Matthew's sweep of vision seems to be broader than Mark's, because Matthew shows the whole span from Abraham to David (Mt 1:1) and through Jesus to the apostles, who have become the Risen Lord's appointed representatives to 'all peoples everywhere'. Matthew has a greater command of the Old Testament scriptures, and a more deliberate and systematic literary style, than Mark. He is able to build upon the narrative foundation which Mark has laid, but he is also able to construct a moving and well-constructed picture much richer and fuller than that of Mark. Matthew adds not only the emergence of Jesus in continuity with the true Israel of the Old Testament, but also the emergence of the Church of the disciples, which is rooted in Jesus and is now the true Israel. The very fact that Matthew has gone beyond Mark at all shows that, although he apparently shares Mark's theological view, he does not feel limited by it— he wants to go further than Mark had gone, and say something that Mark had not said. For this reason we must now look at Matthew's document again, but this

Chapter IX

time we must go deeper than the narrative level and look for his special theological dimension.

1. Can you show three examples of material which Matthew has taken from Mark's Gospel?
2. Can you show how Matthew has adapted or rearranged Markan material?
3. In addition to his obvious citation of Old Testament texts, can you see two or three instances in which Matthew uses traditional Old Testament material without explicitly saying that he is doing this?
4. Are the seven 'panels' or sections of Matthew easily distinguishable?
5. Where did Matthew get the non-Markan material which he has included in his document?
6. Is there anything which suggests that the evangelist who produced this document was not one of the original twelve disciples of Jesus?

Chapter X

The Theological Dimension of Matthew's Gospel: the True Israel

For I tell you, unless your righteousness exceeds that of the scribes and Pharisees, you will never enter the Kingdom of Heaven. *(Mt 5:20.)*

Read through Matthew's Gospel again at one sitting, concentrating especially on his theological message. Notice in particular these theological features:
1) the continuous presence of the Kingdom of God (or Reign of God), from the Old Testament, through Jesus, and in the Church;
2) the opening up of the Kingdom of God to the gentiles, planned and already begun in the Old Testament;
3) the contrast between the 'true Israel' of Jesus and his disciples (the Church) and the 'false Israel' of the Jewish leaders;
4) Mark's picture of Jesus as the 'Son of Man', preserved and adapted by Matthew.

Once we recognize that Matthew has both retained much of Mark's Gospel and also gone beyond it, we can see that he has a purpose of his own—and a message of his own to offer. He has used considerable artistry in constructing his document, and he has added to the basic Markan pattern on both the literary and the theological level. These additions in Matthew, along with the rearrangement of Markan material that we find there, are our best clues to Matthew's special interests, precisely because they indicate where and how Matthew wants to go beyond the Markan message.

Of course, there is a theological core which Matthew shares with Mark as well as with the apostolic preachers who first proclaimed the Gospel about Jesus. This what we have been referring to as the 'Gospel of the Paschal Mystery'—the central message of the primitive Church. We saw it in the kerygmatic discourses in Acts and in St Paul's letters to his new converts, as well as in the whole fabric of Mark's Gospel. Natrually, Matthew has it too, so that, for him, just as for the generation of Christians who lived and died before anyone composed a coherent picture of Jesus' earthly ministry, the Jesus who appears in the Gospel is always the glorious Messiah who has been killed by men and raised up by God, and who will come again. Even in the earlier parts of Matthew's Gospel we see clues which suggest that the whole narrative picture is dominated by this mysterious victory of God which unfolds graphically in the last chapters of his document.

We saw this also in Mark's Gospel, when we made the point that it is not so much a forward-moving history as a backward look at the public ministry of Jesus in the light of his mysterious identity—an identity which becomes intelligible only in his suffering and glorification. The Gospel of the Kingdom of God which Jesus himself preached during his public ministry became the *kerygma* (proclamation) of the apostles: namely, that God had indeed shown himself in Jesus, even though nobody had been able to recognize him as God's Son until he became the Raised-up Lord. Thus the Jesus of the public ministry is always a 'hidden Messiah', as if people's eyes were veiled by their merely-human perspective, which let them see only the external surface of Jesus' earthly life without perceiving the divine reality which was showing itself to them all the time.

Matthew subscribes to all this, as we see, by allowing

himself to be guided and 'steered', so to speak, by Mark. Instead of starting on a whole new path, Matthew merely takes Mark's Gospel, which he has apparently studied in great depth, and supplements it with some of his own source material and some of his own dominant ideas. Right from the Infancy Gospel which forms the opening of his document, Matthew intertwines the two roles which Jesus will eventually have as both the Messiah of the Jews and the one through whom God's rule comes to the gentiles. Even though Mark frequently quotes the Old Testament, Matthew goes far beyond him to show that anyone who is thoroughly familiar with the Scriptures can see the biblical patterns operating in Jesus. This what Matthew means when he says, time and again, that 'this happened in order that the scripture might be fulfilled.' This fulfilment of the Scriptures is not always a mere matching of things point by point, as if it were a matter of mathematics or of material conformity. It means, rather, that the sacred realities which God set in motion in the Old Testament have come to their completion and fullest expression in the person of Jesus, and that this process of God's plan has now moved to a new stage as the apostolic Church, built by Jesus, now witnesses to the things that he taught.

Jews and Gentiles

It appears, then, that there is a line of theological continuity in this document which starts with Abraham and David in the first verse and reaches down to the mixed church of Jewish and gentile converts whom Matthew now invites to await the Raised-up Lord's second coming. The Magi were the first representatives of the wider gentile world, but after their appearance in the Infancy Gospel (Mt 2:1-12) Matthew introduces also the Roman centurion who showed more faith than many members of Israel itself (Mt 8:10). Jesus' satirical parable about the invited guests who refused the invitation to the wedding and were replaced by others (Mt 22:1-14) makes the same point—and so, too, does the other parable about the tenants in the vineyard (Mt 21:33-43). This prepares for the Risen Lord's charge to his apostles to preach to 'all the nations' (Mt 28:19).

The Church

We might well wonder whether Matthew was writing his document for Jews or for gentiles, since he is clearly interested in them both. All in all, however, there is such a pronounced Jewish emphasis throughout his Gospel that it would seem that this evangelist was addressing his message principally to his own countrymen—and to be doing so at a time when, a generation or so after the time of Jesus, Jewish Christians found themselves to be a minority in a Church which had moved away from the unconverted Israel and become a community mainly composed of gentiles. Perhaps these Jewish converts, finding themselves a minority, were vacillating and beginning to wonder whether they should revert to the religion of their forefathers. In order to dissuade them from such a step, Matthew writes to assure them that the true Israel is now the Church which follows Jesus' teaching on the Rule of God as it appeared in the Law and the Prophets. His message is thus a warning against the deceptive and hypocritical formalism of the Pharisees who, apparently, remained as hostile to Christians in Matthew's day as they had been to Jesus a generation earlier.

In fact, it would appear that Matthew's special contribution to the evolving Gospel is not so much a picture of the person of Jesus—Mark has already provided that—as a picture of the apostolic Church as the true Israel and the earthly sign of the Kingdom of Heaven. Against the background of the ancient ancestors whom the evangelist has depicted as the receivers of God's providence in the past, Matthew's picture of Jesus emerges as that of one who brings the fullness of the Law and the Prophets, and thus the essence of the Kingdom of Heaven, in a way in which the leaders of Israel had failed to present it. This is why Matthew never shows Jesus attacking the Law and the Prophets (the Old Testament). Instead, Jesus is portrayed as continually rebuking the scribes and the Pharisees for misleading their countrymen by a distorted teaching which has reduced Judaism to a soulless formalism. (Mt 5:15-20; 23:1ff.)

The healing power of God as a force for help, for life, and for wholeness shows up in Jesus' miracles, which Matthew has grouped as a cluster in Mt 8f. Yet, while Jesus demonstrates by these works that the Kingdom of Heaven is present and operative in his ministry, as an outpouring of favours from a benevolent God, the leaders nonetheless challenge him because his works fail to conform to their expectations and to their lifeless view of religion as a code of observances. The evangelist shows Jesus, in the face of this opposition, organizing and instructing his disciples as his 'church' (Mt 16:16). The core of religion, as Jesus now presents it to his disciples, is not the self-righteousness that comes from performing minute observances designed by human ingenuity, like that of Israel's leaders, but faith in God as Father, and child-like trust in his providence and life-giving power. Jesus is himself the prime example of these qualities.

This is why, as he moves steadily towards Jerusalem, fully aware that he must suffer and die there (Mt 16:21ff; 17:22f; 20:17:ff), Jesus concentrates on instructing the disciples. Even here, as Matthew follows Mark's basic lead, he enlarges the role of the disciples in his Gospel. He gives special prominence to Peter, who does and says much more in Matthew's Gospel than in Mark's (Mt 14:28ff; 16:16; 17:24-7; 18:21ff). Furthermore, Matthew constructs a fourth major 'speech' of Jesus

(Mt 18:1-35) as a 'discourse on community', in which Jesus gives his disciples special instructions on 'how to be church'. (Matthew is the only one of the four evangelists who uses the word *church*). In this instruction Jesus gives them directions on being childlike, on fraternal correction, on praying together, and on mutual forgiveness. In addition to these points, Matthew also reproduces some of Jesus' ethical teachings which he has taken over from Mark: e.g, Jesus' words about service to the brethren as a mark of true leadership (Mt 20:20-28) and of discipleship (Mt 25:31-46), and his words about correcting oneself before criticizing one's brethren (Mt 7:1-5). Some of these words of Jesus come directly from Mark's Gospel, but others have apparently come from the 'Q' source common to Matthew and Luke or from other early Christian texts which were available to this evangelist.

We can also get a good idea of what Matthew considers *not* to be true religion from the scenes in which he shows Jesus sharply rebuking the leaders of Israel. Here Matthew quite evidently wants his Jewish-Christian readers to realize that the teaching of these leaders is hypocritical and self-righteous. That is why he shows Jesus warning his disciples against the 'leaven' or 'bread' with which these leaders purport to feed their countrymen. (Mt 16:5-12; see also Mt 15:1-20.) In another 'speech' section (Mt 23) Matthew brings together into an extended cluster a collection of Jesus' words against these false teachers.

This is the contrast which runs throughout Matthew's message: the false Israel of the Pharisees on the one hand, and, on the other, the true Israel which Jesus practised and preached, and which is now to be found in the church of the apostles sent by Jesus to 'make disciples of all nations', whether they are Jewish or not.

The Stages of the Message
Once we have made the point that the Gospels are not

mere biographies of Jesus in the modern 'historical' sense of that word, but rather documents of 'narrative theology', we can begin to trace the theological pattern which each evangelist has built into his Gospel document. We have said that Matthew's Gospel accepts, more or less as a presupposition, that the paschal mystery of Jesus' death and glorification is the theological core of the New Testament—and of his own document as well. We made the further observation that this evangelist has allowed himself to be guided by Mark's theological message—the message that the mysterious identity of Jesus as the Son of God, unrecognized during his public ministry, can be seen only in the light of his suffering and eventual vindication as the Lord who is both high and low. Given all this, we can now attempt to trace the special theological pattern which Matthew set out to present in his Gospel.

The Kingdom of Heaven in the Old Testament and in Jesus' Infancy (Mt 1f)

As we have seen, the Infancy Gospel shows that the same divine providence which was present and operative in the Israel of the ancient ancestors is operative now, too, in the earthly origin of Jesus. The themes of the prophetic orcales come to life in Jesus' virginal conception, in the homage of the foreigners, and in the star of divine presence. The images of Jacob and Moses, both saved from violent death by God's special protection, emerge in the incidents of Jesus' infancy. All these special interventions by God are so many signs that a unique destiny awaits this child, and that this destiny is summed up in his name, which means 'saviour': 'He shall save his people from their sins' (Mt 1:21). The cruel irony, however, is that his people will respond to their saviour in a negative way!

Chapter X

The Kingdom in Jesus' Ministry (Mt 3-10)

Jon the Baptist is more than a historical accident or coincidence: he turns out to be the forerunner of Jesus, not just because he appears on the scene before Jesus, but even more because he sets the pattern which Jesus will eventually follow—the pattern of the prophet sent by God to call his countrymen to a conversion of heart, but eventually murdered because of his fidelity to the word of God. Jesus accepts baptism and sees the Holy Spirit hovering above him, while his Father's voice declares his special favour and designates him as the 'beloved son'. In the course of his desert retreat Jesus relives, for forty days, the trial which his ancestors underwent for forty years. The difference is that, whereas the Old Testament Hebrews repeatedly failed the tests of faith during their time in the desert, Jesus consistently rebuffs the invitations of Satan, and thereby appears as the paragon of what the true Israel—and a true child of God—should be.

Jesus' public ministry consists in bringing to his countrymen in Galilee the Gospel of the Kingdom of Heaven, in the twofold form of words and works. The works are all benign, signs of God's favour and helping kindness, the actuations of the promises which the Old Testament prophets had given to their people in former centuries. God would pour out on them a torrent of favours which would surpass their expectations and, indeed, anything that they could even imagine. But now these promised favours are living realities in the ministry of Jesus, which turns these past promises into present gifts.

The sermon on the Mount epitomizes Jesus' teaching on what is true religion according to the Scriptures (the Law and the Prophets), and in it Jesus warns his disciples against the misleading doctrines of the scribes and the Pharisees. The Sermon on the Mount does not present a new law, then: it expounds the neglected essence of the one law—an essence which has been obscured by the exaggerated and distorted teaching of the official leaders. This is why Jesus never attacks or rejects the Scriptures—what he attacks is the false Israel, represented by the leaders and by their ingenious human observances, which they pass off as the decrees of God. Instead of seeking the mind and word of God and his providence, these leaders rely on their own resources, building up a self-righteousness which comes not from God but from their own works. In all this Jesus looks like a latter-day Moses, bring to God's people the message of convenant Judaism—a religion made by God to give people peace of soul as they live in trusting dependence upon the providence which he offers them as their daily bread.

The False Israel's Negative Response (Mt 11-13)

The great tragedy is that Jesus meets a negative response. The crowds are enthusiastic about his miracles, but they fail to repond with a conversion of heart to his message. The disciples whom Jesus has assembled to be the nucleus of the true Israel are uncomprehending. The leaders are hostile and decide to destroy him (Mt 12:14-21), but, in the face of this, Jesus remains calm. He is the gentle Servant of God whom the Second Isaiah depicts as a bringer of peace. Nor will the negative response succeed in impeding God or defeating his plan. The apparent weakness of Jesus, the seeming failure of his mission, cannot halt the inner dynamism of God's rule. Like the seed and the wheat, God's plan—and Jesus himself—will be troubled and trampled. There will be death and loss. But eventually success will come: the seed will bear fruit, the wheat will come to harvest, God's rule will show itself. Even though people show no more appreciation of Jesus than they show of a tiny mustard seed, or of a pinch of yeast, there is a power at work in him: it will take its course and bring results which surpass all expectations.

The disciples should not be apprehensive about the apparent failure of Jesus' mission; rather, they should see it as a latter-day occurrence of the experience of Isaiah, who was also rebuffed by his countrymen, even though, in the course of time, events proved that he had been right, and that God's plan showed itself as Jesus had said that it would.

Jesus Prepares the Church (Mt 14-20)

Nevertheless, the die is cast. The false Israel of the leaders has decided to destroy Jesus, and he sees that he is to suffer the fate which the prophets suffered before him—and more. He is not merely to be rejected like Isaiah, but must be murdered like John the Baptist. He continues his ministry, feeds the crowd in the desert region, and reassures his disciples by walking on the water during a storm. Peter, ever the blusterer, must learn a devastating lesson: only the divine power which operates in Jesus can save him. Jesus is truly the Son of God (Mt 14:33)!

Peter's confession of faith in Jesus' true identity is both good and bad. It is good because what he says is true (Mt 16:16): Jesus is the Messiah whom God has sent to his people as his own Son. But Peter, who is to keep the keys of the new household of the true Israel, does not yet understand the whole message—and therefore is not yet ready to witness. Jesus must be, not only the Messiah, but—as the 'Son of Man'— a suffering and raised-up Messiah.

Two new patterns emerge from this section of Matthew's 'narrative theology'. First, there is the necessity of Jesus' being both a suffering servant of God and a glorified Messiah (the 'Son of Man'); and secondly, the disciples, led by Peter, are to be the 'church' after Jesus is taken away by the demands of God's plan. This image of Jesus as the rejected prophet and suffering servant must somehow fit together with the images of him as miracle-worker and transfigured Lord. But, whatever the identity of Jesus, the identity of these disciples is to be that of the church: they are to be the fellowship of brethren, disciples of the Kingdom of Heaven according to Jesus' example, relating to God as trusting children relate to a trusted father. They are to love each other, pray together, forgive each other, and seek always to know and follow the mind of God as it comes through the Scriptures, even though Israel's misguided leaders use these same Scriptures as a plaything in their debates.

This genuine service of God and of one another is something that the disciples have yet to learn. Even the wife of Zebedee has not absorbed the lesson: she want some special mark of prestige for her sons, and still thinks that Jesus is preparing to set himself up as a new king (Mt 19:20-28)! Her sons are optimistic, too, but this is because they have not yet assimilated the instruction which Jesus has been giving them. They are not yet ready to accept a suffering Messiah—or to be suffering disciples! They must either learn the lesson or fade away. Matthew's theological portrait of discipleship comes through clearly here as that of a life-style lived according to Jesus' example, and not as one of merely listening to his words.

In Jerusalem (Mt 21-3)

Even though we tend to speak of Jesus' Jerusalem ministry, a closer look at the Jerusalem chapters shows us that Matthew does not really portray Jesus undertaking such a ministry. It is not so much a matter of ministry as of constant conflict, of a total lack of communication between one side and the other. Even the scene of Jesus' so-called 'triumphal entry', though at first sight a great success, is really a picture of. tragic misunderstanding. Why do the crowds acclaim Jesus with such enthusiasm? It must be for essentially the same reason as the one

Chapter X

which led the blind man (or men) in Jericho to call: 'Lord, Son of David!' (Mt 19:30f). Jesus' reputation as a wonder-worker and healer had preceded him from Galilee, and this encouraged people to expect him to use his superhuman power and set himself up as a new messianic king, like David in the old days. But they completely missed the symbolic meaning of the ass on which he rode—Jesus wanted them to see him as one who is meek and 'without display' (Mt 20:5). Jesus knows that his visit to the capital must lead to his death—and, beyond that, to his vindication. He is to be raised up as the Son of Man, as he has already told the puzzled disciples.

The series of conflicts in Jerusalem shows Jesus engaging in debates with every group of the Jews and their leaders: there are sharp words to the crowds, to the Pharisees, to the Sadducees, and to the priests. Each of these scenes has already appeared in the corresponding sections of Mark's Gospel, so Matthew is not being as original or artistic here as he has been in composing the earlier chapters of his document. Nevertheless, he is successful in showing the crescendo of tension which builds up through the course of Jesus' days in the capital. As he demonstrates the incompatability of Jesus and the leaders becoming so intense as to be irreversible and irreconcilable, he adds, over and above what he has drawn from Mark, the parable of the two sons (Mt 21:28-32) and the double parable of the royal wedding-banquet and of the man who failed to come properly dressed (Mt 22:1-14).

Matthew uses these words of Jesus to give a preview of the future: God's chosen people have failed to respond to his invitation with gratitude and due conversion of heart—and, as a consequence of their defection, the gentiles, who have always been despised as outsiders, will now have an opportunity to receive the favours which are to be the hallmarks of God's dealing with men. The scene of the coin of tribute and Jesus' shrewd reply (Mt 22:15-22) shows that their need be no incompatability between serving God and being a member of the gentile Roman Empire—another opening that the Church will need as it becomes more gentile and less Jewish. The debate with the Sadducees makes it clear that Jesus holds firmly to his expectation that God will raise him from the crucible of death, even though these leaders ridicule the suggestion of life after death.

The final outburst comes as Matthew gathers Jesus' words against the false teachers (Mt 23:1-39). The first of these words (Mt 23:1-12) are Jesus' address to his own disciples, on the contrast between false leadership and true greatness, which consists, not in lording it over others, but in humbly serving the rest of the brethren. This is the kind of religion that Jesus has both preached and practised throughout his ministry. But the conventional teachers of Judaism have reduced religion to a code of formalized externals (Mt 23:13-32) which fail to help their people to relate to God, bring them no joy, and miss the whole essence of true religion!

Matthew broadens the scene in the last verses of the chapter (Mt 23:37ff) by depicting Jesus addressing his last words to the false Israel, represented by the unconverted capital city. There is a hint here of what is to come: Jesus sees himself as one more in a long line of rejected prophets. Others have been abused and killed, and so what awaits him has happened before. He also knows, however, that he will come out successful in the long run, and that the ones who have rejected him will have to admit that he has won through after all. The last verse (Mt 23:39) contains the acclamation of greeting for a victorious king, which the crowds used to sing in the liturgy of celebration (Ps 118:26). This final word of Jesus to his unconverted countrymen is something like the point he has already made in Mt 13: there, in the face of all the negative responses he had just received (Mt 11f), Jesus threw back at them his assurance that, notwithstanding its apparent failure, his mission would eventually succeed. Human action and opposition simply cannot prevent the final triumph of God's fatherly lordship. The Kingdom of Heaven will have victory over human sin.

The Last Instruction (Mt 24f)

Now that Jesus has made his last response to his unconverted countrymen, the evangelist proceeds to show him delivering his 'farewell address' to his disciples. This is one of the most demanding sections of the Gospel to read, and one of the most difficult to understand; nevertheless, the basic lines of Matthew's purpose are fairly clear through the maze. Matthew is probably referring to things that have already happened, although he presents them as predictions, made by Jesus, of events still in the future. Most of the first half of this discourse of Jesus has come from Mark's Gospel (Mk 13:1-37), but Matthew adds some words of Jesus which were also available to him from other sources to emphasize the mood and charge of Jesus' last words to his chosen disciples.

Matthew has shown Jesus rebuking the Pharisees (Mt 23) and leaving them to the punishment which they have brought on themselves by failing to practise religion according to the mind of God. The last message of Jesus to his disciples is much more reassuring, although it is also frighteningly demanding. In all probability the persecutions and even killings of Christians which Matthew here presents as prophecies on Jesus' lips (Mt 24:5-14) have become facts of the recent past by the time he writes. What Jesus predicted in his day is already history in the evangelist's day! The sacred capital city of God's people was destroyed in AD70 by the legions of the Roman army; it appears that Matthew wrote his Gospel, including these words of Jesus, after that event, as if it were the final catastrophe to fall upon the Israelites (Mt 24:15-28). As a consequence, the definitive separation of the Jewish and Christian religions had apparently by now become a fact of history. The Gospel had gone to the gentiles; Jerusalem had been destroyed, and Matthew portrays all this as a sign that God had punished his unbelieving people, even though they were originally his chosen ones.

The one final occurrence that is yet to take place now is the eventual return of Jesus as the vindicated 'Son of Man', to gather together his suffering disciples and bring them to the peace of God's kingdom. This hope and promise must animate Christians as they await their salvation, though they do not know when it will come. The parables which Matthew has added to the discourse (Mt 25:1-30) exhibit the common denominator of an exhortation to the disciples—i.e, in the evangelist's own day, the Christians—to work diligently with what they have received, so that, when the time comes, they may confidently expect a favourable reckoning from God, and then his generous reward.

There is a great deal of blurring of images here. Some of the things which come across as future are already past. Some of the words which Matthew portrays Jesus as addressing to his disciples in Jerusalem are Matthew's own message to his Christian contemporaries. And the picture of the last judgement, with the separation of the sheep and the goats (Mt 25:31-46), fuses the image of Jesus as Son of Man and liberator of his troubled disciples with the image of him as a severe and final judge, sending his inadequate servants to an eternal punishment. Again, the picture of the earthly future is blurred into that of the eternal heavenly future.

It was certainly not the evangelist's intention to confuse his readers, and he seems confident that the oriental imagery and apocalyptic terminology of this discourse would be intelligible to them. It would appear that these readers were, to some extent at least, victims of hostility levelled at them both by Roman pagans and by their fellow-Jews who had remained outside the community of the Church. The ultimate gist of the evangelist's message at this point is the combination of a challenge to these fellow-Christians to endure their tribulations, since these make them imitators of Jesus, and a firm guarantee that the Risen Lord will bring them to share his ultimate victory. Christians who were educated in the Old Testament traditions of Israel before their conversion to Christianity should be able to recognize the biblical patterns of this language, and so transfer it to their own Christian situation.

The Paschal Gospel (Mt 26-8)

Matthew's approach to the Paschal Gospel is more restrained than his approach to the public ministry of Jesus or to his infancy. The principal reason for this may well be that, in this area, Matthew felt himself less free to innovate, since the oral tradition about Jesus' Passion and Glorification had circulated within the primitive apostolic community, in a more or less coherent and set form, for a generation or so. However, even though the basic pattern of the Passion scenes is from Mark, Matthew has drawn the Risen Lord scenes in Mt 28 from other sources, and it is in this last chapter of his document that the evangelist brings out his own theological emphases for the Paschal Gospel.

As far as Jesus' Passion is concerned, Matthew mentions the Scriptures explicitly only once more than Mark does in the corresponding section of his Gospel. This may seem surprising at first glance, since, as we have seen, Matthew mentions the Scriptures frequently in the earlier chapters. However, he has a way of intensifying the biblical element without making explicit mention or quotation of the Scriptures. Matthew has a liking for presenting biblical themes in implicit and graphic form, without direct reference to the texts which they represent; and, in the Paschal Gospel, he introduces many such implicit allusions, inserting them along the way as he reproduces the main lines of the Markan rendering. We see this, for example, in the specific figure of the thirty pieces of silver which Judas received (Mt 26:15); in Jesus' words of acknowledgement, as he calls Judas 'Friend' (Mt 26:50); in the mention of 'legions of angels' (Mt 26:53f); and in the account of Judas' tragic death, where the details are intertwined with biblical phrases from the prophetic books of Jeremiah and Zechariah (Mt 27:3-10). Matthew expects his readers to see these biblical patterns, which he has woven into his narrative, as his way of adding emphasis to the Passion tradition. The same applies to the scenes of Pilate's washing his hands to disclaim complicity in Jesus' death (Mt 27:24), and of the crowd's willing acceptance of responsibility for Jesus' blood (Mt 27:25). This cry of the crowd, incidentally, may be the evangelist's way of suggesting that, whatever guilt may rest on the Roman governor, it was ultimately Jesus' own countrymen who sought his death.

All these elements are in Matthew's Gospel alone, and he uses them to 'historicize' biblical themes as a way of impressing on his Jewish-Christian readers, in terms which they should have been able to appreciate, his point that Jesus' 'Passover' is relevant to them. The same is true for the upheavals in nature—the earthquake, darkness, and other cosmic portents—which come into the scene as Jesus dies (Mt 27:51ff). One or two of these elements are in Mark's parallel rendering, but Matthew has made the whole thing more vivid in order to show that God intervenes and reveals himself at Jesus' death. This lets not only the bystanders, but also Matthew's readers, know that, now they have done their worst to Jesus, God is still supremely in control of the situation.

Going beyond the limits of what human sinfulness can do, the Father brings about a whole new order of things, including the resurrection of the dead 'saints' (Mt 27:53) which flows from the resurrection of Jesus.

Matthew also insists on introducing graphic examples of his own contempt for those leaders who caused Jesus' death. He has not only repeated Mark's depiction of their treachery, but has added the three scenes of the guards—as present at Jesus' burial, as present again at his resurrection, and as being bribed by the Jewish leaders (who are obviously corrupt in their motives here). These scenes add depth and strength to the pictures of Jesus as Son of Man, suffering servant, and righteous victim which have come to Matthew from the earliest stages of the Church's apostolic preaching.

The Risen Lord (Mt 28)

The evangelist has not changed the direction of the Paschal Gospel, therefore; rather, he has tried to enrich it by injecting elements of a peculiarly Hebraic flavour. However, the Risen Lord chapter (Mt 28) reflects more of Matthew's originality, supplementing the Markan base as it does with further special Matthaean features. The women are there, of course, with the angel at the tomb. But the cosmic, or apocalyptic, element of the earthquake is his addition which, like the cosmic disturbances at Jesus' death, suggests that God is showing his presence and his action by these signs. And the Risen Lord himself also appears in Matthew's last chapter, whereas he does not appear in Mark (at least in the original verses Mk 16:1-8).

These concluding verses of Matthew have come from a depth and maturity of theological understanding which surpass those of Mark. It is not only that the Risen Lord presents himself—there are further elements here as well, like the image of the vindicated 'Son of Man' who has received 'full authority' over both heaven and earth. This is Matthew's way of emphasizing that the Risen Jesus is the fulfilment of the Old Testament theme of the 'Son of Man', for the same words occur here (Mt 28:18) as in the apocalyptic scene of Dan 7:14. Again, there is the theological element of 'mission', which the Risen Lord confers on the bemused women (Mt 28:10) and on the hesitant disciples (Mt 28:17-20). This means that it is never enough merely to *know* that Jesus has been raised up: nobody ever comes to experience the reality of the Risen Lord without being sent on mission to *witness* to him! To experience the Risen Lord is to be sent—to be an apostle.

This greater theological depth shows up further in the Risen Lord's injunction to his apostles to baptize (Jesus has not said a word about baptism throughout the whole of Matthew's Gospel, until this final scene). The reference to baptism itself, along with the baptismal formula invoking the three names of the Trinity, is certainly a reflection of the Church's practice in the evangelist's own day, which went beyond the 'baptism in the name of Jesus' of the earlier stages of the Church's practice (Acts 2:38).

Finally, there is too the theological element of universalism, for the apostles are now to go beyond Israel to 'all the nations' and teach what Jesus has taught, waiting for the end with confidence that the Risen Lord has not abandoned them. As he wrote this, our evangelist was well aware that the Church had left behind its Jewish beginnings and gone out to embrace the gentiles. It was probably already some years after the catastrophe of AD70, when the Roman armies suppressed the Jewish attempt at revolution in Palestine, and thus provided the Christians with an occasion for seeing this as God's way of punishing the Jews once and for all for their failure to accept Jesus. The 'things' that Jesus has commanded (Mt 28:20) refer back to all the practical instructions which Jesus had given his disciples throught Matthew's Gospel, in clear contrast to the mislaeading teachings of the Pharisees and other leaders of the false Israel.

Conclusion

In retrospect we can notice that, though Matthew has presented the fulfilment of the Scriptures in Jesus for the benefit of Jewish Christians, his account of the teachings of Jesus on true religion and on how the disciples should relate to God and to each other shows them as universal, practical, and down-to-earth. This means that the evangelist is here offering the Church and Christianity to both Jews and gentiles, not as a philosophy, but as an everyday ecclesial life-style. For Jews it represents the maturation of their ancestral traditions. For gentiles it shows that God calls them too—to the banquet which the invited guests have spurned. These gentiles, who were foreshadowed by the Magi (Mt 2:1-12), are to learn of the Risen Lord from the apostles, who are the true Israel now, instructed by him in real meaning of the Kingdom of Heaven, which follows God rather than the false exaggerations of Israel's hypocritical leaders.

At root Matthew's special theological contribution is his picture of the Church, which has now emerged as the true Israel even though it has become predominantly gentile. This fact of history, as so many of the facts of the Gospel, was anticipated in the Sacred Scriptures of Israel's own tradition, and merely brings that tradition to the completion of what God began long ago. The theological progression of the two evangelists is thrown into relief here by the marvellous interpenetration of the messages of Mark and Matthew. Both present the Gospel of Jesus on the Rule of God, and both present the central apostolic message of the paschal mystery. But whereas Mark, making the first attempt at this kind of 'narrative theology', outlined the mysterious person of Jesus as the unrecognized Messiah, Matthew went beyond him to show the Church and true religion as a life-style willed by God and contained in the Scriptures as interpreted by Jesus. This true religion has moved away from the false Israel and its unconverted leaders, but is now—in the evangelist's own day—clearly reconizable in Jesus, in his apostles, and in the new, larger community of the gentile Church which has grown up and awaits the return of the Risen Lord.

1. Why does Matthew repeatedly show the fulfilment of the Old Testament Scriptures in Jesus?
2. Why does Matthew insist on the contrast between the 'false Israel' of the Jewish leaders and the 'true Israel' of Jesus and his disciples?
3. How does Matthew adapt the miracle-story tradition which he has taken from Mark's Gospel?
4. Did Matthew write for converted (Christian) Jews, to strengthen their faith, or for unconverted Jews, to attract them to Christianity?
5. What is the principal theological feature which Matthew adds over and above the Gospel of Mark?

Chapter XI

Luke's 'First Account'

I thought it would be good to write an orderly account for you. I do this so that you will know the full truth about everything which you have been taught. *(Lk 1:3f.)*

Allow yourself about two hours to read through both St Luke's Gospel and the Acts of the Apostles as a two-part whole. Notice the unity of style and the continuity of the narrative. Read them with an eye to the following special features:-
(a) Luke's frequent mentions of the Holy Spirit;
(b) the gradual but deliberate movement of the Gospel from Israel to the gentiles;
(c) the prominence of compassion, peace, healing, and joy as the chief characteristics of the Kingdom of God;
(d) the favourable light in which Luke portrays the Romans
(e) the presence of 'Q' material, which appears also in Matthew, but not in Mark.

The first point that we can notice about Luke's work, on the literary level, is that he is the only one who has contributed a two-part work to the New Testament. This shows, of course, the broad span of his vision, from the best of the old Israel, represented by Zechariah and Elizabeth in the Temple of Jerusalem at the beginning of his Gospel, to Paul preaching the Christian message in Rome, at the end of Acts. Even if Luke did not have such a plan in mind when he started to compose his Gospel, his finished work nevertheless exhibits the widest and most sweeping view of all the synoptic documents.

In the first verse of Acts Luke refers back to his 'first account', which obviously means his Gospel. These two books therefore represent one mind and one message, as Luke now undertakes to explain Christianity to his friend Theophilus. But in the first verse of his Gospel Luke refers back yet further, to others who have already written earlier works about Jesus. (These earlier works are probably the sources which Luke used, including Mark's Gospel and the 'Q' document.) So Luke does not claim to be the first to interpret the Gospel; rather, his purpose is to bring together the things which are in the Church's early tradition to form an orderly and attractive picture which Theophilus can see as a whole.

As far as his relationship with Mark is concerned, it is evident that he has allowed this document to influence him, but that, at the same time, he has gone far beyond Mark in adding the Infancy Gospel at the beginning and the picture of the emerging Church in Acts at the end. Even reading through Luke's Gospel in a cursory way we notice that this evangelist has combined Markan material with a considerable amount of material which both he and Matthew have taken from the 'Q' document, as well as material which is uniquely Lukan, and which we can therefore call simply 'L'. In the normal course of events we are not aware of what is peculiar to one Gospel or to another, since we are used to thinking of the 'Life of Jesus' in a composite way; but when we study the Gospels one at a time we find clues which draw out the special interests of each evangelist—and Luke is especially generous in providing clues which reveal his mind-set.

It is particularly characteristic of the third evangelist to appear almost anxious to show salvation coming to the gentiles, whom Luke invariably presents in the most favourable light possible. We may wonder why he at the same time shows such a heavy Jewish emphasis in his opening chapters (the Infacy Gospel) and again in the first section of Acts (the emerging Church in Jerusalem). The answer to this has to be the answer of history: the salvation which has come to the gentiles has come to them from God through—as a fact of history—Israel as the channel. A recurrent pattern shows through both of Luke's books: the Gospel comes to the gentiles only after the Jews have rejected it. The pattern appears so often that it can hardly be there by accident—it must be a part of Luke's basic message.

The Lukan Panorama

Luke has not been quite as systematic as Matthew in arranging his source material. He does not provide a regular alternation of narrative and discourse sections, nor does he make so much of Peter's confession—it is not the turning-point of his Gospel as it is of Mark's (Mk 8:26-30). Nevertheless, the flow of his narrative is smoother and gentler than it is in either of the other Synoptic Gospels. Furthermore, Acts follows on from the Gospel so gracefully that we can be sure that Luke's own thinking moves with it, as he shows the Holy Spirit bringing to the gentiles the same 'gospel of peace' that had first been brought to the Israelites, in Jesus.

We cannot do justice to Luke, or understand his message, unless we try to grasp the whole panorama as he has depicted it. Altogether this panorama is quite lengthy (a total of fifty-two chapters), but it is so coherent and even—at least for the most part—that we have little difficulty in reading it through or seeing it as a whole.

The Infancy Gospel (Lk 1f)

The whole first chapter of Luke's Gospel is a 'double diptych'. Luke has constructed parallels of John the Baptist and Jesus, first in the double annunciation/conception scenes and then in the double birth/circumcision/ naming scenes. And yet Jesus is always superior to John. The virginal manner of Jesus' conception surpasses that of John by his aged mother, although both conceptions are miraculous in different ways. Jesus' name ('God saves') conveys a more powerful message than John's ('God is gracious'). All the personalities of the Infancy Gospel represent the best of Jewish piety, serving God humbly and waiting for the peace which God promised to his people through the oracles of the ancient prophets.

The thoroughly Jewish flavour of the first chapter blends with the wider view of the second, which opens with references to the gentile emperor and the time of Quirinius as governor of Syria. In this way Luke suggests to his friend Theophilus, to whom he has addressed both his works, that the Gospel has something to say to the gentiles, and that the Church is also part of the wider family of mankind outside the confines of Israel. The atmosphere surrounding Jesus' birth, infancy, and childhood is touched by the special presence of God, and by a notable gentleness which emphasizes that the God whom Luke represents is a friendly and gracious God. All the four songs which Luke includes here are entirely Jewish, with nothing representing Christianity in any of them, except the context which Luke has provided by placing them at this point. It would seem that they have come to Luke from Jewish sources, and that he has included them in his Infancy Gospel in order that they may now express the faith which animates Luke and his fellow Christians.

Introductory Triptych (Lk 3:1-4:13)

Luke here joins his 'narrative theology' to that of Mark by repeating the three scenes which open the moving picture of Jesus' public ministry: the preaching ministry of John the Baptist, Jesus' baptism in the River Jordan, and his time of retreat in the desert. Even though the

Chapter XI

basic pattern and the sequence of the scenes follow the lead which Mark has given (Mk 1:1-13), Luke has inserted additional elements which make the whole section appealing to gentiles. The first of these additions is the chronological reference to the 'fifteenth year of Tiberius Caesar' (Lk 3:1) and to the other Roman rulers. This again means that what Luke is now about to draw attention to is not something isolated in a remote region, for Israel alone, but something which was a part of the history of the Roman Empire and indeed of the whole gentile world. Even the words of John the Baptist suggest this, when he quotes the oracle of the Second Isaiah to the effect that 'all mankind shall see salvation coming from God' (Lk 3:6, paraphrasing Is 40:5).

The principal feature that Luke adds to this 'Introductory Triptych' is his genealogy of Jesus (Lk 2:23-38). We immediately think of comparing it with the family tree of Jesus which Matthew offers in the opening verses of his Gospel (Mt 1:1-17). Two points at once stand out from such a comparison. First, the two lists are so different that there does not seem to be any possibility of reconciling them. The two evangelists must have used whatever source material they had available, but there are so few names common to the two lists that we simply cannot put them together. The second point is even more important, because it illustrates Luke's theological purpose. Instead of tracing Jesus' family descent forward from Abraham and David, as does Matthew (Mt 1:1ff), Luke goes in the opposite direction, showing that Jesus was descended not only from the great patriarchs of Israel but, beyond them, from Adam himself. Thus, once again, Luke stresses that the gentiles have something in common with the Gospel, since this Jesus is one with them, as a fellow member of the great universal human family, and as a fellow descendant of the common ancestor of all (*Adam* in Hebrew means 'mankind').

In fact, throughout his presentation so far, Luke has shown Jesus to be remarkably human, even though his humanity is unique and special. If he had presented Jesus in spectacular terms, it would have been difficult, if not impossible, for Theophilus, or any other gentile reader, to relate to him. So Luke finds the middle way, which includes both elements: Jesus is always human, a fellow descendant of Adam with every Jew and every gentile, and yet his presence on earth is a special act of God. This has prepared Jesus for an equally special destiny, which will eventually reach beyond the confines of the Israelite people and call for a response of faith from the pagan members of the Roman world as well.

Jesus' Public Ministry (Lk 4:14-9:50)

Though we can readily recognize the familiar lines of Jesus' ministry in this section, there are nevertheless examples of Luke's particular touch in each of these chapters. Right at the beginning of the section Luke has rearranged the sequence of the scenes: whereas Mark presents Jesus' visit to his own home town of Nazareth in the middle of his public ministry (Mk 6:1-6), Luke makes this the first scene of the section, and he also expands it considerably from the simpler and briefer Markan rendering. It is not difficult to see why he has done this. First, the words which Jesus addresses to his fellow townsmen are programmatic for his whole ministry: he quotes the oracle of the Third Isaiah, and announces that he is the fulfilment of this prophecy (Is 61:1f). Jesus' neighbours in Nazareth respond to this with enthusiasm and admiration—but then comes the second part of the episode, as Jesus goes on to announce that his mission is not for Israel only, and that God's favours are for the gentiles as well. It would seem that Luke is 'historicizing' here, by anticipating, even at this early stage of his Gospel, what eventually came to be historical fact—Jesus

Chapter XI

and his message received a negative response from his own countrymen, and this paved the way for the Gospel to be carried to the wider gentile world beyond Israel, where it was much more successful. The welcome which Jesus receives from strangers in Capernaum after the debacle in his home town of Nazareth (Lk 4:31f) is thus a foreshadowing of the same thing.

When Luke describes Jesus' recruiting of his first disciples (Lk 5:1-11), he again enlarges the scene beyond what he had in his Markan base by adding the miracle of the catch of fish and Peter's humble admission that he is a 'sinful man'. Neither of the other synoptic evangelists has given these details, though the miraculous catch of fish is in the appendix to the fourth Gospel (Jn 21:1-11). This, along with some other clues in the third Gospel, leads us to suspect that Luke has somehow been under the influence of the Johannine tradition—perhaps an oral form of it—before the fourth Gospel actually emerged in written form.

The various miracle stories in this section have already appeared in Mark's Gospel: e.g, Jesus' curing of the possessed man and of Peter's mother-in-law (Lk 4:33ff), or the healing of the leper and the paralysed man on the mat (Lk 5:12ff). The hostility of the leaders is also a familiar theme by now, and is clear in the scenes of the paralysed man, the dinner at Levi's house, and the sabbath grain controversy (Lk 5:12-6:11). In these scenes Luke is not being original!

The 'Great Discourse' (Lk 6:20-49), however, is another of Luke's special contributions. Though it has a vague similarity to the Sermon on the Mount (Mt 5ff), it is much shorter, and seems to be not so much Jesus's description of the essence of Judaism—as the Sermon on the Mount is in Matthew—as a collection of Jesus' instructions to his disciples on how to endure the hostility of enemies and persecutors. Both Luke and Matthew have taken this material from the 'Q' text, which was mostly a collection of 'sayings' of Jesus, but they have assembled its elements differently—and there can be little doubt that Matthew has made a better job of presenting Jesus' words in a solemn, well-composed instruction.

Like the 'Great Sermon', the next series of incidents is also absent from Mark's Gospel, and in a similar way they too show some special features of Luke's style and interest. The healing of the centurion's servant (Lk 7:1-10) also occurs in Matthew as one of the cluster of Jesus' miracles (Mt 8:5-13), but Luke's rendering of the dialogue gives further evidence of his sympathy for gentiles, and especially for Roman officials (who always appear in a favourable light in Luke-Acts). Then come the three scenes involving Jesus' gracious relationships with women. The first of these is the scene of the widow of Naim (Lk 7:11-17), which is followed by that of the penitent woman whose humble homage is more acceptable that the shallow hospitality of the Pharisee (Lk 7:36-50). The third scene is more general: it shows Jesus travelling through Galilee, bringing the Gospel of God's peace, accompanied by his disciples and by several women—including Mary of Magdala (Lk 8:2), who has often been identified, though not correctly, with the sinful and penitent woman of the previous incident.

Most of the remaining passages of this public ministry section of Luke's Gospel are from Mark's rendering, and we can see how Luke has allowed himself to be guided by Mark's document. But we can also see what might be called the 'great Lukan omission': Mark's Gospel has two accounts of the miracle of the loaves and of the incidents which go with it (Mk 6:45-7:37; 8:1-26). Matthew has followed Mark here and reproduced both passages (Mt 14:13-16:12). But it is immediately obvious that Luke has simplified the whole narrative by omitting, not only the doublet of the loaves miracle, but most of the material

Chapter XI

which accompanies it in both Mark and Matthew (Lk 8:17f). One reason for this may be that Luke saw this second section as a doublet of the first, and was satisfied with the point made in that first account without feeling the need to repeat it. Another possibility is that in this way Luke is able to concentrate on Jesus' ministry in Galilee, by not mentioning his travels to other areas. Thus Luke omits Jesus' healings in Tyre and Sidon, and in Bethsaida, because later in his Gospel he will move on to show how salvation came to foreigners after Israel had definitively rejected it.

As the narrative progresses, it becomes somewhat more difficult to separate Luke's literary technique from his theological motive. He adds or substracts things according to his overriding purpose, and increasingly we come to see that his purpose is to bring a religious—or theological—message to his gentile friend Theophilus (Lk 1:1-4). Even Peter's profession of faith, and Jesus' first and second Passion predictions, come and go rather smoothly (Lk 9:18-22; 43ff), because they do not have the same importance for Luke's purpose as they have for Matthew and—especially—for Mark.

In fact, we can say that, as Luke ends his presentation of Jesus' public ministry (Lk 9:46-50), the peaceful and gracious atmosphere which marked his Infancy Gospel has come to characterize the whole mission of Jesus among his people. Jesus has brought them a call to conversion, and works of healing power, but the jarring note arises from the fact that he has found a better acceptance among strangers and pagans than among his own people, who consider themselves paragons of righteousness. John the Baptist has receded into the background, and Jesus has become the prophet who knows that he must suffer, die, and be raised up again, as the 'Son of Man' (Lk 9:22, 44).

The Journey to Jerusalem (Lk 9:51-19:27)

The largest segment of Luke's Gospel is this journey section, which occupies about ten chapters—almost half his document! And yet, when we read it through, we see that there is only a thin line of narrative which Luke has used to assemble these fragments under the general heading of Jesus' deliberate decision to go to the capital (Lk 9:51). Mark was the first to write a description of Jesus' journey from his home territory in Galilee down to Jerusalem, but he put it all in a single chapter (Mk 10), which Matthew expanded into two chapters in his Gospel (Mt 19f). And so, when Luke spreads it out to ten chapters, it could seem that he wants to emphasize the journey as the most important part of Jesus' public ministry. But the evidence does not really support that conclusion: rather, this section is little more than a jumble of loosely related fragments which Luke has taken over from the Church's early tradition—and these fragments represent both the oral stage of that tradition and the 'Q' document.

Many of the elements which Luke has placed in the journey section are also in Matthew's Gospel, but not in the context of the journey; in Matthew they are spread around in the various narratives and discourses which the evangelist composed. In the segment of Luke which we call the 'Great Lukan Insertion' (Lk 9:51-18:14) we find those parts of the tradition which are common to Luke and Matthew but are not found in Mark. However, Luke preserves these fragments in a much less orderly way than Matthew, who organizes his material according to narrative and discourse, and according to basic themes. From a comparison of Luke and Matthew in this regard, we can conclude that Luke is not especially interested in showing these elements in a systematic way, or in terms of precise details of time and place. Rather, he has collected them

Chapter XI

in his less organized way simply to preserve them as samples of the 'Jesus tradition'.

In this journey section we notice the familiar parables of the good Samaritan (Lk 10:25-38); the rich fool (Lk 12:16-21); the lost son, lost coin, and lost sheep (Lk 15); the dishonest manager (Lk 16:1-8); the rich man and Lazarus (Lk 16:19-31); and the corrupt judge and the widow, and the Pharisee and the tax collector (Lk 18:1-14). There are also the miracles of the stooped woman (Lk 13:10-17) and the ten lepers (Lk 17:11-19), which are unique to Luke, as are these parables.

Some of the other 'sayings' we have already encountered in Matthew, such as the Our Father (Lk 11:1ff); the confrontation between Jesus and the leaders over Beelzebub (Lk 11:14ff); and the 'woes' against the Pharisees (Lk 11:37-53). Jesus' words about trusting God's providence (Lk 12:22-34) are in Matthew's rendering of the Sermon on the Mount (Mt 6:19-33), and the sayings about watchfulness (Lk 12:35-46) are in the Matthaean form of Jesus' last instruction to his disciples (Mt 24:43-51; 25:1-13). Luke has also placed here, in the journey context, some words of Jesus on the future coming of the Son of Man (Lk 17:22-37) which Matthew positioned in that same last instruction (Mt 24:17f; 26ff; 37-41).

Yet, besides this 'Great Lukan Insertion', there is also the part of the journey narrative which Luke has taken—almost word for word—from Mark (Lk 18:15-43). This section includes Jesus' dealings with the children and with the rich young man; the third Passion prediction; and his curing of the blind man in Jericho who calls him 'Son of David'. The Zacchaeus incident (Lk 19:1-10) is peculiar to Luke—another example of Jesus' gracious kindness towards one who is despised as an outcast and a sinner. The parable of the sums of money (Lk 19:11-27) seems to be Luke's variant rendering of the parable of the silver pieces which Matthew inserted in his version of Jesus' last instruction (Mt 25:14-30).

Jesus' Ministry in Jerusalem (Lk 19:28-21:38)
Though we usually speak of Jesus' time in the holy city, before his Passion, as the 'Jerusalem ministry', the evangelists—including Luke—all give the impression that this period was less a ministry than a clash of two mindsets that never met. The result of this clash is that Jesus' whole time in Jerusalem appeared to have been wasted. True, Luke says that the crowds greeted Jesus enthusiastically, and that they liked to come and listen to him—but he never shows Jesus in a really successful relationship with the capital city, or converting anyone there.

Over and above the basic pattern which he has inherited from Mark, Luke has added a special colouring which prepares for the coming tragedy of the destruction of the city. This actually happend in AD70, when the Roman legions led by Titus occupied the city and suppressed the Jewish revolt which had begun four years earlier. Luke presents Jesus' lament over the city (Lk 19:41-4) in such a way that it appears to be a prediction of things to come; the same theme recurs in the last instruction (Lk 21:20f), and again this may well represent an allusion by Luke to what has already happened. This reflects the early Church's view that the tragic event of the destruction of Jerusalem demonstrated God's avenging wrath, as he punished his chosen people for having rejected the salvation which he had offered them in the person of Jesus.

The series of confrontations between Jesus and the leaders is, in Luke, largely reproduced from Mark's corresponding chapters. In these scenes Jesus disputes with every representative group of religious leaders in the whole Israelite community. There are traders (Lk 19:45); high priests, Pharisees, and elders (Lk 20:1); Sadducees (Lk 20:27); and scribes (Lk 20:46). Moreover, there are further tensions between Jesus and others whom Luke describes simply as 'them' (Lk 20:20, 41). In contrast to the self-righteousness of these false leaders, Luke reproduces from Mark's Gospel the vignette about the widow and her mite (Lk 21:1-4). It is in such people as this poor woman, rather than in the more sophisticated but shallow leaders and teachers, that Jesus sees the true religion, and he gives her high praise accordingly.

The Last Instruction (Lk 21:5-36)
Jesus' final words are briefer in the Lukan rendering. But we have already seen some of the words of Jesus about his future second coming in the earlier journey context (Lk 17:22-37), and Luke places less emphasis on that theme here. For this reason the Lukan rendering of the Last Instruction has a particularly practical tone to it. Like Jesus' words about the 'coming' destruction of Jerusalem, what Jesus says here about the trials of his disciples is really a prophecy after the fact—these things have already been happening to them before Luke writes, and he knows it! When Luke does present Jesus' words about the coming of the 'Son of Man' (Lk 21:25-8), he simplifies the apocalyptic imagery which Mark had used in his rendering of the discourse, and he brings the instruction to a conclusion with a remarkably down-to-earth 'pastoral' exhortation against drunkenness and self-indulgence.

If we see Luke as writing this message after Jerusalem had been destroyed, his version of the last instruction of Jesus takes on the character of an explanation of why that event was not the end of the entire world. We can imagine people asking Luke what was going to happen next, now that Jerusalem had been destroyed. And this is Luke's answer: Jesus' disciples must expect a period of tribulations, and they must keep watch and hope as they wait for him to return as their liberator and their judge. There is no indication of when this will happen. Luke has omitted Jesus' saying about his ignorance of when the end will come (Mk 13:32; Mt 24:36), perhaps because he finds such an admission difficult to reconcile with the image of the 'Son of Man' coming in power as the judge of men (Lk 21:36).

Luke's Paschal Gospel (Lk 22ff)
Some commentators speak of the 'Passion Narrative', but this term does not do justice to what the evangelists had in mind. Each of the evangelists offers not merely a 'narrative'—which can be a neutral word, like 'news report'—but a 'gospel', i.e, *good* news of how God shows himself and his power for life in Jesus. Furthermore, when we refer to the 'passion' of Jesus, we think of his suffering, death, and burial, as if the rest were something separate. But God was present and acting all through these events, and the last chapter is not so much a description of what happened to Jesus, seen as some separate event, as a picture of how the disciples became aware of how God had raised up Jesus. Because Jesus has 'passed over' from death to life, this is his 'Passover' or (in Hebrew) *pascha*. For this reason it is better to speak of the evangelists' intention here as being to render the 'Paschal *Gospel*' in a graphic manner.

Luke presents the Paschal Gospel so independently that he has here deliberately moved away from Mark to follow some other sources. There are some similarities to Mark, of course, but this is simply because the basic pattern of the tradition had been set before Luke came to it—Last Supper, Agony, Arrest, Trial, Execution, Burial, Appearances of the Risen Lord. But Luke is the only one of the synoptic evangelists who mentions Satan as a character in the drama—it is he who causes the failures of both Judas and Peter (Lk 22:3, 31). Luke also includes a fairly lengthy dialogue of Jesus with his disciples at the

Last Supper (Lk 22:14-38). These two features are further clues to suggest that there has been some influence of the Johannine tradition on this evangelist, since the Johannine Gospel also has the long Last Supper discourse of Jesus (Jn 13-17). Luke is also the only synoptic evangelist to mention Jesus' pathetic glance at Peter, who has just denied knowing Jesus (Lk 22:61). If this detail had come from Peter himself, it is difficult to imagine how Mark could have omitted it, since he displays so many other indications of Peter's influence. It is likely, therefore, that this is an imaginative detail which Luke has contributed in order to heighten the emotional and dramatic intensity of the scene.

The appearance of Herod Antipas (Lk 23:6-11) is also a peculiarly Lukan contribution to the Paschal Gospel, and it is quite consistent with the unpleasant relationship between him and both Jesus and John the Baptist, whom he had killed earlier (Lk 9:7ff; 13:31ff). The scene is puzzling, since it is difficult to see why the other evangelists should have omitted it—or Luke included it. The wrenching scene of Jesus' dialogue with the women of Jerusalem (Lk 23:27-31) is another uniquely Lukan feature, but at least this is typical of Luke's interest in depicting women and the gentleness of Jesus' dealings with them. Similarly, Jesus' dying words show his forgiveness and his prayerful manner (Lk 23:34, 43, 46).

Luke's omissions from the Passion chapters are also notable, though we notice them only when we compare the Lukan passages with those of the other synoptic evangelists. Luke gives no scene of Roman soldiers torturing Jesus; this, coupled with Pilate's three attempts to free Jesus (Lk 23:14, 20, 22), reflects Luke's desire to portray the Romans in a favourable light as much as he can. Luke has also omitted showing Jesus praying the opening words of Ps 22 ('My God, my God...'), which both Mark and Matthew give in Semitic form in their

Gospels. Since Luke is writing for gentiles who cannot be expected to appreciate all the subtler meanings of the psalm, he simply omits the phrase and its Aramaic phrasing, though he amply compensates by having Jesus pray in more simple words.

The result of all these arrangements of the tradition by Luke is that Jesus comes across as the innocent sufferer, the victim of Satanic malice, who accepts death calmly and commends himself to God, praying for his killers and consoling the thief who must die with him (Lk 23:43). The Roman soldier at the scene sums up in words that anyone should feel bound to use after hearing or reading this Gospel: 'Surely this was an innocent man!' (Lk 23:47).

The Risen Lord (Lk 24)

But it is in the final chapter of his Gospel that Luke really shows his independence. There is none of the panic and fright which paralyse the women at the tomb in Mark's rendering (Mk 16:8); instead, Luke introduces the fuller picture of two 'men' and their comment about looking for the living among the dead (Lk 24:5). Rather than directing the disciples to go to Galilee, Luke's two men merely allude to Galilee as the place of Jesus' earlier Passion prediction (Lk 9:22).

The Emmaus incident appears nowhere except in Luke's Gospel, even though a later editor alludes to the tradition of it in the 'longer ending' which he added to Mark's Gospel (Mk 16:12). This is one of the most glowingly peaceful elements of the whole Easter tradition, and it is replete with theological overtones: Jesus' Passover was entirely according to the Scriptures (Lk 24:27); and the Risen Lord can be recognized in the breaking of the bread—which is quite clearly a reference to the liturgical (eucharistic) experience of the early disciples (Lk 24:30-35). Finally, there is a certain primacy which accrues to Simon (Peter) because he has experienced the

Chapter XI

Risen Lord—indeed, is apparently the first one to do so (Lk 24:34).

There are also strong apologetic overtones in these scenes, which suggest that Luke intends to reply to some obvious objections from opponents of the apostolic message. This is why he is so careful to include the empty tomb tradition and the witness of the women, of the disciples from Emmaus, and of Simon Peter. The closing verses of the Gospel show that the Risen Lord himself has made his disciples into apostles, entrusting them with the mission of witnessing to him from Jerusalem to 'all the nations' (Lk 24:47). But this witness must be animated by 'power from on high', so that the last verses of this document lead expectantly into the first verses of Acts.

The closing scenes of Luke's Gospel, with the notes of joy and prayer, show the disciples continuing to frequent the Temple (implying that they have no intention of abandoning their heritage in Judaism) and waiting for God's next initiative. We can now move on to Acts, and see how Luke continues his presentation by exhibiting the Gospel in the witness of the Risen Lord's disciples.

1. Can you find in Luke's Gospel three examples of 'Q' material (material which is in both Matthew and Luke, but not in Mark)?
2. What is the most striking feature of Jesus' journey to Jerusalem in the Lukan rendering?
3. How does Luke try to make the image of Jesus and Christianity attractive to gentiles?
4. How does Jesus' 'Great Sermon' in Lk 6 compare with his 'Sermon on the Mount' in Mt 5ff?
5. Do you see how Luke has 'softened' the violence of Jesus' Passion in Lk 22f?

Chapter XII

Luke's Special Contribution: the Acts of the Apostles

You will receive power when the Holy Spirit comes down on you; then you are to be my witnesses in Jerusalem, throughout Judaea and Samaria, yes, even to the ends of the earth. *(Acts 1:8.)*

Taking about an hour or so, read through Acts again. This time concentrate on the theological clues and patterns which Luke has woven into his presentation. Be especially attentive to the following details:-
a) the apostolic preaching (Acts 2:14-36; 3:12-26; 4:8-12; 5:29-32; 10:34-43; 13:16-41);
b) the outward-moving geographical pattern set in Acts 1:8;
c) the dominant influence of the Holy Spirit;
d) the 'we-passages' (Acts 16; 20; 21; 27f);
e) the contrasting reactions of Jews and gentiles to the Gospel.

Though there would surely be an outcry from some people, we could probably make out a good case for a rearrangement of the order of the New Testament books. It would be extremely helpful if we could have Acts appear immediately after Luke's Gospel, for in that way we could appreciate how smoothly his second work flows on from the first. In the opening verse of Acts Luke repeats the address to his friend Theophilus (whoever he may have been), and then refers back to 'my first account', which quite obviously means his Gospel. Acts is thus the second part of Luke's message to Theophilus. In addition to putting this reference at the beginning of the book, Luke has also given a brief summary of the things which he has already presented in his Gospel. These two features lead us to infer that some time may have elapsed between the composition of his Gospel and the composition of his second book. Nevertheless, even if this is the case, we cannot help but admire the evenness of the narrative, and the joyful optimism which characterizes both books.

Luke-Acts is the largest of the synoptic works, and we therefore need to spend enough time on it to get a view of it as a whole. This necessarily means that we must expect to go through it more than once, noting various features as we go. This time we shall continue to concentrate on the literary and narrative features of Luke's second book, just as we have done the first time through for all three of the synoptic Gospels. Then we shall go through Luke's whole work again at a deeper level, concentrating on the special theological features which are the real unifying elements in the evangelist's message to his friend.

Transition: the Church Awaits the Spirit (Acts 1:1-26)

Acts 1:1-14 Perhaps the best way to appreciate these opening verses of Acts is to re-read the last chapter of Luke's Gospel immediately beforehand. Some interval of time has apparently elapsed, and Luke now undertakes to continue where he left off, explaining to Theophilus how the Gospel of salvation which Jesus brought to the Israelite people has passed on to the gentiles. That is why these first verses of Acts are a kind of 'literary seam' in which Luke gives a resume of the last part of his Gospel. We see a large number of features alluded to again or even repeated here: Theophilus himself (recalling Lk 1:1); the Risen Lord; the puzzlement of the disciples as Jesus teaches them about the Kingdom of God; and their mistaken optimism as they expect to see Jesus now establishing some kind of new kingdom (Acts 1:6), which means that they have not yet come to understand his identity or the purpose of his earthly mission. There is also their own mission, as the Risen Lord sends them to witness to him; the promise of the Holy Spirit and the Ascension of Jesus; and the scene of the apostles at prayer. The element of universalism also carries over: in Lk 24:47 the Risen Jesus sends the apostles to 'all the nations', and here he specifies that they are to be witnesses 'in Jerusalem, throughout Judaea and Samaria, and even to the ends of the earth' (Acts 1:8).

There are also a few new features here, such as the scene of the 'two men in white' ('angels', as we usually say) and their words to the apostles (whom they call 'men of Galilee'), assuring them that Jesus will come again in his *parousia*. Mary's appearance here, constantly at prayer with the disciples, is the last occasion on which we see her in the Gospel tradition. The mention of the 'forty days' is also unique here, since none of the Gospels mentions this time element in relation to the Risen Lord and his sojourn with his disciples.

Perhaps the most significant feature of this resume is the little scene in Acts 1:6ff. Here Jesus tells his disciples that they should not allow themselves to be preoccupied about when they will see the splendour of God's kingdom. They should instead wait for the gift of the Holy Spirit, and then put their energy into the task of being witnesses to Jesus—and here we should notice the geographical factor. The disciples, who are now apostles ('those who have been sent'), are to witness first of all in Jerusalem, and then—in progressively widening circles—in Judaea and Samaria, and finally all the way to the ends of the earth. As the narrative pattern of Acts unfolds, we shall see that this is exactly what Luke shows. The Holy Spirit has been given, transforming these confused disciples into convinced and confident apostles. They then witness to the Risen Lord precisely according to theis geographical scheme, eventually—through Paul's journeys—reaching as far as Rome, which, for people in Luke's part of the world, was equivalent to reaching the 'ends of the earth'.

In this geographical-theological clue we can already see the pattern which Luke will present in Acts. It is a twofold pattern, working on two levels. First, there is the theological pattern: the Holy Spirit has been given, and this Holy Spirit is the real protagonist of Luke's drama. (We could also make out a case for renaming this book 'The Acts of the Holy Spirit', since he is the one who dynamizes the apostles and works through them to bring the Gospel of healing and salvation to the gentiles beyond the confines of Israel's homeland in Palestine.) The second level of Luke's pattern is the more obvious, geographical level: he shows the witness of the apostles in three stages—first in Jerusalem, then in Judaea and Samaria, and finally in Rome.

Acts 1:15-26 Now that he has prefaced the work with this resume of what was in his 'first account', and also given a clue to what he intends to show in this second document, Luke presents the first entirely new scene of Acts: the election of Matthias to succeed Judas. The whole scene is thoroughly Jewish, as is all the Jerusalem material. This shows that Luke has used what we may call a 'Jerusalem Jewish-Christian' source for this part of Acts. The apostles appear eager to keep the number of their members at twelve, evidently because that was the number of the tribes of the old Israel, now to be replaced by the new 'twelve' of Jesus' apostles. The whole incident does not appear to have much significance in the long run, however, because Luke is writing for his gentile friends who would not be likely to appreciate the subtle meaning of this sacred number. Nevertheless, the prayerful preparation, the leadership role of Peter, the citations of the Old

Testament Scriptures, and the references to Judas' tragic failure, as well as the description of Jesus' earthly mission, framed between John the Baptist and the Ascension—all these elements convey the character of the early Jerusalem tradition which Luke has inherited. And the vivid and well-detailed narrative, with its highly-stylized scene of the formal assembly of the brethren and Peter's solemn discourse, constitutes a good preparation for the kind of pictorial style which Luke will maintain consistently throughout Acts, right up to the last verses of the book.

The Promised Spirit Comes (Acts 2:1-13)

There are several scenes which Luke present as special highlights, as turning-points, in the narrative of Acts. This is the first of them. Later on, the dramatic pictures of Saul's conversion experience (Acts 9); of Cornelius' conversion and baptism (Acts 10); of the Council of Jerusalem (Acts 15); and, finally, of Paul's voyage to Rome as a prisoner, with the added detail of the shipwreck (Acts 27), will come to be some of the most memorable scenes that we have anywhere of the early days of the Church.

Luke has also used his Jewish-Christian source material here. We can recall a familiar pattern from the Old Testament, which we may call the 'prophetic investiture', or the 'prophet's inaugural experience'. There are examples of this pattern in Is 6, Jer 1, and Ezek 1. Perhaps the best-known instance is that of God's calling of Moses at the burning bush (Ex 3), but there are other Old Testament passages that are relevant here as well (e.g, Num 11:25; 1 Sam 10:10; Joel 2:28; 3:1). All these texts show that, in his own way, God takes the initiative in making people into prophets, taking possession of them and sending his Spirit into them so that they become his spokesmen and say what he wants them to say. The elements of this pattern are present in the Pentecost scene, as the apostles collectively experience their 'prophetic investiture'. There are symbolic features, too: the 'great wind' and the fire, as well as the ecstatic outburst as the apostles speak in 'tongues'. Merely human language is strained at this point, because Luke is trying to describe the effect that the Spirit of God has on the lives of the apostles and, eventually, on the life of the whole Church. The universalism of Luke's plan is clear here, too, in the variety of places and peoples which the crowds represent (Parthians, Medes, Cretans, Arabs, etc.). Yet, at the same time, there is a limiting factor, since these are all Jews who have come to Jerusalem to participate in the liturgy of Pentecost, or 'Weeks'. Gradually, as we move through Acts, we shall notice that Luke sprinkles small clues such as these, to serve as advance notice of what is to come later. They are all Jews now, because that is how the Church started. But eventually the Gospel will move away from Israel and come to the gentiles, who are here represented implicitly in the homelands of these visiting Jewish pilgrims. The real essence of prophecy appears here, too: it is not primarily a matter of predicting the future, but rather one of 'speaking forth' under the influence of God's Spirit.

Luke has embellished the scene with some extra details, such as the point that the Jews from various lands understand the prophetic outbursts in different languages, implicitly suggesting—as some commentators argue—that this understanding reverses the tragedy of division which came to men in the incident of the Tower of Babel (Gen 11:1-9). Again, there is the very normal reaction of some of the bystanders, who think that the apostles are merely drunk. This provides a 'down-to-earth' touch to the scene, and means too that these bystanders do not understand the significance of the situation or give God credit for being at work in it. They need someone to explain to them just what is going on and what it is all about. In this way they serve as a foil for Peter's first kerygmatic discourse, which comes next.

The Witness in Jerusalem (Lk 2:14-8:3)

Acts 2:14-5:42 The geographical pattern which Luke hinted at in Acts 1:8 now begins to work out. The evangelist draws more scenes from his Jerusalem Jewish-Christian source to point the first stage of the Church's witness, as the apostles offer the Gospel of the paschal mystery to their fellow Jews in their own capital city. Though the title of the book is *The Acts of the Apostles*, we may nevertheless take notice that only a very few of the apostles appear in it as active: apart from Peter and John, there are James, Philip, and Paul—but none of these latter three were certainly members of the original group of twelve. Matthias is chosen in Acts 1, but he never appears again! Luke is not really trying to be comprehensive, therefore, or to give a complete account in the way that we might expect a modern historian to do. The scenes and characters of this second Lukan work are selective, and typify the various things which they represent. The same applies to the 'highlight' or 'turning-point' scenes to which we referred earlier, and which will recur in their proper places. These scenes *represent* major changes or advances in the situation, and this is why Luke introduces them, even though in historical terms they may not have been as prominent as he makes them out to be.

Peter always has the image of being the one whom Jesus named as the leader or 'manager' of the apostolic Church, so it is natural that Luke should portray him as the first proclaimer of the *kerygma*. This Greek word *kerygma* (meaning 'proclamation' or 'heralding') has become widely used and known in recent years, and well represents the original message of the apostles which we have been calling the 'Gospel *about* Jesus', or the 'Gospel

Chapter XII

of the Paschal Mystery'. Peter, who had consistently failed to understand Jesus, who had lied and even run away, is now transformed by the Holy Spirit. He now presents himself bravely in the public square and witnesses to what God has done: God has brought the new age of his goodness, which the prophets had described in their Old Testament oracles. He has shown his power for goodness and for life, supremely, in raising Jesus from the dead by his own right hand, so that Jesus is now Christ (or Messiah) and Lord. Then comes his challenge: for this very reason, the people in the crowd before him should receive the message, be converted, and accept baptism in the name of the raised-up Lord Jesus. If they do, they too will be dynamized by the Holy Spirit, just as the apostles have been dynamized. This will ensure that they receive the salvation which God has planned for them, and they will be separated from the great majority of their fellow Israelites who have not accepted Jesus or his Gospel of the Kingdom of God.

The scene is vivid, dramatic, and graphically powerful. The presence and active power of the Holy Spirit is almost palpable as we read the text and hear Peter preaching in our 'mind's ear'. Three thousand converts respond on the first day, and the Church is off to a flying start! In the next two chapters (Acts 3f) Luke shows more preaching and more conversions. But a new element appears, in the form of opposition from the official religious leaders. Nothing can stop the forward momentum of the Gospel, however. Miracles occur; thousands more join the Church. All this represents 'Acts of the Holy Spirit', and the unfaith of the official leaders is powerless to stop it.

Acts 6:1-8:3 Stephen and the other six deacons (Acts 6:1-6) are Hellenistic Jews with Greek names. Moreover, when the mob kills Stephen, Saul is present and approves of their action (Acts 7:587-60; 8:3). In these details Luke foreshadows the eventual shift of the Church to the gentiles. But the long discourse of Stephen is one more of the many monologues which are a principal literary feature of Acts. It would appear that Luke has adopted this feature as a device for presenting his theological message in a way that will be more interesting and attractive than it would have been if he had simply put it in the form of abstract statements. In Stephen's discourse we see the same heavy Jewish emphasis on the Old Testament Scriptures which we saw earlier in Peter's Pentecost discourse (Acts 2:14-41). Biblical citations and images flood forth in a profusion which is rapid enough to bewilder. We may wonder whether Luke really expected his gentile friends to recognize all these biblical allusions! In all probability he did not worry about this too much, and merely contented himself with arranging and presenting what he had in his source material.

The principal message to emerge from all these scenes is that the Holy Spirit is offering the Gospel of Christian salvation to the Jews first. Most of them, including their official leaders, reject it, and there are already signs that it will soon move to those who are outside Israel. Persecution and resistance actually appear to help the spread of the Gospel, as Luke shows in the several summaries which he sprinkles through these chapters (Acts 2:41-7; 4:4; 5:12-16; 6:7). He shows it, too, in the subtle point which he makes in Acts 8:1ff: precisely because of the murder of Stephen (the first martyr of the Christian Church) many Christians fled from Jerusalem to the country districts of Judaea and Samaria. But they took the Gospel and their new faith with them, and now became witnesses in these new areas—just as the Risen Lord had said that they should do (Acts 1:8.)!

There is also an echo of Jesus' own attitude here. We recall that Jesus not only showed no hostility towards his own killers, but even prayed for them to the Father (Lk 23:34)—and, incidentally, that Luke is the only evangelist to make this point in his Gospel. Now Luke presents the parallel, as the followers of Jesus—all of them Jews so far—remain loyal to their religious ancestry, and display no animosity towards their unconverted countrymen, in spite of the pressure they undergo from fellow Jews. This pattern recurs several times in the course of Acts, and so we are correct to infer that it is no accident but rather an inherent part of Luke's message. We may, of course, wonder whether it is properly a literary feature, or belongs more appropriately to the theological level—but, either way, it is certainly a Lukan point that Christianity is not a hostile or antagonistic religion.

The Witness Widens: Judaea and Samaria (Acts 8:4-9:42)

The evidence now begins to suggest, for the first time, that Luke has drawn upon other sources, such as, perhaps, a 'Philip' source, since Philip appears three times here, in connection with Samaria (Acts 8:4-8), with the Ethiopian (Acts 8:26ff), and with Gaza, Azotus, and Caesarea (Acts 8:39f). He could have been one of the original twelve, of course (Lk 6:14); but there is also a Philip among the deacons (Acts 6:5), and there is a 'Philip the Evangelist' living at Caesarea in Acts 21:8. Tradition has a way of smoothing over distinctions, so that several persons with the same name can come to be considered as just one person. It may well be that Luke did not even know or think about who Philip was, but simply used the material of this 'Philip' source to show the advance of the Church's witness beyond Jerusalem into Samaria. The names of Peter and John also recur here in connection with Samaria, as well as the name of Simon the magician, who has to learn the hard way that the Gospel is a matter of salvation and not of money-making (Acts 8:9-24)! These incidents could possibly represent a 'Samaria' source, since the common denominator seems to be the place rather than any single person or incident (Acts 8:25).

A Christology begins to take shape here, as we see a whole collection of titles being applied to the person of Jesus. From the first kerygmatic scene (Acts 2) to this point a number of Old Testament terms have come to be associated with him. He is Messiah and Lord (Acts 2:36); the Servant of God (Acts 3:13; 4:27, 30); the prophet like Moses (Acts 3:22); the Son of Man (Acts 7:56)—and now (Acts 8:32f) Philip speaks of Jesus as the sheep led to the slaughter, the suffering servant mentioned in the Isaian oracle (Is 52f) and elsewhere. The early Jewish-Christian tradition which Luke is quoting here had employed the vocabulary of the Old Testament to describe Jesus, above all in terms of the Christ of the paschal mystery who has been brought low by men and raised high by God.

Acts 9:1-30 Another highpoint in Acts is the scene of Paul's conversion. He appears as a rabid Pharisee at first, rushing from Jerusalem to Damascus to find all the Christians that he can and bring them back to the capital in chains. How many artists and preachers have interpreted this scene! Its basic content must have come to Luke from Paul himself, long after the event, with Paul describing his conversion experience to his friend and travelling companion. Later in the same book (Acts 22; 26) Luke will portray Paul explaining his conversion from Judaism to Christianity as a traumatic reveral of his fundamental convictions and loyalties.

Three powerful realizations come to Saul (Paul) here. First, he comes to see that this crucified Jesus is really alive and glorified as Lord. Secondly, he recognizes that, in persecuting the Christians, he is persecuting Jesus himself, so that he sees an intimate link uniting Jesus with the Church of his disciples (Paul was to develop this point later on when he came to write his epistles, in which he discusses the Church as the Mystical Body of Jesus). Thirdly, Paul realizes that he has himself been chosen by Jesus to be his witness to the gentiles! Luke well captures the devastating impact which these realizations have on Paul as a traditionalist Pharisee. The evangelist is evidently retrojecting on to this scene things which Paul came to understand only gradually, since, as the narrative progresses, Paul begins his apostolic ministry by going first to the Jews rather than to the gentiles. Furthermore, he does not speak at all in Acts of the special link between the Risen Lord and the Christians. This point emerges only in his later epistles, as he develops his theological teaching about the Church as the Mystical Body with Jesus as its Head. These clues all suggest to us that Luke's purpose here is to prepare the way for his presentation of Paul's apostolic ministry by means of a scene which is powerful and impressive in proportion to the dynamism and importance attaching to Paul's ministry as it unfolds in the chapters ahead.

For all the importance of his conversion, the Jews now reject Paul as a traitor, and the Christians are suspicious of him because of his recent reputation as their avowed enemy. Here again, though, Luke shows the Holy Spirit drawing good out of bad: the Gospel moves ahead geographically, and the Church draws interior consolation from the ever-active Spirit of God (Acts 9:31).

Acts 9:32-40 Peter returns briefly as a wandering apostle. Luke has already portrayed him bringing the Church's expanding witness to Samaria (Acts 8:9ff); now, in keeping with the theme of Judaea and Samaria (Acts 1:8; 9:31), he includes a few scenes which may have come to him from a 'Peter' source, showing as they do Peter's apostolic ministry 'star-studded' with healing miracles in the outlying areas of Judaea. If we follow these journeys on a map, we can see that Peter has moved from the capital of Judaism northwards to Samaria (Acts 8), and now to the area between there and the Mediterranean Sea. Lydda, where Peter heals Aeneas, is the site of the present-day airport of Lod, in Israel, where contemporary visitors coming to the Holy Land by air arrive and depart. Joppa (or Jaffa), where Peter raises the dead woman Tabitha (Acts 9:36ff), is now Yafo, a suburb of the modern Tel-Aviv on Israel's Mediterranean coast.

By showing Peter in Joppa, Luke has also prepared for the following section in which he will describe the conversion and baptism of Cornelius. This well-disposed Roman officer hears that Peter is staying nearby, and sends for him.

The First Witness to the Gentiles (Acts 10:1-14:28)
Acts 10:1-11:18 Gradually Luke has shown the Church beginning to spread and to move away from Jerusalem. Now he presents another incident which stands out for its 'typical' value as one of the great 'milestone' events of his theological narrative. His description of the conversion of Cornelius and the members of his household is a masterpiece of this kind of literary form. The pace is even, the scenes are carefully detailed, and there is a gracious balance between monologue and dialogue. The principal character of this section as a whole is manifestly theological, as we can see in the visions of Cornelius and Peter (Acts 10:3-16) and in the no fewer than eight references to the Holy Spirit. The incident provides another occasion for Luke to show Peter preaching the *kerygma* of the paschal mystery (Acts 10:34-43) as he invites the centurion and his family in Caesarea to join the new Church. Salvation has come to the gentiles!

An interesting tension is built up as a result of this action of Peter, despite the fact that he is the recognized leader of the brethren. The conservative Jewish Church of Jerusalem resents his action because it has broken down the wall which separates Jews from gentiles (whether Christians or not). But Peter's explanation convinces them, and they are satisfied that this was indeed an act of the Holy Spirit, and they then accept it as such.

The whole episode has a major place in Luke's evolving drama. It signifies that the Church has now come to realize that the time is ripe for a major advance. Up until now it has been a Jewish church, even though Jesus had told the disciples that they must witness to all the nations. The vision of the ritually clean and unclean animals all mixed together convinces Peter that he must make a decisive break with one of the basic principles of his Jewish upbringing and must now accept gentiles as his equals before God! The change occurs on two levels: first, there has to be an understanding at the level of faith that this must be so, and, secondly, that internal understanding has to express itself at the level of the external, concrete act of baptizing Cornelius and his household and staying with them for a few days as a willing guest.

The step has now been taken, and from this point on Luke's picture shows the Holy Spirit bringing the Gospel of salvation to the pagans by leaps and bounds. The resistance of the Jewish Christians has crumbled in the face of the assurance that what Peter has done has been directed by the Holy Spirit. But the unconverted Jewish brethren will continue to oppose the spread of the Gospel. No matter—nothing can prevent God's plan from taking its course.

There is another clue to be found here, in the shape of the cordial way in which Luke describes Cornelius (Acts 10:1f). It reminds us of the similar goodwill which Luke displayed towards the Roman centurion in his Gospel (Lk 7:1-5; 23:47). Luke also shows Pontius Pilate as a good man who three times declares Jesus innocent and endeavours to have him released (Lk 23:14, 20, 22); and, furthermore, there is no scene in Luke's Gospel of the Roman soldiers torturing Jesus. It would seem that Luke is more than accidentally interested in making the Romans look as good as possible. This suggests that Luke expects the readers of his bipartite work to be Romans, and that he is eager to attract their goodwill by showing their countrymen to have been well-disposed towards his religion.

Acts 11:19-12:25 While there has been success over Cornelius and his household, the Jerusalem Church nevertheless remains strongly conservative, and uncomfortable about the new association with gentiles, even if they are now fellow Christians. In contrast to this hesitant attitude in Jerusalem, there is, as Luke now goes on to show, a new mixed Church of Antioch in which the Jewish and gentile leaders get along very well together. Barnabas goes to bring Saul (Paul) from his hometown of Tarsus in Cilicia (part of present-day Turkey), and together these two become agents of the Antiochene community, bringing a gift from Antioch to help the poorer mother-church in Jerusalem.

The centre of gravity is gradually shifting now—away from the conservative Jewish mother-church of the capital, and towards the more flexible mixed church of Antioch. The Christians of this Hellenistic metropolis were apparently more accustomed to mixing with strangers and foreigners, and this made them better able to relate to gentiles than the traditionalists of the Jewish capital. This shift of emphasis also prepares for the narrative which is to come, because in the following chapters Luke will show Paul and Barnabas undertaking their great missionary effort as representatives of the 'outreach' programme of the Church of Antioch.

Chapter XII

Acts 13f When we try to follow Paul's missionary travels throughout the eastern Mediterranean, we should use a map to trace his routes and stopovers. Luke again emphasizes that it was the Holy Spirit which was the real force behind this missionary project (Acts 13:1ff).

Though this first missionary journey was the shortest in terms of the distance covered, it was the longest in terms of the time taken. Luke does not give a precise indication of the years, but from various clues we can conjecture that this effort lasted from about AD45 to AD49, i.e, for the best part of five years. The pattern shows Paul consistently going to his fellow Jews in town after town, because Luke wants to make the point that the Gospel and the Church have not rejected Judaism—it is always vice versa! The major contrast in this section comes between the hostile reaction which Paul and Barnabas receive from the Jews of Antioch in Pisidia (Acts 13) and the cordial, even enthusiastic reception which they get from the pagans of Lystra and Derbe (Acts 14). This is another incident which shows Luke's careful arrangement of the narrative scenes in order to underline the theological point he is making (Acts 13:44-9).

As this narrative moves on, we may now find ourselves beginning to forget about the Jewish Church of Jerusalem, and even about the original group of apostles. The spotlight falls upon Paul from this point on, even though—for Luke—Paul is never more than the agent of the Holy Spirit and a typical representative of the Church's witness. This is probably because, as we have already seen, Luke selects from the source material available to him to construct a moving drama with its own theological pattern. The result is a picture which is by no means a complete account of 'the acts of the apostles', even though it is a definitive picture of *the action of the Holy Spirit*, bringing a Gospel of God's friendship to strangers who welcome it after it has been refused by the original members of the household. This Gospel comes through the ministry of the apostles, and it is this ministry which Paul represents from now on.

The Judaizers and the Council of Jerusalem (Acts 15:1-35)

Despite the fact that it is not very long, this section is another of the 'milestone' passages which Luke has worked into Acts. It has all the elements of high drama—a crisis, an urgent conference, a debate, the pros and cons, a decision, and an after-effect. The speeches of Peter and James stand out most of all, while Paul and Barnabas, though present and active, are not portrayed by Luke as actually speaking.

It is not surprising to see the Judaean Christians still clinging to the Jewish tradition here, and insisting that even gentile converts to the new faith must accept circumcision. This means that the Jerusalem brethren see Christianity as merely a sect of Judaism, and not as really a new religion. But the success which Peter has had with Cornelius, and the many successes which Paul and Barnabas report from their first journey, prove decisive. James goes for a compromise, waiving the circumcision rule for gentile converts, but demanding that they be required to observe some of the lesser provisions of the Mosaic code. It would appear that Luke has here blended together two meetings and two decisions which were probably distinct. There is no further reference anywhere to the compromise proposed by James: a respectable school of thought holds that the apostles simply voted to waive the circumcision rule, and that this was all there was to the Council of Jerusalem—Paul mentions this meeting in his Epistle to the Galatians (Gal 2:1-10), but says nothing about James' compromise proposal.

Interestingly, the evangelist again displays an emphasis

on the basic influence of the Holy Spirit in the letter which he records the apostles as composing and sending to the brethren in Antioch. They say that 'the Holy Spirit and we' have worked out this decision (Acts 15:28). This first major conference of the apostles as a group—the first ecumenical council, so to speak—is confident that when they deliberate and decide together, they have the guidance of God's Spirit.

Luke seems to have constructed this scene largely on the basis of what has come to him in the early oral tradition. If he had drawn on written sources, these would certainly have mentioned more details of the conference. The James who appears in this chapter (Acts 15) is undoubtedly the same as the James who appears also in Acts 12:17 as the leader of the Christians in Jerusalem after Peter's departure from there. This James was probably a relative of Jesus, but not necessarily one of the two apostles who had the same name.

The whole point of the Council of Jerusalem is that the way is now clear for the floodgates to open, allowing the Gospel of Christian salvation to pour out to the gentiles unburdened by the irrelevant and obsolete practices of the old religion. This is also why Luke makes a point of setting out the text of the letter to Antioch—the mixed church there was getting along very well without James and his restrictive policies. Now that the 'Judaizing controversy' has been successfully resolved, Jerusalem and its conservatism recede into the background, and the more vibrant community of Antioch becomes the springboard for Paul's second and third missionary journeys. When Jerusalem does reappear (Acts 22), it will be as a scene of trouble, when Paul is mobbed by his own people. But even then, out of that trouble God will produce good.

The Witness to the Ends of the Earth (Acts 15:36-28:31)
We have already said that Luke does not record the 'acts'

of all the disciples; he is selective, and the only one of the original twelve to have any real prominence in this book is Peter. And yet the person who dominates more than half of Acts is Paul, the 'apostle of the gentiles', who joins the Church because he has been pulled into it by the Risen Lord! The whole of the third phase of the Church's witness—'to the ends of the earth', as Jesus says in Acts 1:8—appears here as the work of one man, and a latecomer at that. The reasons for this are twofold: first, Luke uses what he has available, and it would seem that his 'Paul source' was ready to hand from his own association with Paul—quite likely as his travelling companion; and secondly, whether he portrays one apostle, or two, or all twelve of them, the number 'twelve' has no special significance for Luke's gentile readers, since they would be unlikely to see the parallel between them and the twelve ancient tribes of Israel. Furthermore, there are also other witnesses involved here in addition to the original twelve—e.g, Barnabas, John Mark, Apollos, Silas, and Timothy—, so that the main point is that the Church's witness to the Risen Lord is spreading out ever wider to the gentiles and 'to the ends of the earth'. The real protagonist, as Luke repeatedly insists, is the Holy Spirit. The other basic pattern which the evangelist weaves in here is the picture of the gentiles accepting the Gospel with enthusiasm, and in marked contrast to the violence with which the original chosen people reject it.

More and more definitely Luke now shows the Gospel witness approaching Rome. He never suggests that Paul was the one who first brought it there—indeed, Luke shows that there were already some Christians in Rome who welcomed Paul there as a prisoner. The underlying emphasis is that Jerusalem and Judaism have now taken a back seat—the Church has now become truly universal, just as Rome, the centre of the Roman Empire and the cultural world, is universal.

Chapter XII

Acts 15:36-18:22 Luke's excellent style makes this whole sequence read like a travelogue of the eastern Mediterranean region. It is easy enough to follow the route on a map—from Antioch to the new churches which Paul had established on his first journey (at Derbe and Lystra); then on to Troas, in the north-west of present-day Turkey; the crossing from Asia into Europe, with major stops at Philippi, Thessalonica, and Beroaea in northern Greece; and then to Athens and Corinth in southern Greece. From Corinth Paul returns to Antioch by way of Ephesus, Caesarea, and Jerusalem.

But, if we see no more than a travelogue, we miss the real substance of Luke's intention. On the literary level alone, there are the famous 'we' passages, which begin in Acts 16:10 (there will be several more, in Acts 20, 21, and 27f). The most obvious explanation of these sections is that, at least during this part of his apostolic career, Paul had Luke as a companion, so that Luke can describe these adventures from his own memory. Some commentators say that they are the record of another companion of Paul, and that Luke is therefore using the material without saying whose it is. It does not matter: either way, they add an authentically personal note to the picture.

Luke is careful to insist that the whole enterprise is the work of God (Acts 16:5, 6, 10, etc). This is a further reason for saying that it is not simply an account of Paul's travels, but is rather the story of the spread of the Gospel witness by the initiative of God's Spirit working through human agents.

There are elements of high drama which make this narrative as interesting as any adventure thriller: strangers; imprisonment; earthquake; an admixture of popularity and rejection; high and low social classes; Roman officials; pagan temples—and even a sea voyage. The Roman officials, as we have already seen, always appear in a good light in Luke's scenes. In this section the principle applies to the magistrates at Philippi (Acts 16:35ff) and to Gallio, the proconsul in Corinth (Acts 18:12ff), who are ever scrupulous to safeguard justice and legality. Luke again seems eager to emphasize the contrast between the hostility of the Jews, both in the homeland and in the dispersion, and the disciplined and honourable decency of the Romans. This must certainly have been pleasing to Theophilus (see Acts 1:1)!

The highpoint of this section is Paul's kerygmatic discourse to the pagans at the Areopagus in Athens. The Areopagus is still in existence—it is quite close to the famous (indeed, rather more famous) Parthenon—and visitors to Athens can visit it. A large bronze tablet now there contains the Greek text of Paul's speech to the Athenians, taken straight from the text of Acts 17. What a thrill it is for any Christian to stand there and imagine himself or herself hearing Paul's classic message for the first time!

There is also a subtle theological point which Luke makes here. The earlier kerygmatic addresses were replete with Jewish (Old Testament) terminology, which is understandable enough, since they were spoken to and for Jews (except for Peter's address to Cornelius—but in this case the inclusion of such terminology would seem to represent the Jewish pattern of Peter's thought). Here in Athens, however, Paul is careful to avoid the use of biblical language, since he is well aware that these pagans, sophisticated as they may be, can hardly be expected to grasp the significance of Old Testament terms. Instead, in a masterpiece of tact, Paul quotes Greek poets (Acts 17:28) to present the Christian Gospel to the Greeks.

But the reaction is mixed, and Luke here offers another of the contrasts of which he is so fond. Whereas the more cultured pagans of the capital city of Greece give the Gospel a welcome that is no more than mediocre at best, the lower classes of the great port of Corinth accept it with open arms! Even here, however, their acceptance comes only after the Jewish residents of the city have shown their hostility. Eventually, of course, Corinth became one of Paul's favourite churches: he later wrote several letters to the people of Corinth, which indicates that he had every intention of keeping in vital contact with his converts and disciples.

In a neat and orderly way Luke makes the point that Paul now heads back to his home base which, be it noted, is Antioch, not Jerusalem. (Acts 18:18-22.)

Acts 18:23-21:16 The third journey is perhaps less interesting. By now the pattern is clear, and Luke becomes a bit repetitive, even though there are some fresh incidents. Apollos, a Jewish intellectual from Egypt, joins the Church and proves a valuable asset. Probably the best piece of dramatic narrative in this section is the lengthy scene in which Luke describes Paul's close call in Ephesus. Although Ephesus was later to become another of Paul's favourite churches, he was almost killed there by the pagan mob. And, sure enough, the Jews here are as Luke has depicted them elsewhere—unconverted, and hostile to the suggestion that they and the gentiles should share the same religion.

This time, however, there is a threat from the gentiles as well. The silversmiths see that their source of livelihood will disappear if people become Christians: they will stop visiting the pagan Temple of Diana and buying silver souvenirs! Again Luke shows that the civil officals—evidently Romans—are scrupulous exemplars of legality, cool-headedness, and decency, challenging the rioters to press valid charges against the Christians or end their demonstration. Truth wins out, and the Gospel triumphs against pagan chaos!

But black clouds are on the horizon. In Corinth Paul learns that his countrymen are plotting against him

(Acts 20:3). He is becoming a Christ-figure! He is not surprised, however, since he has been dogged all along by this kind of hostility (Acts 14:22). But now Paul faces a dilemma: should he avoid going to Jerusalem and so escape the trouble, or should he follow the example of the Master and undergo the supreme test in that capital city? How ironic that Jerusalem is not kind to Paul, just as it was not kind to Jesus or to the other early witnesses of the new Gospel! Either the conservative mother-church there represents the kind of intolerable restrictions which were eventually thrown off at the Council (Acts 15), or the unconverted brethren there are ready to destroy Paul as a punishment for his ignoring the ancient wall of separation between their people and the rest of the world.

Paul decides to go to Jerusalem anyway, and he travels the long way, revisiting northern Greece overland, and then eventually embarking at Troas. (Another 'we' passage comes in here, in Acts 20:5-15, and a third in Acts 21:1-18.)

A dramatic tension comes to dominate the atmosphere during the return of this third missionary journey. This is certainly no accident, since Luke builds up our expectations of something big about to happen to Paul. Besides the superb narrative of the riot at Ephesus, Luke also surpasses himself in capturing the pathos of the scene in which Paul gives his farewell words to his friends from Ephesus. They meet briefly as the ship puts in for a short stopover at Miletus (Acts 20:17ff). Paul speaks to them as if he were himself a patriarch—we are put in mind of Jesus' last instruction to his disciples, which Luke interprets in his Gospel (Lk 21), or of the unique Last Supper discourse of the fourth Gospel (Jn 13-17). Paul is sure that he will never see these friends again, so he charges them to preserve their new faith and to avoid any weakening or compromising of it. He repeats the names of God and the Holy Spirit so often here that he appears

Chapter XII

totally abandoned to whatever fate awaits him. He is more concerned with the good of the Church that he is with his own safety. Luke must certainly admire Paul to have portrayed him in such heroic terms.

The point has been made, the pattern is set—all that remains is for Paul to proceed, in the face of repeated warnings, to the capital, and into the centre of a hostile force of his own countrymen. Underneath the narrative, another constant and persisting theological pattern is operating here, as it has throughout both of Luke's works: the Gospel of salvation, which Paul now represents, never rejects Judaism—it is always Judaism which rejects the Gospel and exhibits hostility towards the emerging Christian cause. Yet, from this evil God always brings good: more and more gentiles come to embrace the Gospel and its healing freedom (Acts 19:20).

Acts 21:17-28:31 It would be easy enough to see this final segment of Acts as Luke's account of Paul's imprisonment and subsequent voyage to Rome. Indeed, this may have been the original intent of the source material which Luke had to work with. But we must bear in mind the difference between the external narrative which Luke constructs out of his source material and the deeper theological pattern which he set from the beginning of his work, and which is about to draw towards a conclusion. It is not primarily a biography of Paul, therefore, much less a travelogue—it is a picture of the Holy Spirit animating the Church's witness and guiding it until it extends 'to the ends of the earth'.

There are a number of well-constructed speeches here: Paul addresses the Jewish mob in the Temple courtyard in Jerusalem (Acts 22), the Roman procurator Felix (Acts 24), and then the visiting puppet-king Agrippa (Acts 26). In between these speeches are the rabid threats and plots of the Jews, who go on a hunger-strike and intend to stay on it until they have succeeded in killing Paul. Again, as before, the Roman officials are ever honourable and worthy of respect for their careful regard of legal procedures, and for maintaining law and order. It is the Romans to prevent the mob from lynching Paul, who protect him against the planned assassination, and who finally respect his right to be sent as a Roman citizen to present his case before the imperial court in Rome itself.

Acts 27f In the voyage and shipwreck section Luke produces his last piece of high drama. The 'we' form returns and clearly intensifies the vivid personal character of the account. Paul's earlier visions of the Risen Lord (Acts 18:9; 23:11) have prepared him for his universal witness, and they have also shown the basic purpose of his voyage to Rome—not to plead in a pagan court, but to witness to the Lord Jesus in the capital of the Empire! During the stormy voyage Paul has another vision (Acts 27:23), and we are reminded of the many other vision-scenes in Acts. Indeed, there are so many of these vision-scenes that they are evidently another of Luke's favoured ways of presenting theology in narrative form, rather than in abstract formulas which would be much less interesting.

The fact that even as a prisoner Paul continues to preach and witness in Jerusalem, Caesarea, and Rome— as well as on the high seas!—shows that this is really the theological emphasis of Acts: Paul personifies the Church's witness, sent and directed as he is by the Holy Spirit to the world of the gentiles, and now specifically to the people of Rome. The final verses of Acts show for the last time the irreconcilable gulf which has arisen between the unconverted Jews (even in Rome) and the Gospel which Paul represents.

We can only wonder and conjecture whether Luke was

satisfied to end Acts with what seems to be an abrupt and incomplete summary of Paul's Roman ministry (Acts 28:30f). Did Luke write a further section which has been lost? Or did he perhaps plan to write more and then fail to finish it? Or did he write the whole work—his Gospel, as well as Acts—as a defence of Paul and of his apostolate? These questions have all been asked before, and various answers to them offered; in the end, all we can do is accept what we have, and recognize that, with Paul's arrival and preaching in the capital of the Empire (in about AD61-3), the Church's witness had reached what, at least from the point of view of Theophilus, represented 'the ends of the earth'. Even in the last verses of Acts, as he says that Paul was unhindered in his preaching, Luke shows his appreciation to the Romans, whose goodwill he hopes to attract to the new faith.

1. Do you see clues in the text of Acts which suggest that it came from the same writer as the one who produced the third Gospel?
2. What significance does Luke attach to the conversion of Cornelius (Acts 10)?
3. Why do you think Luke wrote Acts?
4. Do the 'we' passages (Acts 16:10; 20:5-15; 21:1-18; 27:1-28:16) come from the experience of the author himself, or has he taken them from the experience of someone else?
5. How do you think Luke tries to portray Roman officials in his two books?

Chapter XIII

The Essence of Luke's Theology: Peace and Goodwill to All Men

Glory to God in the highest, peace on earth to those on whom his favour rests. *(Lk 2:14.)*

If we see Theophilus as a pagan whom Luke hopes to attract to Christianity, then Luke is the only one of the four evangelists who is genuinely kerygmatic. Mark and Matthew, as well as the writer of the fourth Gospel, were all writing for people who were already Christians, in order to strengthen their new faith, and to challenge them to persevere as disciples of Jesus in the face of pressures. Luke is different from them in several ways. He is fuller than any of them, in that he has produced two books which have a single unified theological thrust. He is the only New Testament author who shows how the Christians lived and how the Church grew after Jesus had finished his earthly mission. He is the only one who shows the whole beginning of Christianity as an action of the Holy Spirit, and likewise he has tailored this interpretation of the Gospel to make it applicable to members of the wider gentile world outside the community of Israel. It is this purpose—to convert those who are not yet Christians—which characterizes Luke-Acts as the most properly kerygmatic literature of the New Testament.

Scholarly experts have debated for several years in order to find an answer to the question whether Luke is principally a historian who writes theologically, or a

Chapter XIII

theologian who writes historically. In the long run it seems that this kind of terminology comes close, but it does not quite suffice to explain what Luke is doing. The basic reason for this is that the best word to describe Luke is neither 'historian' nor 'theologian', because he is, first and foremost, an *evangelist*—his conscious intention is to offer to Theophilus an attractive and interesting message and he wants it to come across as *good news*, or 'gospel'. In this he has been much influenced by the example of his friend St Paul, who has given him not so much a narrative or biography of Jesus, but rather an attitude about him. Paul was an apostle, an evangelist, and a missionary teacher, who was always anxious to show his new converts that Christianity is a life-style for people in the present, rather than merely a story about people in the past. Furthermore, Paul gradually came to understand that God had chosen him to be the apostle for the gentiles, and so he had to work to find ways of presenting what was originally a Jewish Gospel so that it would be interesting and attractive for people of different cultural backgrounds. This universalism of the Gospel characterizes Paul's letters, and it has obviously rubbed off on Luke, whose message is consistently a universal gospel designed to show convincingly that Christianity, even though it was originally Jewish, is really for everyone, and that this is God's plan and no accident.

Luke evidently has a special admiration for Peter, since he shows him as particularly prominent in both of his books. In the Gospel, of course, Peter gropes, stumbles, and falls more than once. But in spite of all this, by the time the flow of the narrative reaches Acts, and the Risen Lord has returned to the Father, there can be no doubt that Peter has undergone a transformation. He becomes a confident and articulate apostle who effectively leads the infant community, and he is the first and principal proclaimer of the Christian *kerygma*. Surely a partial reason for Luke's interest in Peter is the fact that he has used Mark's Gospel, which shows Peter as the most prominent of the disciples, whose special importance comes from Jesus' special interest in him. But beyond Mark's influence, Luke has seen in the life of the primitive apostolic Church the fact that Peter was known and recognized as the accepted leader of the Christians, both by the brethren who lived, worked, and suffered with him, and also by the hostile leaders of Israel who implacably opposed him, as they had opposed Paul—and Jesus.

In all of this the personalities of these two chief witnesses of the Gospel are typical of what Luke wants to present to his gentile friends. They come across as men of God entirely absorbed in the work of being apostles and evangelists of the paschal mystery, rejected by their own people as Jesus was before them, but who nevertheless have something worthwhile to offer to Theophilus, and whoever else may read Luke-Acts.

Therefore we can be confident that our view is correct when we say that Luke is the most kerygmatic of the four evangelists, and that his purpose is not so much to show the history or biography of Jesus—still less that of the first generation of the Church—but rather to illustrate graphically the character of the religion which this new Church professes. Necessarily, Luke must show the Jewish background and the Old Testament matrix out of which Jesus and his Church have come, but this is simply a matter of the historical fact. The Gospel which has come to the gentiles was originally a Jewish Gospel, even though from the beginning it was the plan of God that it should pass beyond Israel and reach 'to the ends of the earth'.

This is why Luke intertwines so thoroughly his Jewish source material (such as, for instance, his Infancy Gospel [Lk 1-2] and the chapters on the infant Church in Jerusalem [Acts 1-7]) with details which relate to the Roman empire (the names of the emperors in Lk 2:1 and Lk 3:1

Chapter XIII

and those of the various Roman officials in Acts). The result of all this is that, even with the obvious emphasis on Israel's past and its hopes, there is nevertheless a constant and irresistible forward movement from the beginning of the Lukan Gospel to the end of Acts, which is constantly resisted, but which simply cannot be stopped or prevented by any human power. The message which comes to Mary and the shepherds, preceded by the message to Zechariah in Lk 1, comes more fully in Jesus to his own people; but they fail to grasp or accept it, in spite of the fact that it is a message of joy, healing, and salvation which comes from a friendly, loving, and fatherly God—the God of their own fathers! Then, rejected and even opposed and hounded by those to whom it was first offered, it moves on, impelled by the same Holy Spirit who brought it originally to Israel, to be the dynamizing force which now animates the newly-emerging Church, and eventually is offered to the larger world-community of Rome's gentile empire, where it is accepted by men of goodwill.

This is why the Jewish elements of Christianity are always presented by Luke as passing more and more into the background. John the Baptist appears at the beginning as a prophet sent by God to be a moralizer and proclaimer of the coming of God. But, once Jesus comes on the scene as the awaited prophet, whom God has anointed and filled with his spirit to offer a message of healing, peace and favour, John disappears, and does not reappear. The temple of Jerusalem, and indeed the whole city of Jerusalem, are prominent at the beginning of Luke's Gospel, along with the special personalities of the the Infancy Gospel—Zechariah and Elizabeth, Mary and Joseph, the shepherds, Simeon and Anna, and the doctors of the Law of Moses. They all represent the best piety of Israel and the sanctifying power of the Old Law. But now the new age has come, and Jesus moves in his journey to

Jerusalem (Lk 9-19), which now becomes both the place of the paschal mystery and also the city which rejects the Gospel. Throughout Acts the Jerusalem scene is always hard on the work of the Gospel, and eventually the mixed Jewish-gentile Church of Antioch comes to the fore as the focal point. It is the Church of Antioch which engages Paul and Barnabas, and sends them out on the work of outreach, to undertake the three great missionary journeys. When these are finished, Jerusalem again is hostile, this time to Paul (Acts 21); the Gospel goes with him into imprisonment, first in Caesarea, and then finally in Rome. Even in the capital of the Empire (Acts 28:17-28), the Jews reject the Gospel one last time—the Gospel which Paul offers to them in terms of their own tradition. Then Luke concludes Acts showing Paul preaching freely to all comers, meaning to all gentiles of goodwill.

In this forward movement Luke depicts the character of Christianity. He does this not so much by articulating at length any special exposition of doctrine as if for its own sake, but rather by showing personalities and scenes which are typically representative of the Gospel, and of the kind of people to whom, and from whom, the Gospel comes. Naturally enough, and necessarily, the Gospel is centered in Jesus. But, from the first, the Gospel which is centered in is a message of salvation, which is even implied in the Jewish meaning of his name (Saviour). This is why the first word of God's message to Mary (Lk 1:28) is 'Rejoice'. Similarly, the messenger tells the shepherds that his word is 'good news of great joy for everyone' and the heavenly singers proclaim 'peace on earth for God's friends' (Lk 2:10-14). Jesus himself begins his public ministry at Nazareth, by presenting himself as the prophet filled with God's Holy Spirit, sent to proclaim liberation, forgiveness, and favour from God. After the trauma of death has turned into the radiance of victory, the Risen Lord sends his disciples to preach a message of forgiveness and the loosing of sins (Lk 24:48), and this is just what Peter does as a result of the Pentecost experience (Acts 2-4).

Luke is remarkably successful in this effort. The character of Christianity shows up clearly as a religion of goodness and help from a God who wants to relate favourably to his people. The Jewish specifics recede into the past, as Luke emphasizes those features of Christianity which are likely to impress the universal family of all men. Jesus' family tree (Lk 3:23-38) relates him not only to Abraham and Israel, but even further back, to Adam, and through him to everyone. The message which Jesus preaches is not merely an exposition of the teaching of the Law and the Prophets, as Matthew shows it to be in the Sermon on the Mount (Mt 5-7); rather, it is the 'good news of God's rule' (Lk 4:43) as Jesus presents it, and the 'good news of peace' when Peter explains the essence of Christianity to the Roman centurion at Caesarea (Acts 10:36).

In order to emphasize this character of Christianity, Luke carefully prunes out some of the harsh elements which have come to him in his Markan source document. Luke shows no prearranged plot on the part of the leaders to kill Jesus (Mk 3:6); he omits Jesus' cursing of the fig-tree (Mk 11), the perversity of Judas (Lk 22:3), and the Roman torture of Jesus during his Passion (Mk 15:16-20). Likewise, the miracles which Luke presents are always helpful, life-giving, and peaceful. Nevertheless, Luke is quite willing to allow the miracle tradition to speak for itself, and for this reason he does not intensify it as Matthew does. Matthew, as we may recall, doubles the cure of the blind man of Jericho to a cure of two blind men, and then goes on to describe the same incident again; he also doubles the number of possessed men whom Jesus heals in the land of the Gerasenes, and records twice the healing of the possessed mute, but in all of these instances Luke is content to reproduce the substance of the tradition as he receives it from Mark. As for Jesus' feeding of the crowd of five thousand in the desert, Luke omits the cluster of details which accompany the scene in Mark, as well as the doublet which makes it look like a second feeding (Mk 6:45; 8:26). The result of this is that Jesus appears as a miracle-worker, but Luke's purpose is not served by intensifying the scenes, or by doubling them, as Matthew decides to do.

With regard to the kinds of people who receive the benefits of salvation in Jesus and in the Gospel, Luke shows an interesting variety of types. They range from the rather traditional Jews typified by Zechariah and Elizabeth, Mary and Joseph, the widow of Naim, and the disciples such as Peter and Paul themselves, to sophisticated Romans like the centurions of Capernaum (Lk 7) and Caesarea (Acts 10), the well-intentioned jailer converted at Philippi (Acts 16), and the sleepy young boy whom Paul restores to life at Troas (Acts 20). These personalities represent a full spectrum of every imaginable type—Jewish and gentile, rich and poor, powerful and weak, young and old, simple and sophisticated. But the common denominator which Luke wants to illustrate is present in all of them—they are all open to accept God's invitation to be taught, helped, and healed by the mystery of Jesus.

The Holy Spirit has such a special importance in Luke's theology that, were it not for the firmness of our Christian tradition with regard to the names of these New Testament books, we might be inclined to go along with those who suggest that we should rename them 'The Acts of the Holy Spirit, Part One (in Jesus) and Part Two (in the Church)'. We may easily miss this thread the first time, but we would do well to read through both of Luke's books again, this time with a coloured marker, and mark out each mention of the Holy Spirit. From the first chapter of his Gospel to the last chapter of Acts, Luke consistently presents the Holy Spirit as the animating force which is constantly operative and bringing God's plan to its completion. It is the Holy Spirit who comes to John the Baptist, Zechariah, Elizabeth, Mary, and Jesus himself. And, of course, at Pentecost the Holy Spirit is given now to the new generation of Christian converts, both Jewish (Acts 2:38-41) and gentile (Acts 8:29ff; 10:44ff; 15:8). Even when the apostles meet at the Council of Jerusalem and make their momentous decision to go beyond the old Jewish formalities in accepting gentile converts to the Church, they are confident that the Holy Spirit has guided them to this decision (Acts 15:28).

We would miss the whole point of Luke's message, therefore, if we thought that he was trying to be no more than a good historian. Indeed, people have argued at great length, and carried out considerable research, in order to show that Luke is a reliable historian; but, by worrying so much about this, they have failed to recognize the 'Spirit' character of his language and the overall nature of his theological message. What Luke wants Theophilus to see is that Christianity is a good and helpful religion, offered by God to everyone—to the Jews first, and then to the gentiles—through the powerful activity of the Holy Spirit.

We may wonder whether Luke thought of the Holy Spirit as a person of the Trinity, distinct from the Father and the Son (he does not use the word 'Trinity'—but nor does any other New Testament author). Perhaps it would be more realistic to say that Luke represents an intermediate stage of the Church's growth in understanding. He inherited the Old Testament tradition which sees the Spirit as the 'breath' of God—a life-giving and animating force, as much divine as the God who sends it forth. However, the images of fire, wind, and ecstasy which Luke used to depict the active power of the Holy Spirit at Pentecost (Acts 2) may also suggest that he had not arrived at the more mature understanding which came to the Church several centuries later. Moreover, if we read carefully, not only Luke's message to Theophilus, but also the rest of the New Testament as well, we will see why the Christians of the Eastern churches insist that the Holy Spirit proceeds from the Father but not from the Son. Their grounds for this insistence are good, since the New Testament writers—including Luke—do not say that Jesus is the source of this gift. In summary, we may conclude that Luke, along with Paul and the fourth evangelist, shows a much fuller appreciation of the Holy Spirit than Mark or Matthew, but that they all represent a level of theological understanding which was to evolve further in later centuries, as the Church continued to reflect on the mystery of God's work in Jesus and in itself.

As this 'gospel' purpose of Luke's message becomes more familiar to us, we see better how and why he has blended together two pictures, or images, of Jesus. The Church's Gospel of the paschal mystery is central for Luke, as it is for the other apostolic preachers. After all, how could Luke have allowed himself to be influenced by Paul and Mark without accepting their basic insistence on the centrality of Jesus' Passion and Glorification? Yet, in this central mystery, there is still a compenetration of images: Jesus is simultaneously the exalted Lord and Christ (or Messiah), and the lowly Suffering Servant and rejected Prophet. Luke knows this well, and he brings it out clearly, although it may not have struck us very forcefully on our first reading through. Let us recall the Infancy Gospel and the two angelic messages: the first message tells Mary that her son will be great, son of King David and heir to his royal throne—indeed, Luke even introduces Joseph as a member of the royal house of David! The second angelic message tells the shepherds at Bethlehem that the one born there is a saviour, and that he is Christ the Lord. And yet, despite this exalted terminology, Jesus is born in poverty and obscurity, surrounded by beasts and visited only by these wandering shepherds! Throughout his Gospel Luke presents Jesus as the prophet sent by God but unappreciated and ultimately rejected by his own people, in spite of the miracles which have shown God's power working in him. Jesus accepts the agony of this rejection as the innocent sufferer, commending his spirit to God, praying for his killers, sympathizing with the women who try to comfort him, and promising paradise to a confessed thief! The soldier at Calvary personifies the reaction that Luke wishes to elicit from any gentile of goodwill: 'Surely, this was a good man!' But, in contrast once more, the mystery of God's power for goodness and life is made supremely manifest in the exaltation of Jesus as the Risen Lord, and in the inexorable forward movement which brings his name and his Gospel of salvation to the ends of the earth.

Theophilus should be impressed. He should be able to see that the new religion which has spread so far and so fast can only be understood as something which is good, given to all men by a loving God. Such is the character of Christianity, of its God, and of its life-style. Such is also the character of the Church, attacked and persecuted, but always patient, prayerful, joyful in the consolation that it feels in being guided by the Spirit of God, always polite and respectful towards enemies and friends alike. This Church is not at all disruptive of public order, although its enemies cause riots to oppose it, nor is it hostile towards the Empire and its government—indeed, the Roman governor found no guilt in its Lord, and various other Roman officials repeatedly found no breach of law in its principal witnesses.

Luke's gracious manner towards the gentiles in general and towards the Romans in particular shows that he was a careful diplomat as well as a dedicated and persistent evangelist. Jerusalem had apparently fallen some years before he wrote, under the attack led in AD70 by Titus and his Roman legionaries. This event marked the definitive separation of Christians from unconverted Jews. But for those who lived outside the religious structures of both Jews and Christians, some explanation was necessary to show how and why the Christians came to follow such a religion, and to try so hard to propagate it. People may also have wondered how and why Christianity had come to be composed of a gentile majority spread so widely throughout the Empire. The destruction of Jerusalem and of its Temple was the end of Israel's claim to temporal sovereignty as a nation, but it was by no means the end of the new Christian movement. These Christians, now more separated from Judaism than they had ever been before, were carrying on as good citizens of the Empire, and waiting for an end of the world and the return of their Raised-up Lord, which they did not know when to expect, in the meantime eager to share the basic values of their life-style with their pagan neighbours in peace. This peace is what Luke wants Theophilus to discover and share.

1. Does Luke seem to be writing for Jews or for gentiles?
2. Does Luke put as much emphasis on the expected return of the Risen Lord as do Mark and Matthew?
3. What are the characteristics of Christianity which Luke seeks to offer to Theophilus?
4. How does Luke portray the Holy Spirit in his two-part work?
5. What significance do you see in Mary as she appears in Luke's work?
6. Of the three synoptic evangelists, which is your favourite? And why?

Conclusion

The Gospel and our Life-Style

This, however, is not the way it is among you. If one of you wants to be great, he must be the servant of the rest; and if one of you wants to be first, he must be the slave of all. *(Mk 10:43f.)*

When all is said and done, at least this much should come across to us clearly—that there is in essence one Gospel, and that it is a personal message rather than some kind of historical record as we would normally understand that. This one Gospel is what was foreshadowed in the oracles of the Old Testament prophets, what Jesus preached during his public ministry, and—finally—what the apostles and their friends witnessed during the first generation of the Church's life. The 'good news' is that God is a God of goodness and life, that his power is greater than the power of evil, and that he shows this power in Jesus—supremely in the raised-up Jesus, in whom the sinfulness of his killers is defeated by the life-giving power of the Father.

Because this Gospel is the central core of the whole Christian reality, it is the common denominator which we find pre-eminent in every one of the twenty-seven books of the New Testament. We tend to miss this point, because we tend to think of the word 'gospel' in a restricted way, as if we could apply it only to the four documents of Matthew, Mark, Luke, and John. But, as a message proclaiming this power of God for goodness and life in Jesus, the 'Gospel' pervades the whole of the New

Testament. The apostles had the challenging task of offering this 'good news' to the people of their generation, as they declared that in the raised-up Jesus they had received from God the supreme sign of his power and favour.

The Gospel had to pass through a number of stages as it came first to the Jews, and then to the community of gentiles who lived in the wider world of pagan culture, outside Israel. In the first chapters of the Acts of the Apostles we have the picture of Peter and his fellow apostles preaching the Gospel to Jews in Jewish terms—in their own language, and in their own capital city. But gradually, with the apostolic ministry of Paul and Barnabas, the Gospel came to gentile pagans who did not share the same culture, and who did not understand the terminology and the references of the Jewish Scriptures. This new situation led to growth, with Paul searching—successfully—for new ways of presenting the Christian message without using biblical terminology and imagery. Instead, he quoted the Greek poets, and took examples from the world of nature, which anyone of goodwill would have been able to recognize.

In this preaching of Peter and Paul, as well as of the other apostles, a further feature becomes evident: namely, that the Gospel message which they had to offer is a challenge to people's lives and therefore demands a vital response. It is never enough merely to hear the Gospel—there is always a call, and an insistent one at that, to absorb the Gospel at the level of faith, and to express this reponse in the form of a life-style. This is why Christianity is essentially a religion of practical life, why it must be worked out in terms of people's everyday activity. It can never be lived exclusively on the intellectual level. Christians who do not build and maintain a Christian life-style cannot remain as active members of the Church, because

Conclusion

they soon wither away and are separated from the vitality of the community's shared experience of God.

St Paul's letters make it clear that he was profoundly aware of this fact. He wrote to the various groups of his converts in the local churches, according to the particular problems which emerged as they worked to learn how to live out their new faith. But the answers and the instructions which this apostle of the gentiles gave to his new friends were on two levels. In terms of formal doctrine, or theology, Paul explained the deeper and fuller meaning of the *kerygma* (the proclamation) which he had brought to them, and which they had accepted by their response of conversion. But there also the practical or moral dimension to his letters, and the reason for this is that Christians had—and have—to work out the practical application of their response by developing an appropriate new life-style.

For converted Jews this involved moving away from an exaggerated dependence on the formalities of the old traditions of Moses, and being guided instead by the indwelling Holy Spirit who had now been given through the Risen Lord. For gentiles who had accepted the Gospel, it involved abandoning the maze of superstitions and rituals, as well as the earthy licentiousness, which dominated paganism and its culture. These new gentile Christians had also to learn how to recognize the full power of divinity as it came to them from Father, Son, and Holy Spirit: such a dynamizing principle was bound to encourage and animate them to free themselves from the useless idolatry which had previously blinded their vision. The love which they had received from God they were now required to share with each other, so that this charity could liberate them from the fear of demons or of any human masters—even of the Emperor!

In all this it is the Risen Lord Jesus, and the paschal mystery of his passover from earthly death to heavenly glory, which is at the centre of the Gospel and of the Christian life-style which responds to it. The vitalizing appeal of this Gospel was something that had never previously hit the ancient world, and the spread of this message—so far, and so fast—was itself an obvious sign of the presence of a superior God.

Then, as time moved on to a point some years (we may assume) after the deaths of both Paul and Peter, the synoptic evangelists took up what was at root the same project: to present, to their own contemporaries, the living Gospel message of Jesus and of his great passover to glory. The great difference was that Mark, Matthew, and Luke all used a new literary form, beyond the purely oral preaching of the first apostles and distinct from the letter-writing form which Paul had used so successfully. They adopted what we have been rather accustomed to see as a biographical, or 'life of Jesus', form and style. We call these three evangelists 'synoptic' because they 'see together', or appear to stand together, inasmuch as, when we look at their Gospels set out alongside each other in parallel columns, we can see just how much they seem to work from the same perspective and to present what appears to be, more or less, the same picture.

There is certainly a common core to the documents which these three evangelists have produced. Indeed, we can say that this core common to their three messages comes across on two levels. The first, and by far the most important, level is the theological one. If the apostolic Gospel of the paschal mystery was the core of the early Church's faith, then surely it must also have beeen the theological core common to these three synoptic messages—and so indeed it was! For, even though—on the narrative level—the story of Jesus' death and glorification comes only in the final chapters of these three documents, this paschal mystery is nonetheless the controlling reality which gives shape and purpose to them, and to the Acts of the Apostles as well.

The second level on which these evangelists share a common core is that of the narrative pattern. We credit Mark with being the first composer of such a 'narrative theology' of the Christian Gospel, recounting the flow of movement from the ministry of John the Baptist, through the public ministry of Jesus, to the Jerusalem setting of Jesus' Passion and the Easter experience of the women at the tomb. Both Matthew and Luke inherited Mark's document, and used it in their different ways, so that Mark's Gospel is also the literary—or narrative—core of the synoptic messages.

However, we do a grave disservice to these evangelists, and to ourselves as well, if we fail to appreciate the special individual touches which each has brought to the Gospel tradition in the course of applying it to the life-situation of his own contemporaries. We saw Paul demanding a response in the form of a Christian life-style from those who were to receive and read his letters, and the same goes for these three synoptic evangelists. Their purpose was by no means so mild or so simple as merely to tell an edifying story about the Jesus of the past! Rather, their intention was to get their friends to live and act according to the demands of the paschal mystery in the present. The Gospel is *now*!

This brings us to the variations between the three individual evangelists interpreting the same Gospel to three different groups of receivers. They speak with three distinct voices—in three different theological 'accents', so to speak. One of the most promising projects for our own generation, but perhaps one of the most challenging and difficult projects as well, is that of discovering the special meassage of each of the synoptic evangelists for us, and of working out the practical consequences of their messages in terms of our own life-style. This is the 'biblical spirituality' of our time: to make the Gospel the dominant force in our life.

In order to grasp this point, and to work out these consequences, we must learn to see each of the three synoptic messages as a whole. Although we may not appreciate it, the greatest help for us in this task is the Sunday liturgy based on the current (new) form of the Lectionary. We now have a three-year cycle of biblical readings, with one of the synoptic Gospels as the principal Gospel for each of these three years: Matthew's Gospel is the one for the first year (Year A) of the cycle, Mark's for the second (Year B), and Luke's for the third (Year C). There are interruptions, of course, especially for Advent and the Christmas season, and then again for the entire period of Lent and the Easter season (which lasts for about thirteen weeks, from Ash Wednesday to Pentecost). However, aside from these times, there are about thirty Sundays—most of them falling between Pentecost and Advent—on which we follow one of these synoptic Gospels. And so, even though we have only a short passage of a few verses each Sunday, over the course of these thirty-or-so Sundays we have an excellent opportunity of imbibing the special 'flavour' of the synoptic evangelist of the year in question. Despite the fact that we have in the past been accustomed to putting all three Gospels together to form a sort of 'composite' picture of Jesus, this exercise has never really succeeded. The 'picture' which emerges is unreal—which is not surprising, because it is not the picture which any one of these inspired evangelists tried to present. We are much better off, therefore, if we take the synoptic Gospels one at a time, following the cycle of the Lectionary, and concentrating on absorbing the particular message of the 'evangelist of the year'.

This process is also much more interesting, because we not only get a single, coherent 'story of Jesus', but also a

Conclusion

grasp of the style and rhythm of the evangelist concerned. Of course, to benefit in this way, we must do more than listen passively to the Sunday reading. We need to re-read it at least once during the week, and then also to study a reliable commentary. But this effort will bring us a richer and deeper appreciation of the living reality of the Gospel, and, as the Gospel takes more and more of our attention, this must certainly have an effect on our life-style.

Besides this, of course, there is nothing at all to prevent us from sitting down and again reading through one of the synoptic documents as a whole. As we have already seen from working through the earlier chapters, this exercise does not have to take a long time: Mark's Gospel is some fifty normal book-pages long, and the longest one (Luke-Acts) is only about 170 normal book-pages long. We can read any of them in about an hour or an hour and a half, especially if we make it a point to keep on reading and not to stop for problem texts (we can always make a not of such passages and come back to them later). When we do this, we should start with Mark's Gospel—the earliest of the three documents—and for preference read it at least twice, in order to get the 'feel' of it. Even so, we will probably not really begin to sense the impact of this exercise until we go on to read Matthew's Gospel a couple of times, and to notice how it is both similar to Mark ('synoptic') and at the same time remarkably different from it. Luke-Acts is also based on Mark, and also both similar to and different from Mark and Matthew. And, of course, Luke's unique contribution becomes evident to us when we read his two books as a single whole.

This effort will lead us to see the individual message which comes across as each evangelist interprets the same core Gospel for different people. *Mark* wrote for gentile Christians, presumably in Rome, shortly before the tragic destruction of Jerusalem. It was the time of Nero and his anti-Christian campaign, which had already brought death to Peter and Paul and to many other Christians as well. Mark wrote to show his friends how Jesus is really the Son of God, even though nobody recognized him as such. It was only after Jesus had died as the Father's Suffering Servant that God showed his endorsement and acceptance of his perfect service: the Roman soldier at Calvary said what no Jew had said, 'Surely this man was God's son!' Thus Mark made clear in his 'narrative theology' that Jesus could never be fully understood as a prophet or a teacher or a wonder-worker: the only true key to the identity of Jesus is the paschal mystery—Jesus is the Son of Man, killed by men but raised up by God. And then comes the demand for a practical response! For the pressed Christians of Nero's city, discipleship was a matter of walking the same path, carrying the same kind of cross, and being brought by the Father to the same vindication. The new Christian life-style was thus essentially a case of living out the paschal mystery.

Matthew's message builds on that of Mark, but is tailored to Jewish Christians. He constantly quotes from the Old Testament Scriptures to show that the fullness of Judaism is now present in Jesus, just as it had been before in the old Israel. Two Israels now emerge in the evolving dynamic of Matthew's picture: the false Israel of the leaders, and the true Israel, once found in the Old Testament period, then later in Jesus, and most recently in the Church of Jesus' disciples. The former was a matter of formalism and practices lacking true piety, but the latter was a matter of the covenant relationship of interpersonal communion between Father and children, which was present in the Law and the Prophets (i.e, in the Old Testament), but which the leaders had neglected to bring to their people. The fullness of the Kingdom of God, formerly located among the ancient ancestors of Israel, now appeared in the words and the works of Jesus,

Conclusion

but the false Israel was unable to make the adjustment which Jesus demanded. Rather than change its life-style, it preferred to destroy the challenger. The reality of the mystery reached its peak when the supremacy of God's reign of goodness and life overcame the sinfulness which could do no more than kill his Son. Finally, Matthew shows the true Israel as now present in the Church of the apostles, and in 'all the nations' who, from this point on, were to follow, not the teachings of the false leaders, but the things which Jesus had taught them.

At first sight Matthew's theological message might appear irrelevant, since he emphasizes Judaism and the Jewish character of Christianity. But he has a great deal to offer to gentiles, since his overall theme is that the true Israel was not a matter of the obsolete formalism of the leaders, but rather the living covenant relationship which bound God to his people—and his people were now gentiles as well as Jews. It is a simple fact of history that by Matthew's day (about AD 80-85) the Church had become mostly gentile, and that the early Jewish-Christians may therefore have felt themselves uncomfortably in a minority. Some of them, it would seem, resented the situation strongly enough to have been inclined to abandon the new faith and revert to their ancestral traditions. It is in the face of this reaction that Matthew interpreted the Gospel to them in such a way that they might see that to be Christian was their best route to arriving at the fulfilment of the true Israel. For gentiles—such as ourselves—this also works in reverse, because it means that the gentile members of the Church can trace their spiritual ancestry back, not merely to Jesus and his apostles, but to two thousand years before them—to the ancient patriarchs of God's people, as Matthew shows in the first verses of his document.

The *Lukan* form of the Gospel tradition is unique in several ways, in spite of the fact that it shares the common core of the paschal mystery on the theological level and of Mark's Gospel on the narrative and literary level. To this common core Luke added a large amount of new material, and as a result his special handling of the material shows up in the wider sweep of his view—a view which does not end with the picture of the Risen Lord, but continues through the Acts of the Apostles, as the Holy Spirit brings the Gospel to Rome through the witness of St Paul. The prominence of the Holy Spirit is another unique feature of Luke's theology, and we can all too easily miss it if we limit ourselves to seeing only the narrative or literary level of his message—if, in other words, we make the mistake of turning him into a historian rather than allowing him to be the evangelist he intended to be. The whole Lukan thrust is to emphasize those aspects of Christianity which should be appealing and attractive to gentiles: the kindness and healing power of God, manifested first in Jesus and then in the Church which witnessed to him; and the patience, forgiveness, and compassion which Jesus exemplified as the unappreciated Lord and innocent sufferer. All the individual fragments of the tradition are brought together to form this portrait, though we may, if we are not careful, fail even to recognize the whole because we concentrate to hard on its parts.

The task which faces us is that of absorbing more of the challenge of the Gospel in order to work it through into our practice to the point where it becomes the dominant influence in our life-style. To do this we must get beyond the 'material' level, and become constantly aware that what we are relating to in these documents is not merely a kind of modern historical record or scientific account. Historical records can never bring us to experience the healing power of God, or challenge us to pay the price of renouncing all in order to taste the freedom which only

Conclusion

the Gospel can give! When we do experience this healing power and the purification which it brings, we will will be able to go on and do what Jesus told the healed man to do (Mk 5:5:19): 'Go and tell your people how the Lord has been good to you!' That will mean that we have moved far beyond the stage of passive hearing of the Gospel, and ourselves become apostles and witnesses. When other people can see this in our life-style, it will mean that the Gospel has done its work and become the most important force in our lives. This is what God wants it to be.

Appendix

Appendix

Suggestions for Further Reading

The following series and titles are suggested for further reading on the Synoptic Gospels. All the commentaries listed are written by competent biblical specialists, but they have been designed to be helpful without being too technical.

Image Books Series
ACHTEMEIER, PAUL J., *Invitation to Mark*, Garden City, N.Y., 1978.
KARRIS, ROBERT J., *Invitation to Luke*, Garden City, N.Y., 1977.
KARRIS, ROBERT J., *Invitation to Acts*, Garden City, N.Y., 1978.
SENIOR, DONALD, *Invitation to Matthew*, Garden City, N.Y., 1977.

New Testament Reading Guide Series:
FLANAGAN, NEAL, *The Acts of the Apostles*, 1960^2.
SLOYAN, GERARD, *The Gospel of St Mark*, 1960.
STANLEY, DAVID, *The Gospel of St Matthew*, 1963^2.
STUHLMUELLER, C., *The Gospel of St Luke*, 1964^2.

Pelican Gospel Commentary Series
CAIRD, G.B., *Saint Luke*, Harmondsworth and New York, 1963.
FENTON, J.C., *Saint Matthew*, Harmondsworth and New York, 1963.
NINEHAM, D.E., *Saint Mark*, Harmondsworth and New York, 1963.

New Testament for Spiritual Reading Series
KUERZINGER, JOSEPH, *The Acts of the Apostles*, London and New York, 1969-71.
SCHNACKENBURG, RUDOLF, *The Gospel according to St Mark*, London and New York, 1971.
STOEGER, ALOIS, *The Gospel according to St Luke*, London and New York, 1969.
TRILLING, WOLFGANG, *The Gospel according to St Matthew*, London and New York, 1969.

Daily Study Bible Series
BARCLAY, WILLIAM, *The Acts of the Apostles*, Edinburgh, 1953.
BARCLAY, WILLIAM, *The Gospel of St Luke*, Edinburgh, 1953.
BARCLAY, WILLIAM, *The Gospel of St Mark*, Edinburgh, 1954.
BARCLAY, WILLIAM, *The Gospel of St Matthew* (2 vols.), Edinburgh, 1956-7.

GRECH, P., *The Acts of the Apostles Explained*, New York, 1966.

A Panoramic View of Mark's Gospel

3 Basic Theological Assertions
1) Jesus is Real, but unrecognized Son of God.
2) Discipleship
3) Immanent Parousia

INTRODUCTORY TRIPTYCH Mk 1:1-13	JESUS IS THE
	BEGINNING OF JESUS' PUBLIC MINISTRY Mk 1:14-3:6

Opening verse 1:1
 	
Preaching Mission of John the Baptist 1:2-8
 	
Baptism of Jesus; the voice of the Father 1:9-11
 	
Jesus' trial in the desert 1:12-13
	Summary formula 1:14-15
	
	Call of first disciples 1:16-20
	
	Ministry at Capernaum 1:21-39
	   Narrative setting; summary 1:21-2
	   The Synagogue; exorcism of the demoniac 1:23-8
	   Peter's mother-in-law cured 1:29-31
	   Summary: success and acceptance 1:32-9
	
	Cure of a leper 1:40-45
	
	Conflicts with the Leaders 2:1-36
	   The paralytic cured 2:1-12
	   Call of Levi; eating with 'such as these' 2:13-17
	   Fasting; sayings on patches and wineskins 2:18-22
	   The standing grain; the Sabbath 2:23-8
	   Cure of the man with the withered hand 3:1-5
	   Conclusion: Jesus' true identity is unrecognized; the leaders plan to destroy him 3:6

REAL BUT UNRECOGNIZED SON OF GOD Mk 1:14-8:30

SECOND PHASE OF JESUS' PUBLIC MINISTRY Mk 3:7-6:6a	FINAL PHASE OF JESUS' PUBLIC MINISTRY Mk 6:6b-8:30
Summary formula 3:7-12	Summary 6:6b
Choice of twelve disciples 3:13-19	Mission of the twelve 6:6-13

Jesus' Identity is not Understood 3:20-35
  His family 3:20-21
  The Scribes: 'Beelzebub' 3:22-30
  Jesus' 'true family' 3:31-5
	Parenthesis: Herod's killing of John; his fear of Jesus 6:14-29

	The apostles return 6:30-33
	Feeding of the 5000 6:34-44
Jesus' parables are not understood 4:1-34	Jesus walks on the water 6:45-52

Some Miracle Stories 4:35-5:43
  Lake storm calmed 4:35-41
  Gerasene demoniac exorcized 5:1-20
  Jairus' daughter raised from death 5:21-4; 35-43
  Woman with the haemorrhage cured 5:25-34
	Arrival at Gennesaret; cures 6:53-6

	Confrontation with Pharisees; defilement sayings 7:1-23
	Tyre exorcism; Decapolis cure (Ephphatha) 7:24-37

	Doublet of the Preceding Sequence 8:1-26
	  Feeding of the 4000 8:1-10
	  Pharisees demand a sign 8:11-13
	  In the boat; the leaven of the Pharisees and of Herod 8:14-21
	  Bethsaida; the blind man cured 8:22-6

Conclusion: rejection at Nazareth; Jesus' true identity is not appreciated by his neighbours 6:1-6a	Conclusion: Peter's mistaken enthusiasm; Jesus enjoins silence upon the uncomprehending disciples 8:27-30

JESUS MUST BE THE SON OF MAN: HE INSTRUCTS HIS DISCIPLES AND HEADS FOR JERUSALEM Mk 8:31-10:52	
JESUS EXPLAINS HIS IDENTITY AND SPEAKS OF DISCIPLESHIP Mk 8:31-9:50	THE JOURNEY TO JERUSALEM Mk 10
Jesus speaks of himself as the Son of Man; first Passion prediction; Jesus and Peter rebuke each other 8:31-3 Sayings on discipleship; cross-bearing; sacrifice and the Kingdom of God 8:34-9:1 *The Transfiguration 9:2-13* On the mountain 9:2-8 Descent from the mountain; discussion about Elijah 9:9-13 Exorcism of the boy 9:14-29 *Journey through Galilee 9:30-50* Second Passion prediction 9:30-32 Discussion on true greatness 9:33-7 The strange exorcist 9:38-41 Some sayings of Jesus 9:42-50	*Going to Judaea 10:1-31* Narrative setting; summary 10:1-2 Pharisees; discussion on divorce 10:3-12 The children 10:13-16 Rich man; the danger of riches 10:23-7 Sayings on rewards 10:28-31 *Final Stages of the Journey to Jerusalem 10:32-52* Third Passion prediction 10:32-4 James and John; rank and precedence 10:25-45 Jericho: blind Bartimaeus cured 10:46-52

JESUS' TRUE IDENTITY IS UNRECOGNIZED IN JERUSALEM Mk 11-13	
BEGINNINGS OF THE JERUSALEM MINISTRY; CONFLICTS IN THE CAPITAL Mk 11:1-12:44	THE LAST INSTRUCTION TO THE DISCIPLES Mk 13:1-37

Jesus' Messianic entry 11:1-11
 	
Jesus curses the fig-tree 11:12-14
 	
Cleansing of the Temple; the leaders plot against Jesus 11:15-19
 	
The withered fig-tree; some words of Jesus on faith and prayer 11:20-25
 	
Conflicts in Jerusalem 11:27-12:44
  Priests, scribes, elders; the dispute on Jesus' authority 11:27-33
  Parable of the tenants 12:1-11
  Narrative appendix 12:12
  Pharisees and Herodians; the coin of tribute 12:13-27
  A scribe; the greatest commandment 12:28-34
  Jesus criticizes the scribes; the crowd approves 12:35-40
  The wealthy; the widow and her mite 12:40-44
	Narrative setting 13:1-4
	
	Calamities and persecutions will afflict the disciples 13:5-13a
	
	Exhortation to perseverance; assurance of salvation 13:13b
	
	Apparent triumph of evil; the supreme test 13:14-23
	
	Coming of the Son of Man; salvation of the chosen 13:24-7
	
	The signs of the times 13:28-31
	
	Sayings on watchfulness 13:32-7

JESUS IS VINDICATED AND GLORIFIED IN HIS PASSION Mk 14-16

Prelude 14:1-42
  The leaders' plot 14:1-2
  Bethany; the Anointing 14:3-9
  Judas' betrayal 14:10-11
  The Supper; the Eucharist 14:12-25
  On the way to Gethsemane: predictions of denial and of resurrection 14:26-31
  Gethsemane: the Agony 14:32-42
 	
The arrest 14:42-52
 	
The Jewish trial 14:53-65
 	
Peter's denial 14:66-72
 	
The Roman trial; Pilate 15:1-15
 	
Crucifixion 15:21-36
 	
Jesus is vindicated as he dies; signs; the women 15:37-41
 	
Burial 15:42-7
	THE RISEN LORD Mk 16:1-8
	
	The women at the tomb 16:1-3
	
	The stone 16:4
	
	The messenger 16:5
	
	The message 16:6-7
	
	The women's reaction 16:8
	
	THE LONGER ENDING Mk 16:9-20
	
	Apparition to Mary Magdalene 16:9-11
	
	Apparition to two travellers 16:12-13
	
	Apparition to the Eleven; the mission 16:14-18
	
	Ascension and Session 16:19
	
	The Eleven preach; signs accompany their witness 16:20

A Panoramic View of Matthew's Gospel

1. Preparation of the Kingdom of Heaven in Israel; Jesus is the Messiah in his Birth and Infancy Mt 1-2

Genealogy: Jesus is Messiah/Christ; Son of David; Son of Abraham 1:1-17

Joseph and Jesus; Jesus is Emmanuel (Is 7:14) 1:18-25

The Magi (Mi 5:1; 2 Sam 5:2; Num 24:17; Is 60:5f) 2:1-12

The flight into Egypt (Hos 11:1) 2:13-15

The Innocents (Jer 31:15) 2:16-18

The return from Egypt; Nazareth (Ex 4:19; Jdg 13:5, 7; Is 11:1) 2:19-23

2. THE KINGDOM OF HEAVEN COMES IN JESUS' TEACHING; ITS CHARACTER Mt 3-7

Introductory Triptych 3:1-4:11
  John preaches 3:1-12
  Jesus is baptized; the Father's voice 3:13-17
  The desert trial 4:1-11

John arrested; Jesus withdraws and preaches in Galilee (Capernaum) 4:12-17

First disciples called 4:18-22

General summary 4:23-5

THE SERMON ON THE MOUNT Mt 5-7

The setting 5:1-2
The Beatitudes 5:3-10, 11-12
The disciples are salt and light 5:13-16

The Essence of the Law and the Prophets 5:17-48
  Introduction 5:17-20
  Justice 5:21-6
  Chastity and lust 5:27-30
  Marital fidelity 5:31-2
  Sincerity 5:33-7
  Talion and love 5:38-42
  Love of all 5:43-8

True Piety 6:1-18
  Almsgiving 6:1-4
  Prayer 6:5-15 (with 7:7-11)
  Fasting 6:16-18
Appended sayings on related themes 6:19-34

Various Sayings 7:1-23
  Judging 7:1-5
  Pearls 7:6
  Prayer 7:7-11 (with 6:5-15)
  The golden rule 7:12
  The narrow gate 7:13-14
  False prophets 7:15-20
  Good works and their reward 7:21-3
Conclusion: the two houses 7:24-7
Epilogue: the crowd's reaction 7:28-9

3. THE KINGDOM OF HEAVEN COMES IN JESUS' MIRACLES; HIS DISCIPLES ARE TO CARRY ON HIS MISSION Mt 8-10

Three Healing Miracles 8:1-15
    The leper 8:1-4
    The centurion's servant 8:5-13
    Peter's mother-in-law 8:14-15

General summary (Is 53:4) 8:16-17

On following Jesus 8:18-22

Three Miracles 8:23-9:8
    Stilling the storm 8:23-7
    Two Gadarene demoniacs (the pigs) 8:28-34
    The Capernaum paralytic 9:1-8

Call of Matthew; dinner and fasting discussion; three parables (bridegroom, cloth, wineskins) 9:9-17

Four Healing Miracles 9:18-34
    Woman with blood; the official's daughter 9:18-26
    Two blind men 9:27-31
    Possessed mute 9:32-4

Jesus sees the people's need (Num 24:13) 9:35-7

Jesus summons his twelve disciples 10:1

The mission; introduction to the Missionary Discourse 10:5a

The Missionary Discourse 10:5b-42
Go to Israel! 10:5b-6

Preach the Gospel of the Kingdom of Heaven! 10:7

Heal! 10:8

Travel light; trust God's providence 10:9-10

Stay with worthy persons 10:11-15

Saying on sheep/wolves and serpents/doves 10:16

Expect persecution 10:17-25

Confess fearlessly 10:26-33

Division in families 10:34-6

Extent of the renunciation demanded by discipleship 10:37-9

Conclusion 10:40-42

Epilogue and transition 11:1

4. THE KINGDOM MEETS NEGATIVE RESPONSES FROM ISRAEL, BUT WILL PRODUCE ITS FRUITS NEVERTHELESS Mt 11-13

John is puzzled; Jesus witnesses to himself and to John 11:2-19

Jesus reproaches the unconverted generation 11:16-17

Reproach to the unconverted towns of Israel 11:20-24

Sayings on the Father and the Son; Jesus' yoke 11:25-6, 27-30

The Pharisees; Sabbath grain controversy 12:1-8

Sabbath withered hand cure; Pharisees' plot 12:9-14

Jesus is the gentle Servant of God (Is 42:1-4) 12:16-21

Blind-dumb demoniac cured; the Pharisees: 'Beelzebub'; Jesus rebukes their unfaith 12:22-37

Scribes and Pharisees ask for a sign; the 'Sign of Jonah' 12:38-42

Sayings on the unclean spirit 12:43-5

Jesus' true family 12:46-50

Parables of the Kingdom 13:1-52
The setting 13:1-3

    The sower 13:4-8
    Appended saying 13:9
    Jesus and the disciples; the reason for parables 13:10-17
    Explanation of the sower parable 13:18-23
    The weeds 13:24-30
    The mustard seed 13:31-2
    The leaven 13:33
    Comment on Jesus' use of the parable form (Ps 78:2) 13:34-5

    Explanation of the weeds parable 13:36-43

    The hidden treasure 13:44

    The merchant's pearls 13:45-6

    The net 13:47-50

Conclusion: 'Every scribe learned in the Kingdom of God...' 13:51-2

5. THE KINGDOM IN THE CHURCH OF THE DISCIPLES HEADED BY PETER; JESUS INSTRUCTS THEM ON DISCIPLESHIP Mt 13:52-18:35

Jesus rejected at Nazareth 13:53-8

Herod; the killing of John 14:1-12

Jesus withdraws, feeds the 5000 14:13-21

Jesus prays, walks on the water (Peter) 14:22-33

Arrival at Gennesaret; acceptance; healings 14:34-6

Confrontation with the Pharisees over essentials of religion 15:1-20

Jesus heals Canaanite woman's daughter 15:21-8

Jesus returns to Galilee and heals 15:29-31

Feeding of the 4000 (doublet) 15:32-9

Pharisees and Sadducees: the 'Sign of Jonah' 16:1-4

Warning against the leaven of the leaders 16:5-12

Peter's confession; Jesus' Messianic identity; the Church; the keys 16:13-20

First Passion prediction; sayings on cross-bearing and the coming Kingdom 16:21-8

The Transfiguration 17:1-8

Discussion on Elijah 17:9-13

Possessed boy cured 17:14-21

Second Passion prediction 17:22-3

Peter; Temple tax; fish-coin 17:24-7

Discourse on Discipleship and Community 18:1-35
   'Who is the greatest?': Jesus speaks on childlikeness 18:1-4
   On giving and taking scandal 18:5-9
   Regard for 'little ones'; the ninety-nine sheep and the one 18:10-14
   Fraternal correction in the ecclesial community 18:15-18
   Prayer: 'where two or three are gathered...' 18:19-20
   Forgiveness (70 times 7 times); parable of the unmerciful official 18:21-35

Conclusion and transition; Jesus heads for Judaea 19:1-2

> 6. CONFRONTATION WITH ISRAEL'S HOSTILE LEADERS BRINGS A CRISIS WHICH PREPARES FOR THE SUPREME MANIFESTATION OF THE KINGDOM OF HEAVEN Mt 19-25

Journey to Jerusalem 19-20
    The setting 19:1-2
    Discussion on divorce and marriage; celibacy 19:3-12
    Jesus and the children 19:13-15
    Rich young man 19:16-22
    Danger of riches 19:23-6
    Reward of renunciation 19:27-30
    Parable of the labourers 20:1-16
    Third Passion prediction 20:17-19
    Zebedee's sons; true greatness 20:20-28
    Jericho: two blind men cured 20:29-34

Jesus in Jerusalem 21-22
    Jesus enters Jerusalem 21:1-11
    Temple cleansing 21:12-17
    Fig-tree cursed 21:18-22
    Priests and elders 21:23-7
    Sons and tenants parables; leaders react 21:28-46
    Royal wedding parable 22:1-14
    Coin of tribute 22:15-22
    Discussion on resurrection 22:23-33
    The greatest commandment 22:34-40
    David's Son 22:41-6

Rebuke of the Pharisees 23:1-39
    The setting 23:1
    Hypocrites; sayings to the disciples 23:2-12
    Seven 'woes' against the leaders 23:13-31
    Their coming punishment 23:32-6
    Jesus' last words to 'Jerusalem, Jerusalem!' 23:37-9

The Last Instruction 24-5
    The things which will precede the end 24:1-14
    The onset of the *parousia*: calamities and signs 24:15-28
    The *parousia* of the Son of Man 24:29-31
    Exhortation to watchfulness 24:32-6
    Added watchfulness sayings; householder and servants 24:37-51
    Parable of the maids 25:1-13
    Parable of the talents 25:14-30
    The Last Judgement; final rewards and punishments 25:31-46

7. THE KINGDOM IS MANIFESTED SUPREMELY IN JESUS' SUFFERING AND VINDICATION; THE RISEN LORD INAUGURATES THE MISSION OF THE APOSTLES TO ALL THE PEOPLES Mt 26-8

Prelude 26:1-46
   The plot against Jesus 26:1-5
   Bethany anointing 26:6-13
   Judas' betrayal 26:14-16
   Last Supper; eucharistic memorial 26:17-35
   Gethsemane: the Agony 26:36-46

The arrest 26:47-56

Jewish trial; Peter's denial 26:57-75

Roman trial and torture 27:1-31

Execution of Jesus 27:32-56

Burial 27:57-61

Th priests arrange to get guards at the Tomb 27:62-6

The women at the Tomb; earthquake; the Angel; the Risen Lord; the mission 28:1-10

The priests bribe the Tomb guards 28:11-15

The Risen Lord sends his disciples/apostles on mission 28:16-20

A Panoramic View of Luke-Acts

INFANCY GOSPEL Lk 1:1-2:40	INTRODUCTORY TRIPTYCH Lk 3:1-4:13

Prologue 1:1-4
 	
Annunciation Diptych 1:5-56
  a. of John to Zechariah 1:5-25
  b. of Jesus to Mary 1:26-38
  b. Visitation; Mary's *Song* 1:39-56
Birth Diptych 1:57-2:40
  a. of John; joyful wonder of parents and neighhbours 1:57-80
  b. of Jesus; joyful wonder of the local shepherds 2:1-40
  b. Angels' *Song* 2:13-14
  a. Circumcision; naming of John 1:59-64
  b. Circumcision; naming of Jesus 2:21
  a. Zechariah's *Song* 1:68-79
  b. Presentation; Simeon and Anna; Simeon's *Song* 2:22-38
  a. 'The child grew' 1:80
  b. 'The child grew' 2:40
  b. Jesus lost and found in Jerusalem 2:41-52
  b. Jesus 'grew' 2:52
	Preaching mission of John the Baptist 3:1-18
	
	(Herod and John) 3:19-20
	
	The Baptism of Jesus; the Father's voice 3:21-2
	
	Genealogy of Jesus 3:23-38
	
	The desert trial 4:1-13

Jesus' Galilean Ministry Lk 4:14-9:50

At Nazareth 4:14-30

At Capernaum 4:31-44

Call of Peter; catch of fishes 5:1-11

Cure of leper 5:12-16

Conflicts with the leaders 5:17-6:11

Call of the Twelve 6:12-16

Healings 6:17-19

The Smaller Lukan Insertion 6:20-83
   The Great Discourse 6:20-49
   Centurion's servant healed 7:1-10
   The widow's son at Naim 7:11-17
   Messengers from John 7:18-35
   The sinful woman; anointing 7:36-50
   The woman who helped Jesus 8:1-3

Sayings of Jesus 8:4-21

Four miracle stories 8:22-56

Mission of the Twelve 9:1-6

Herod's curiosity 9:7.9

Feeding of the 5000 9:10-17

(The Great Lukan Omission)

Peter's confession; first Passion prediction 9:18-22

Sayings on following Jesus 9:23-7

The Transfiguration 9:28-36

The boy exorcised 9:37-43

Second Passion prediction; sayings 9:43-50

THE JOURNEY TO JERUSALEM Lk 9:51-19:27

The Great Lukan Insertion 9:51-18:14
  In Samaria 9:51-6
  Sayings on discipleship 9:57-62
  Mission of the Seventy 10:1-20
  Sayings of Jesus 10:21-4
  Good Samaritan parable 10:25-37
  Martha and Mary 10:38-42
  Sayings on prayer 11:1-13
  Jesus and his opponents 11:14-54
  Exhortations and warnings 12:1-13:9
  The stooped woman 13:10-17
  Sayings on the Kingdom 13:18-21
  'How many will b saved?' 13:22-35
  Jesus in the Pharisee's house 14:1-24
  Parables of God's mercy 15:1-32
  Parables about riches 16:1-31
  Four sayings of Jesus 17:1-10
  The ten lepers 17:11-19
  The Day of the Son of Man 17:20-37
  Parables about prayer 18:1-14

The Common Section 18:15-43
  The children; the rich ruler; sayings on riches 18:15-30
  Third Passion prediction 18:31-4
  Jericho; blind man cured 18:35-43

Zacchaeus of Jericho 19:1-10

Parable of the sums of money 19:11-27

JESUS' JERUSALEM MINISTRY Lk 19:28-21:38	THE PASSION GOSPEL Lk 22:1-23:56
The Messianic entry 19:28-38 Jesus' lament over Jerusalem 19:39-44 The cleansing of the Temple 19:45-8 Jesus teaches in the Temple; conflicts with the leaders 20:1-21:4 The Last Instruction 21:5-36 Summary 21:37-8	The plot 22:1-6 Preparation of the Passover 22:7-13 The Last Supper 22:14-38 The Agony 22:39-46 The arrest 22:47-53 Peter's denial 22:54-62 The guards; the Jewish trial 22:63-71 The Roman trial 23:1-5 Jesus before Herod 23:6-12 Pilate and the crowd 23:13-25 The crucifixion 23:26-43 Jesus dies; the signs 23:44-49 The burial 23:50-56

THE RISEN LORD Lk 24:1-53	TRANSITION: THE CHURCH AWAITS THE HOLY SPIRIT Acts 1:1-26

The women at the Tomb 24:1-12
 	
The Emmaus incident 24:13-35
 	
The disciples; apparition, instruction, and mission to witness 24:36-49
 	
The Ascension of the Risen Lord 24:50-51
 	
The disciples in Jerusalem 24:52-3
	Resumé of the 'First Account' 1:1-14
	   Reference to the 'First Account' 1:1-2
	   Jesus promises the Holy Spirit 1:3-5
	   The Ascension of the Risen Lord 1:6-11
	   The disciples in Jerusalem 1:12-14
	
	Matthias becomes the twelfth witness 1:15-26

The Promised Holy Spirit Comes to the Apostles in Jerusalem Acts 2:1-13	The Church Witnesses in Jerusalem Acts 2:14-8:3
The prophetic investiture 2:1-4 The apostles prophesy; the crowds understand the tongues 2:5-11 Reaction of wonder and interest; suspicion 2:12-13	Peter's Pentecost discourse 2:14-41 Summary 2:42-7 Cure of the crippled woman; Peter's second discourse 3:1-26 Peter and John arrested; they witness before the Sanhedrin 4:1-22 The Prayer of the Church 4:23-31 Summary 4:32-5 Barnabas 4:36-7 Ananias and Sapphira 5:1-11 Signs and wonders 5:12-16 The persecuted apostles protected by God 5:17-42 The seven deacons 6:1-7 Stephen accused and martyred 6:8-7:60 Sequel: persecution in Jerusalem; Christians are dispersed 8:1-3

THE WITNESS WIDENS TO JUDAEA AND SAMARIA Acts 8:4-9:43	THE BEGINNINGS
	FIRST WITNESS TO THE GENTILES Acts 10:1-14:28

Philip in Samaria 8:4-8
 	
Simon Magus; Peter and John 8:9-25
 	
Philip and the Ethiopian eunuch 8:26-40
 	
Saul's conversion 9:1-19a
 	
Saul witnesses in Damascus 9:19b-22
 	
Saul in Jerusalem 9:23-30
 	
Summary 9:31
 	
Peter witnesses and heals in Lydda and Joppa 9:32-43
	Peter and the baptism of Cornelius 10:1-48
	
	Peter explains his action to the Church in Jerusalem 11:1-18
	
	The mixed Church in Antioch; the mission of Saul and Barnabas 11:19-30
	
	Herod persecutes the Church in Judaea; Peter miraculously freed from prison; the death of Herod 12:1-23
	
	Summary 12:24
	
	Barnabas and Saul return 12:25
	
	Paul's First Missionary Journey 13:1-14:28
	   Commissioning of Barnabas and Saul 13:1-3
	   Witness in Cyprus 13:4-12
	   In Antioch of Pisidia; the turn to the Gentiles 13:13-52
	   Paul and Barnabas in Iconium; the Jews 14:1-7
	   In Lystra; the Gentiles 14:8-18
	   Witness in Derbe; return to Antioch 14:19-28

OF THE CHURCH'S WITNESS TO THE GENTILES Acts 10-28

THE JUDAIZING CONTROVERSY AND THE JERUSALEM COUNCIL Acts 15:1-35	PAUL WITNESSES TO THE ENDS OF THE EARTH Acts 15:36-28:31

The Judaizers cause a crisis 15:1-2
 	
The apostles confer in Jerusalem; Peter, Paul, and Barnabas speak 15:3-12
 	
James speaks 15:13-21
 	
The decision and the letter to the Church of Antioch 15:22-9
 	
The reaction in Antioch 15:30-35
	Paul's Second Missionary Journey 15:36-18:22
	  Cyprus and Asia Minor revisited 15:36-16:10
	  To Greece; Philippi (prison); Thessalonika; Beroea 16:11-17:15
	  Paul in Athens; the Areopagus 17:16-34
	  Corinth 18:1-17
	  Return to Antioch 18:18-22
	Paul's Third Missionary Journey 18:23-21:16
	  Paul in Asia Minor 18:23
	  Apollos converted 18:24-8
	  Paul in Ephesus; the riot 19:1-41
	  To Greece; return to Troas; Eutychus; to Miletus 20:1-15
	  Paul at Miletus; the farewell 20:16-38
	  Tyre and Caesarea 21:1-14
	  Arrival in Jerusalem 21:15-17
	Paul Witnesses as a Prisoner 21:17-28:31
	  Paul attacked in Jerusalem 21:17-22:21
	  Imprisonment in Jerusalem 22:22-23:11
	  Imprisonment in Caesarea 23:12-26:32
	  The journey to Rome 27:1-28:16
	  Paul in Rome; his witness to the Roman Jews 28:17-28
	  Conclusion: Paul witnesses in Rome to all comers 28:30-31